Praise

"William Cook - writer, poet, artist, editor. This talented man has no illusions about the horror that is human nature. His exploration of torture, murder and mayhem combines the scientific precision of a scientist dissecting a specimen with the creative flair of a sculptor working with words. Something tells me that he is just getting started and we'll be seeing a lot more of his dark crafts in the future."

– Anna Taborska, author of *For Those Who Dream Monsters*, director of *The Rain Has Stopped, Ela, The Sin, My Uprising, A Fragment of Being*

§

"William Cook is an uncompromising horror writer. Be prepared to slink down into the underbelly of the world as visions are revealed that can't be unseen. Blood Related is a true horror novel. Strong stomachs required here folks!"

– Rocky Wood, President of The Horror Writers Association and Stephen King biographer.

§

"A world-creator who fuses the psychosis of character with literary poetics. William Cook will disturb you, enlighten you, and entertain you."

– Vincenzo Bilof, author of *Necropolis Now* and *Dark Rising*

§

"William Cook's work hits like a ton of bricks: the horror is intense, the poetry is deep, and the artwork grabs hold and sinks in."

– Donald White, author of *The Visions of Sandy Brown*

§

"William Cook is an author to watch."

– Mark Edward Hall, author of *The Lost Village* and *The Holocaust Opera*

"William Cook is a damn good writer. His style of writing and how he composes a story is exactly what horror readership is starving for and why horror movie fans should start reading him if they don't already. They don't know what they're missing. His stories are part Tarantino in their brilliance, Thomas Harris in raw violence, and utterly William Cook in originality."

– Nicholas Grabowsky, author of *Halloween IV* and *The Everborn*

§

"William Cook is one hell of a writer. 'Blood Related' is a swirling cocktail of blood and mayhem, a thrilling ride of unrelenting terror. Cook is a force in the industry; he has given horror a new voice, a brutal roar across the literary landscape."

– Jason Gehlert, author of *Red Triangle* and *Contagion*

§

"William Cook creates madness with the unsettling candor of yanking a hair out all the way to its root. He gets right to the point with a bloody scalpel edginess and an EEK factor attached."

– Lori R. Lopez, author of *An Ill Wind Blows* and *The Fairy Fly*

§

"William Cook knows horror from Fiction to Nonfiction, and he has a gift for blending the two genres seamlessly. You pray his fictional horror is not real, and hope his nonfiction horror is fiction. No matter what book of Cook's you read, you'll be hoping and praying. Here is Horror that you revel in with fascination and repulsion."

– Anthony Servante, author of *East Los* and *Killers and Horror: Ink Black, Blood Red*

Also by William Cook

Fiction

Dreams of Thanatos: Collected Macabre Tales
Death Quartet
Dead and Buried

Poetry

Corpus Delicti: Selected Poetry

Non-Fiction

Gaze Into The Abyss: The Poetry of Jim Morrison

Edited By

Fresh Fear: Contemporary Horror

BLOOD RELATED
WILLIAM COOK

KING BILLY PUBLICATIONS
Wellington, New Zealand
Copyright © 2015, William Cook.

Artwork © Steve Upham
Book cover design © by 3cagency
http://3cagency.co.nz

Blood Related (A Novel)
©William Cook – 3rd edition, 2015.

[1. Fiction 2. Psychological Horror 3. Thriller]
Please visit the author's website at:
http://williamcookwriter.com

And who made terror, madness, crime, remorse,
Which from the links of the great chain of things
To every thought within the mind of man
Sway and drag heavily, and each one reels
Under the load towards the pit of death;
Abandoned hope, and love that turns to hate;
And self-contempt, bitterer to drink than blood;
Pain, whose unheeded and familiar speech
Is howling, and keen shrieks, day after day;
And Hell, or the sharp fear of Hell?

From Prometheus Unbound by Percy Bysshe Shelley

Prologue:

Charlie has big plans for me. He's thinking crazy thoughts and talking crazy talk. He keeps telling me about his recurring visions and his 'mission.' Apparently, he has occasion to talk to God. During one of these conversations, God granted him absolution in hell, free from the tyranny of everyday pain and suffering if Charlie did his bidding. This particular vision also revealed that God and Satan were the same, as were heaven and hell. For Charlie, he saw this as a sign that he would be sitting at Satan's side on a throne made of human bones, once he was mortally dead.

He would be a god.

I could tell he was delusional.

He was gone.

I knew this because there was no God.

God was dead and so was Charlie.

I hear Charlie's voice now, clear as a bell. My consciousness clears and my surroundings come into sharp focus. I see his face clearly in my mind. I shake my head, trying to rid myself of his image. I wrap my bleeding fist in a towel and step gingerly over the broken shards of mirror littering the wet tiles on the bathroom floor. I make my way to the kitchen and search the cupboards, looking for some tape or Band-Aids to stem the flow of blood from the lacerations across my throbbing knuckles.

"God," Charlie whispers to me, "has given me life—to do my deeds upon this earth before he takes me to the next level."

"Another life," he continues, "will not allow me the freedom of choice you have with your future Caleb. Some things we cannot change. Some lives are not led by natural laws, but by unnatural processes—events."

"My life, your life …" Charlie says, "is a road map to hell."

I remember the last time I looked in his eyes when he was alive. He was crazy then and the voice in my head shakes with equal insanity as an image of him floats before my eyes. His face appears gaunt, skeletal. The vision ebbs in and out of focus as I start to tremble with a mixture of naked coldness and fear. I remember him as if he is with me now and he is, in his own twisted way. My mind reels with tangents and the bending of physical laws.

He used to seem very confused to me.

He now seems very logical to me.

He still seems very dangerous.

He is my twin brother and he has returned home.

I see him in my own eyes.

I feel that he is now part of me.

Blood related.

The missing piece of the jigsaw puzzle has been found. It is a moment of realization that we are two parts of the same equation. Standing there alone in a stranger's house, nude as a newborn, thoughts swirling through my adrenaline-charged brain.

I realize that with the puzzle complete, the revealed image is far more bloody than romanticized. Like two halves of something that shouldn't be together. It is a vision of apocalyptic proportions that unfurls in my mind's eye. Despite my realization, I feel like shit more than ever.

Back in the bathroom, I look once again at my crazed reflection in the broken shards of mirror on the floor, before I smash myself in the face with my fist. I hear Charlie gasp as I do. The sum of our union is chaos. Death. Destruction. Violence. And loneliness.

We are hollow men.

Empty men.

The walking dead.

We are one.

With some ammonia-saturated cleaning spray, I spray the droplets of blood on the remains of the cabinet mirror, vainly attempting to clean my presence from the room. I look at the floor covered in bloody footprints. My bloody footprints. I look at the woman in the bathtub, her glazed lifeless eyes staring vacantly at me. Her bruised neck is set at a strange angle. One bare arm dangles over the side of the porcelain tub. Her alabaster fingers delicately lay palm up on the floor, in a glistening pool of dark blood. A bare breast exposed, floats whitely like an island of chalk amongst the maroon water in the tub. At this point, I give up any attempts to conceal my indiscretions.

I look through the doorway at the clock on the mantle in the living room. It's time to go and I've come ill prepared. This was, after all, a 'crime of opportunity' as they sometimes are. I complete my task and take my trophy from the body, arranging the remains in my careful way. I remove my clothes from the backpack and replace them with the head, neatly wrapped in a plastic bag. I wipe the remaining smears of congealing blood from my body, careful not to get the viscous liquid on anything else as I shed my unease and dress hurriedly in the hallway. All the while, my gaze is fixated on the broken work in the bathroom. She appears to move as her limbs stiffen a fraction with the onset of rigor mortis.

My heart starts beating again and I think of Lucille, as I make my way to the gas hob in the kitchen. I check that all the windows are shut tight, light a candle in the living room and in the hallway, and turn all the gas rings to high. In my head, Charlie remains quiet as I gently close and lock the back door, before making my way across the yard and over the fence at the rear of the property.

I walk slowly down the poorly lit alley that runs behind the North-Shore Boulevard. It takes approximately six minutes of pacing my steps in the dark night, counting the seconds as I go, until I hear a muffled thump behind me as the house explodes in a ball of flame. Charlie starts to laugh. A frightening maniacal noise, which sounds like someone hacking at a tree-trunk with an axe. It only takes a brief minute to realize that the crazed laughter is not Charlie's, but my own.

I
Into The Abyss

The very emphasis of the commandment: Thou shalt not kill,
makes it certain that we are descended from
an endlessly long chain of generations of murderers,
whose love of murder was in their blood,
as it is perhaps also in ours.

Sigmund Freud

It takes two to make a murder.
There are born victims, born to have their throats cut,
as the cut-throats are born to be hanged

Aldous Huxley

1

Pa, Ma, Charlie and I, all lived together in a rundown rooming house inherited from Grandpa. Pa's father had been a wealthy manufacturer and founder of the nearby Eden Park industrial estate in Portvale. He made his millions and retired to the country to spend his days tending to pigs on his farm, leaving the house to Pa's care with the promise of inheritance if he kept it well maintained.

The house is one of the largest residences on the dockside end of the avenue that borders the east side of Eden Park. Essentially, it's a rectangular building with two levels plus a large basement and garage. The main building sits back slightly from the street with a large balcony and entrance in the front of the house, and a substantial paved rear section with drive-on access from both the front and rear of the property. The exterior of the house is a dark red brick, almost black in appearance, and the lower windows have metal bars over them, presumably to prevent burglaries but more likely, to prevent escapes.

When the house operated full-time as a rooming house, it advertised twelve rooms, built specifically for the housing of guests and available for short-term tenants. Pa had seen a business opportunity and had subdivided the large ground floor rooms to accommodate paying visitors, leaving the floor upstairs, for our family. It was an old rundown building and had its share of ghosts and bad history, all the local kids used to call it the 'Dead Zone.' They probably thought we were a bunch of freaks but that didn't stop the crack heads and whores from taking advantage of the cheap rent when it was a rooming house.

I was aware of my own differences from the other kids when I went to public school, it seemed as though I couldn't relate to anyone. After a spell in reformatory with other young men not dissimilar to myself and my exclusion from any normal schooling thereafter, I knew that my life was destined to be lived on the fringes of society. It was a lonely dark place to be and much of my time was spent alone outside the house or listening to my parents beat themselves, or other people, senseless. I resented society and I hated my parents, both for who they were and for bringing me into such a shitty world.

Things have changed now and my parents are both dead to me, even though one is still alive and squawking. After Pa died, Ma was indifferent to me living with her. I wasn't sure whether she didn't care if I was alive or dead, or she just tolerated my presence because she had some last vestige of a maternal connection, ticking away in the back of her demented brain. I think in some ways I reminded her of Pa and she sure reminded me of my dead mother, except she was still alive, barely.

Anyway, I helped around the place, 'earned my keep' as she liked to call it. Take the trash out, collect the rent off the few remaining tenants, sweep the yard, and shoot stray cats—that kind of shit. I lived in the garage in a loft, it was secure and afforded me a base from which I operated. Despite living in a garage, anything was better than living with a suicidal mother who dripped nightmares as a candle drips wax.

When he wasn't locked up, my brother Charlie would return to savor the comforts 'home' had to offer and would live in the house with Ma. Despite the fact that Charlie and I were identical twins, he was definitely her favorite. She spoilt the ass off Charlie and I sometimes hated him for that. When he was at home, Charlie would come and go as he pleased, often disappearing for long periods before returning without explanation. Vera used to say with disgust that she saw more of me than she ever did of him.

Despite our difficulties, Ma and I seemed to exist together amicably enough, especially when we could avoid meeting or talking with each other. While I lived in the loft, I would plan it so I could use the rooming house facilities when Vera went to the casino or the liquor store, the main reason being there was no toilet or shower in the garage. I barely set foot inside the main house itself if I could avoid it. The old place stank inside and reeked of bad memories. It smelled like a damp graveyard stained with cat's piss and dead mice. It had the smell of death about it, that strangely familiar stench, like old farts or stale paraffin. Malignantly malodorous.

Despite officially closing down as a rooming house in 1997, the year Pa died, Ma still advertised for 'tenants' to keep money coming in. The few occasional tenants occupied the old rooms downstairs while Ma had the run of the top floor. She never cleaned anything, except a path from the kitchen to the sofa in front of the TV and another leading out of the living room to her bedroom and then diagonally across the hall to the bathroom.

The floor was stacked chest high with moldy old piles of newspapers, TV guides, and junk mail brochures. In between the stacks of papers, the floor was littered with old clothes, dirty dishes, and cigarette butts and the occasional dead mouse or rat. And that was just the top floor, the downstairs rooms were thick with grime and stained yellow with years of tenants' cigarette and crack smoke.

While Ma is not the most attentive house cleaner, she had been an obsessively imposing and influential force in my early life. Her and her sky-blue hair curlers and bent cigarettes dangling between her thin wrinkled lips. By the time I hit puberty she was a haggard middle-aged woman, the years of alcohol abuse and the ravages of prostitution had aged her well beyond her years. Her paisley skirt would sweep the floor as she tucked the sleeves of her brown cardigan up, as if she's going to start swinging, as she would chase my brother and me out of the house. When she wanted our attention, she'd stand at the top of the stairs that run down the outside of the rear of the rooming house and shriek in her ungodly voice in the general direction of the garage. Her wizened hag of a face screwed up, her furrowed brow, dark with bad intentions while her rotten teeth snapped dryly as she bayed for our blood. Time had not dulled her bitter nature and now with Pa gone and Charlie in trouble with the law all the time, she had become even more insidious as the years ticked by. Yeah, as far back as I can remember, Ma was a real hoot!

Lately, she'd been telling me she wanted me 'the hell out!' I told her back, if I had somewhere to go, I'd be there. Hell, I know I'm no angel. She's got my number, but it's a sweet deal now she's turning soft in the head, despite all the years of nagging. I keep out of her way and she ignores my small indiscretions. Despite the headaches and the memories, the old place is somewhere to live until my own plans bear fruit

My living quarters in the loft were quite comfortable although it was freezing in the garage during wintertime. The long concrete-block garage sat against the east fence of the property and was approximately thirty meters in length. It had been built with a high stud and could quite easily accommodate a large semi-trailer truck and trailer unit. When Pa was at home he used to have the garage piled high with all sorts of trash—mainly cars and machinery. The garage was divided internally in two, by a block wall that quartered the north end off from the rest of the building. It was in this section that the loft floated above the motley assortment of grease stained engine blocks and 40-gallon drums full of assorted fastenings and spare parts. A heavy plywood floor lined the loft and a basic timber frame enclosed it from the rest of the garage.

Over the years as I got handier with tools, I insulated the walls and floor and lined everything with plywood. My mattress sat on a bed-base I had constructed from old wooden packing cases and the walls were covered in posters and pictures ripped from library books and magazines. The various pictures juxtaposed with each other, the naked bodies of centerfold models set alongside the images of naked corpses of concentration camp victims. Favorite movie posters like *Evil Dead, Taxi Driver, Halloween* and *Texas Chainsaw Massacre* took pride of place with their symmetrically positioned spaces on each wall. Later, I would remove the pictures from my walls, preferring the 'minimalist' look with the realization that physical manifestations of my fantasies were potentially incriminating. It was a place to sleep and a place to plan; this was my aboveground home. My true dwelling was deep in the bowels of the old underground tunnel system that crisscrossed deep beneath Portvale, this I called my 'lair.'

As I mentioned, Charlie and I grew up in Portvale. We were born ten minutes apart on June the 15th, 1974. Our early days were unhappy ones, as Ma and Pa were incapable of kindness or paternal nurturing. We were brought up hard and were expected to look after ourselves, which we did to the best of our ability. When we could walk and talk we began to feel the wrath of our sadistic parents, I withdrew into myself while Charlie became temperamental and uncontrollable. As a result, he would bear the brunt of Pa's fists and belt more than I would.

Apart from visits to our Grandparents' house in mid-west Fey County and a few stints each in various reformatories up and down the East Coast, Portvale and the torture chamber we called home was all we knew. Charlie of course had his time away in the 'big house' and the sanitarium, but other than that, we had never strayed very far from our birthplace.

Portvale is a small borough, half industrial/half residential, on the lower east side of one of the largest East Coast cities; built during a once-lucrative manufacturing boom, now largely exhausted by cheap overseas labor and imports. The old production factories and warehouses now either house makeshift business premises, or crumble along with the rest of the area. Today, residential Portvale is the result of an unsuccessful council experiment that managed to convert 1950s urban planning and new suburbs into typically degraded places, reminiscent of inner-city ghettos but on a slightly smaller scale. Portvale is sort of like an extra limb, parasitically attached to one of the sprawling southern arterial routes that feed into the Metropolis.

Everything is unkempt—paint peels off buildings and trash blows down the long wide avenues and streets in the smog-laden breeze. The winter winds blow snow through the docks to chill the bones of the hardiest inhabitants. Graffiti is the only relief from the drab houses and apartment buildings that sit nestled between chop shops and flophouses. In fact, just about every available street surface had been overlaid and tagged with colorful graphic images. Death motifs largely proliferate. It's a ghost town basically, despite the living residents.

I constantly wonder what life would be like outside of this place and answer myself with the same response every time:

Anywhere would be better than here!

When I was a kid, before I started visiting the small Portvale library, I had no idea that there was another world outside the confines of the city. Upon discovery of the quiet refuge of the library, in an otherwise culturally barren neighborhood, I would spend hours reading old National Geographic magazines and be enthralled with the accounts of the Arctic Circle and South America.

The other thing I discovered at the Portvale library was one whole wall devoted to literature about the various world wars. These books exploded my mind as to the capacity for evil inherent in humans. Graphic picture after picture of emaciated naked corpses, piled high on pyramids of carrion. Black and white photos of Auschwitz and Belsen; the massive chimneys spewing clouds of incinerated corpse-smoke into bleak European skies. I lined my walls in the loft with the pictures from these books; however, my most important discovery was located directly next to the shelves stacked with war books. 'True Crime' literature was my next step into the dark corners of the human mind—my own mind, to be exact. I quivered with excitement and guilty pleasure as I thumbed through the volumes filled with the most horrible aspects of humanity. I recognized myself between the lines. I found kindred spirits on these pages; new heroes filled my world as I read voraciously, devouring the methods and the means to avoid detection and to make my mark on the world.

I had a rating scale for the most impressive serial killers. 'One' being best overall and 'ten' being good enough to be in the rating, but not quite good enough to make the top nine. Here are the results:

1. Ted Bundy
2. Green River Killer, Gary Ridgeway
3. The Ice Man, Richard Kuklinski
4. H. H. Holmes
5. The Yorkshire Ripper, Peter Sutcliffe
6. The Zodiac Killer
7. The Dusseldorf Monster, Peter Kurten
8. The Mad Butcher of Kingsbury Run
9. The Night Stalker, Richard Ramirez
10. Jack the Ripper

My preferences were dictated by my own biases and experience. Others did not make the list because of a displeasing aspect of their characters or their work. The ones on the list did not earn their place because of the quantity of their deeds, rather the quality, style, or the emission of an intelligent type of evil, evident in their work.

When I was a kid, one day, I naively resolved, I would actually see the world. I would travel to Europe, to South America and India. I wanted to go everywhere and do everything. I wanted to expand my world and domain. I especially wanted to visit the international places and historic crime scenes that I had read about in the books. One day, I too would take my place amongst the pages of those True Crime annals as the master of all rogues. I aspired to be a 'Super Killer.' Number one. However, 'one day' was a long way off and everywhere was far away from number seven Artaud Avenue, in the Portvale suburb of Eden Park. Now I am older and so much has happened, I have achieved some of these goals and 'that day' does not seem so far away. My plans to travel remain firm and probably have become even more relevant now, than ever before.

It is time to plan my exit. Time to put my own plans into motion. I know I have to leave soon. Too many things are starting to surface. Too many people are starting to talk. With Pa dead and Charlie AWOL again, the police have started a surveillance program—I see them sitting outside in their unmarked cars, making no attempt to be discreet. Despite the surveillance, my business is expanding and as I have indicated, I'd like to 'go global' soon.

2

W hen I was younger, I had a few caseworkers appointed by the courts. One of them felt it her duty to 'reveal some information about my parents' to me. She was a typical newbie–plain looking, nose-stud, glasses and suitably inexperienced. She was still wet behind the ears, fresh out of a graduate program. I wanted to rip the pen out of her hand and stab her to death with it. She adjusted her frameless spectacles on her ski-jump nose, drew a breath through her crooked teeth and relayed with obvious relish that "Errol Wieland Cunningham was born in 1953 to an abusive father, who had owned a manufacturing plant in Portvale. He also had an alcoholic mother who eventually committed suicide ... Throughout his life he had many different occupations: Soldier, Landlord, Mechanic, Cabbie, Construction specialist."

Don't forget, 'Hot cock,' etcetera. Etcetera.

The stupid bitch didn't know the half of Pa's story. But I knew. It goes something like this. Pa was in the Armed Forces for three years in the early seventies but was discharged due to a possible mental breakdown. After his release from the army, he found that he had inherited his father's large mansion-like house in Artaud Avenue. He wasted no time in quickly converting it into a passive income by renting the rooms out to lodgers. Pa married Vera shortly after, in a small ceremony at a registry office sometime in 1973.

Not coping well with life as a civilian, he tried on a number of occasions to commit suicide, and spent a lot of time in different county mental institutions in-between wandering aimlessly around the country. During Pa's stints in and out of various institutions, Ma proved a formidable proprietor in his absence.

He underwent various psychological tests during his periods of incarceration and while most of the records are still bound by doctor/patient confidentiality legislation, certain details have inadvertently been made public by way of media release.

He had been tested with an IQ of 146, this intelligence usually only evident in his financial decisions. Despite a lack of education and bad beginnings, Pa managed to build a portfolio of real-estate investments off the back of his inheritance, which saw his net worth stand at over a million dollars. Even with his wealth, he chose to live in squalor and was repeatedly hospitalized for suicide attempts and general mental instability through his adult life. Towards the end, Errol was under increasing police and media scrutiny due to his position as 'number one suspect' in the infamous 'Dockside Ripper' serial killings. The investigation ended with Pa's apparent suicide in 1997, a week before my brother Caleb's twenty-first birthday. The killings seemed to stop for a few years then mysteriously began again exactly five years after Errol's death.

Like my naïve caseworker, the cops only knew a fraction of what Pa had done and seemed completely ignorant of my own crimes. Over the years, I learnt a lot about Pa from my own experiences. I had a good idea of who he was and what he'd done. It was obvious, with the increasing amount of attention he was receiving from the authorities, that they had their own suspicions about him. I remember, with the constant harassment and police surveillance, Pa started to break. He started drinking more heavily than usual and smashing furniture around the house. He was now in the grip of an obvious full-blown mental breakdown and began arguing with himself as he paced around the house swigging wildly from a 40oz bottle of Bourbon. He would sit at the kitchen table, mesmerized by the light glinting off the blade of a large butcher's knife. His deep-set eyes empty of life. He cut all the phone lines in the building and moved a mattress into the cellar where he began to spend most of his time. Occasionally, when he had a moment of sobriety, Errol would venture out to the garage and fire up the Ford for a run to the liquor store.

I went to ground literally, when Pa was under scrutiny from the feds. I spent the better part of a month in my subterranean lair in the storm drains and sewers under Portvale. I had time to explore the bowels of the city and to perfect my own nocturnal practices. I worked out a plan for the inevitable end-time, which felt closer with every passing day. I would leave Portvale when things had passed, when things had happened that were bound to happen. When I finally emerged back above surface, my skin was the pallor of a corpse from lack of sunlight and Pa was dead.

When Pa died, Ma hit the bottle more than usual. With Pa's life insurance money, she disappeared for a while and left me on my own. With the house now empty, my curiosity began to get the better of me. I ventured inside and began to explore those dirty dark memories, hidden for years in the shadows and recesses of the interior. Under a loose floorboard, in a trunk, under Pa's old bed, I found a tatty old cardboard suitcase, held together with laced shoelaces and an old brown belt I recognized with disgust.

I took my switchblade from the pocket in the back of my jeans and proceeded to hack the old belt, the cause of so much pain when I was a kid, into small pieces. It was as if I was watching myself from the cobwebbed ceiling in the corner of the room, transfixed with every thrust and pull of that knife.

In the trunk, I found a bunch of papers, some porno mags and maps, some liquefied speed in a moldy plastic baggie, three handguns, a massive roll of cash and three old journals bound with some pantyhose. I stroked one of the handguns—a .44 Magnum nearly as long as my forearm. It gave me a hard on so bad it felt like I had a two-by-four down the front of my jeans. I took the diary from the bottom of the case and a dirty envelope fell on the floorboards, scattering Polaroid photos in a horrific rainbow splash of florid reds and pinks and black bodies, gaping wounds, taut terror-stricken faces, clawing at the camera lens. I started counting the photos and gave up after fifty.

I stood amongst Pa's harem and knew exactly where those pictures were taken. The brick walls of the basement were evident with Pa's yellow and black dartboard mounted on the back wall, with a tall dark wooden block in the center of the room. The pictures screamed my suspicions with clear and irrefutable evidence. I leant down and pocketed the wad of cash.

After my discovery of Pa's trunk, I removed it immediately from its original hiding place under his old bed and concealed it in a hidden chamber I had discovered in the tunnels beneath the house. I remembered the day I showed Charlie what I found in Pa's trunk, he had only been released a few weeks earlier but I felt I needed to show him what I'd found. I remember spreading the contents on the floor of the garage for him to see. He stood behind me, hesitant at first but I heard his breathing quicken when I held Pa's Magnum clenched in my fist, tilting it in the stark fluorescent light as I admired the sheen on the long steel barrel. Charlie bent down and picked some of the photos off the floor.

"I knew Pa's secret," he said to me earnestly.

"Yeah, me too" I replied angrily.

"Yeah but you fucking stayed" he said.

"Yeah well you never fucking left, you son of a bitch" I spat back.

He looked at me with his black eyes. The scar almost glowed white, its jagged path reaching from his forehead, across his cheek down to his jaw line. He smiled a crooked smile and bounced on his haunches as he crouched there, sprung tight like a mongoose.

"I'm gonna have me a homecoming party soon," he said and laughed. I rubbed my temple with the muzzle of Pa's .44 Magnum and pictured Charlie's brains splattered across the ceiling. I cursed him again as I turned my back and started looking thru Pa's papers and belongings, turning secrets into answers as I went.

According to the house plans I found in the suitcase, there was a substantial cellar that ran the length of the house with a small boiler room to operate the heating system for the large building. The plans were marked as lodged with the local borough-housing department when the house was constructed in 1862. I had only ever been in the basement on a few occasions and had subsequently tried my hardest to eradicate those memories from my brain. It would only be years after Pa's death that I would have the courage to confront the demons that lurked in the deep, dank shadows of that malevolent place. Seeing the photos in Pa's diary had bought the memories of that dark pit of fear flooding back. It was like taking the lid off a bottle of air from Chernobyl. Poisonous, evil, and extremely dangerous.

Since Pa's death, I can't remember the last time the basement was cleaned out. He was the only one who ever used it. He used to bring his freak jailhouse brothers over and they would party until dawn. The whole fucking house would be shaking on its foundations.

I was pleased as punch, when I made the move to the loft in the garage at fourteen years of age. No more did I have to endure jamming a pillow around my ears so I didn't have to go to sleep listening to that bastard and all his fucking scumbag cronies, screaming and smashing around the large brick enclave under the house. Then there were the muffled petrified screams of young women. The noise would break though the still night on occasion, from the bowels of the rooming house.

Even after the old man died, I swear I could still hear, late at night, music and shouts, clinks of bottles across the yard and frightened whimpers and screams. I could see the small rectangular basement fanlight window glow red, clouds of blue smoke billowing from the bottom of the house like hot water steaming on ice. Nothing would prepare me for what I discovered in that basement. The basement was one of the seven gateways to hell, filled with ghosts of the dead!

The basement plans weren't the only interesting pieces of paper in Pa's old trunk. Another set of maps revealed the subterranean tunnel system I had already begun to explore beneath the Portvale streets. Clearly shown on the old city sewer and storm-water technical plans, were all the entry and exit points around the city, including man-hole covers and viaduct entrances. The disused subway systems were also shown, inextricably linked to the warren of underground tunnels.

On the main set of plans, a red circle marked in ink on the old paper map, highlighted a vertical man-sized pipe that exited directly under the house. Clearly visible, was the drain entrance situated in the corner of the property which I already knew well.

Another revelation was visited upon my eyes.

With the maps spread out before me, I suddenly felt connected to the whole city. It was like looking at the vascular system of some great beast flayed bare.

I was plugged in.

My whole body and mind glowed as if an H-bomb had been detonated in my very core, filling me with a warm fire as I in-and-outed the whole fucking city. My underground world had suddenly flowered and grown.

An urge burnt with hot fire in my gut.

I ached to explore.

Before I found the Polaroid photographs in Pa's case under the bed, I didn't really know or care how bad things had been. All I knew was that I had found out he had killed on many occasions and used to like to bring his work home with him after dark. It explained a lot about the old man and a lot about my brother and me. The memories came flowing back, tumbling over themselves like great black waves of death.

I remember Ma and Pa forcing us downstairs on occasion. The feeling of fear enveloped me once again as I remembered the terror, which lurked down the concrete steps in the dim light. They held Charlie and me down there until we stayed on our own accord, without a beating. Ma and Pa both made us watch their sick games.

Then we helped them find them.

Then we joined in.

Then cleaned up and then did it all over again.

I was glad Pa was dead.

I wished I had laced the old man's bourbon with Secanol. I wished I had killed him before he gassed himself in his car parked in the garage. I would have loved to stick that fucking hose from the exhaust pipe down his dirty throat. I would've got carried away and given him the knife and the twist and turn and slice a hole in his fucking neck trick as well. But I didn't, I just continued to cower like a beaten puppy and prayed to a faceless God that he would at least die, horribly. At least my prayers were answered eventually. But by my reckoning, God had nothing to do with it.

From A Sordid Life: The Life and Crimes of Errol Cunningham (London: Lowdown Press, 2003)

When Errol Cunningham died, he was a 44-year old ex-con from Portvale who, amongst other things, had constructed an underground concrete bunker in the basement of his house. Passers-by and neighbors reported hearing screams coming from the Cunningham residence late at night. After his death by suicide on the 6th of June 1997, he was linked to as the key suspect in as many as 50 murders.

The victims were mainly young women who answered ads for models and 'actresses' for homemade porn films. When the women showed up at the hostel, he would usually offer them refreshments laced with sedatives and throw them down into the deep chamber he had constructed in his basement. He would usually kill them with a hammer or let the women choose between being beaten to death with his fists or electrocuted until dead. After committing his heinous murders, he would then either dump the bodies or burn them in the furnace in the basement of the hostel. The series of murders came to be known as the Dockside Ripper killings.

On April 29, 1980, at approximately 2:00am, a patrol officer discovered the nude body of Teresa Carlyle, 46, in an alley behind the Eden Avenue Sea Food Market. She had been stabbed more than 30 times in the face, chest, and lower abdomen. Her head and face were mutilated beyond recognition. In addition, her stomach had been slashed open from groin to sternum, and her intestines coiled around her head and shoulders decoratively, as if the shape of a crude wig. Her hands were covered in deep cuts, as if she had tried valiantly to fend off her assailant. The rookie police officer that found her body had been responding to an attempted burglary reported by a security company who monitored the business alarm system. It was established that Carlyle had been murdered sometime after 12.30 and before 1.50am.

A potential second victim of the serial killer was a woman named Sally Jessie. Her corpse was found three months after the first victim had been identified. At age 37, she worked at Joe's fast-food restaurant on Dockside Avenue and moonlighted as a hooker. Her record showed a long list of drug and prostitution convictions. Sally Jessie's naked body was found beaten, stabbed seven times and decapitated, then dumped beneath the North Shore Harbor Bridge on the Portvale side. The coroner estimated she had been dead for six days. High-level indicators of alcohol and cocaine were found in her body. Her occupation and the geographic location of her corpse indicated that she was a possible victim of the Portvale Slasher. The lack of severe mutilation indicated that the killer was disturbed during the attack or that another killer was responsible for the murder.

One month later, Transit workers found the body of a decapitated woman around 8:30 A.M. on the morning of August 26, 1981. The headless corpse lay between the rows of stacked railroad ties at the train yard, at Dock and Container Lane in the lower northeast section of Portvale. The victim was nude from the waist down and was posed in a sexually provocative position, with legs open and her blouse pulled up to expose her mutilated breasts.

By the next day, investigators had identified the victim as one Maria Frost, who came from Woodville, a town in nearby Coyote County. She was 52 when she died, and while it was clear to the police that she had been stabbed many times, it took an autopsy to determine the official cause and manner of death. Maria Frost had been sexually assaulted and had died of 47 stab wounds to her head and chest. Like the first victim, she had been disemboweled and her internal organs arranged around the head area.

It was determined that Maria was last seen at her home on August 19, as reported by Patrick Frost, her former husband. Patrick Frost identified the body and affirmed that the murdered woman was Maria. Despite the fact that they were no longer married, they lived together in their Coyote County home, although Frost claimed that his wife had left the week before without mentioning where she was going. This was not out of the ordinary, as they lived separate lives. (In fact, those who knew her around the Portvale area were surprised to learn that she had a home outside the city.)

Patrick Frost was initially investigated as a suspect but his alibis checked out and he was taken off the growing suspect list. According to reports, Frost frequented the bars in the Portvale area, especially on the strip—police subsequently began to question the long list of dockside workers and truckers who frequented the red-light district.

Over the next year, more victims surfaced and the local newspapers gave the killer the name of the Dockside Ripper. One disturbing aspect of the killer's MO was the vicious mutilation and the way the victims' internal organs were arranged around the body, reminiscent of the gruesome crimes of Jack the Ripper a century earlier.

Fear gripped the industrial suburb as the killer spread his reign of terror deeper into suburbia and the middle-class North Shore suburbs. No longer concentrating his blood lust on prostitutes, females from all types of backgrounds began turning up dead. It seemed as though the killer had adapted his MO, or a new player had begun a deadly killing spree.

After New Year celebrations for 1982 had died down, so too had the murders. Police were thinking that their boy had moved on, been jailed, or hopefully had committed suicide as the weeks ticked by with no new victims. Then the body of Anita Pieta, 72, was discovered. Anita lived in Portvale, on the corner of Ritalin and Staple Streets.

It was a cold winter's morning in February when she was found lying face down on the floor of her bedroom, the door to her apartment standing open and the hall entrance ankle-deep in snow. She was nude from the waist down and had been stabbed over thirty times in the back and head.

What stood out to investigators at the scene was the ferocity of the attack. In particular, a massive post-mortem wound that stretched from breastbone to pelvis. Her intestines and other internal organs had been left displayed on her blood-soaked bed. No murder weapon was discovered at the scene. It was evident from her injuries that she had been tortured. A 10cm puncture wound at the base of her neck indicated that a sharp instrument, probably a knife, had paralyzed her from the neck down.

The horrific wounds were mostly rendered

before the time of death according to the autopsy
report. At first police believed it was the work of
another killer, as she was not decapitated. After
revising their case files, they discovered that
they had equal unsolved cases of non-decapitated
victims that fit the same MO.

Carla Ouspensky, 56, was found dead in
her apartment a fortnight later in similar
circumstances to the other victims. She had been
stabbed repeatedly in the face, rendering her
once pretty features barely recognizable. She
lived on Eden Street, five blocks over from the
first reported murder scene.

A year later, another victim was discovered.
Nicole Muir lived on the streets and most nights
slept rough close to where she worked as a hooker
on the main strip. She was 28, a chronic sufferer
of narcolepsy and a potentially easy victim for
rape or murder. Her body was found by a security
guard in a skip in a Dock Street alley, east of
Portvale Avenue. She had been violently stabbed
in the chest over 80 times. Her body was found
not far from where Maria Frost had been killed and
left lying in a pool of blood, nude from the waist
down, with her legs spread.

Blood spattered against a nearby wall
indicated she has been stabbed with considerable
ferocity during the attack. Autopsies indicated
both victims had been sexually assaulted. Once
again, the arrangement of the victim's internal
organs around the body was evident.

One investigator noted that the placement of
the heart, kidneys, lungs and liver, connected
with cut lengths of long intestine, resembled the
outline of a five-pointed star or pentacle. Both
victims were not decapitated, although Muir's

neck had deep slashes that nearly severed her
spinal cord. Over the course of the next four
years, the body count grew to a staggering forty-
six brutal homicides attributed to the Dockside
Ripper. It was at this point that the bodies of
women who continued to go missing stopped turning
up. Police assumed the killer/s had either died,
moved location, been incarcerated, or had changed
their disposal method.

A week after Errol Cunningham's death by
suicide in 1997, another body turned up under
the harbor bridge, as did another twenty-three
mutilated corpses over the next decade. Locals
thought that perhaps authorities had suspected
the wrong person. After all, Cunningham did not
resemble the young male that witnesses saw talking
with some of the other victims shortly before
their deaths.

Hopes were raised as the third month came to a
close without any fresh homicides. More women
walked the streets at night and local police began
to pray that the killer had moved to a different
city or had committed suicide.

This proved to be a false hope with the
discovery of a freshly mutilated corpse; it
appeared the killer had simply had a short break
from his terrible hobby or that a new killer was
at large. Fear gripped the district once again.

Authorities had been certain that Errol
Cunningham was the Dockside Ripper. They had
realized that the murders following his suicide
were the work of another killer and now they
faced the grim probability that they had another
prolific serial killer operating in the same area.
Investigators were no closer to finding their
suspect than their colleagues had been a decade

earlier. It seemed as though Portvale was rapidly becoming the Serial Killer capital of the world.

3

According to Pa's journal, he was the recipient of a regular type of post-war upbringing. A native of Portvale, he was born May 26, 1953 and baptized as Errol Wieland Cunningham. He was the only son of Samael Caleb Cunningham, a foul-tempered manufacturing tycoon who treated his boy to regular ass-whippings, often supplemented with bondage and blindfolds, as punishment for real or imagined infractions of his almighty law. When not working his underpaid factory staff to near-death, Errol's father trapped and killed stray cats and dogs in his backyard, enjoying their agonized death throes and often forcing his son to participate in the culling.

Meanwhile, Samael's wife, Cassandra Cunningham, was long on excuses for Grandpa's weird behavior and short on support for her battered son. She suffered a nervous breakdown at home when Pa was nine years old, the fresh trauma apparently contributing to his failure of third grade. His diary went on to describe how school counselors labeled him as suffering from an inferiority complex, with aggressive tendencies and poor impulse control.

By early adolescence, Pa was apparently a chronic bed-wetter and a heavy drinker. Caught red-handed with a jug of wine at age thirteen, he was so badly beaten by his father, that he was confined to the county hospital for two full weeks to recover. Soon after his release, he ran away from home, but soon returned, establishing a pattern of abortive flight that followed clashes with his father.

The writing in his journal was very jagged and would become quite small and hard to read, especially when describing his perceived failings as a son to his father. I persevered and came up with some more interesting information about Pa.

Failing high school in his sophomore year, Pa dropped out and joined the armed services at the age of seventeen. He started well, responding to the discipline and camaraderie of military life. After 3 years active service in Vietnam and two tours of duty, his chronic use of drugs and alcohol resulted in a disciplinary hearing and a premature medical discharge in 1973. The early discharge was apparently due to a psychiatric diagnosis of an unspecified personality disorder. After meeting and marrying Ma the same year and fathering Charlie and I, Pa left us largely to look after ourselves while he barhopped up and down the east coast "looking for work" and trying to avoid the law.

As I continued to read Pa's journals, my stomach churned. Not because of what he'd done, it was nothing I hadn't seen or done myself. It was more to do with the knowledge that this was where it started—that if my parentage had been different—if the circumstance of my youth was not what it had been—then I may have been different. It wasn't nature or nurture that dealt me the cards I played with now, more of a divine providence that gave me the tools I had at my disposal. These same tools allowed me to step into Pa's mind's eye through his words and see what he saw, feel what he felt.

The descriptions of his life experiences became more lurid and extreme as I delved deeper into his journals. One particular incident he described took on a life of its own in my imagination. I could smell the hotdogs and cheap perfume of the carnival he described. I could hear the sounds of the screams coming from the roller coaster, as they surged across the noise and bustle of the carnival to Pa's keen ears. Pretty teenage girls and their preppy dates floated from one stall to the other. Young men played for soft toys and cheap tokens of their machismo for their women. I could feel Pa's excitement rising from the page as his written scrawl became tighter, more exact.

Pa took it all in; he even described a cigarette dangling from his mustachioed lips, leather jacket collar up against the cold night. He looked at the kids hanging upside down on the roller coaster called 'The Demon.' Loose change spilling from their jeans as it corkscrewed into the shadows and round again until it squealed to a halt next to a flimsy scaffold platform. He watched the gorillas unlock the cages as ashen-faced girls in bobby socks and flared mini-skirts held onto their boyfriend's skinny arms, as they tried to look pleased with themselves, for not puking simultaneously. And like me, he saw them, as they would look after years gone dead, in a drain, under a bridge on the outskirts of town, stripped bare—bleached bone or burning in the basement furnace.

He described smelling some cheap sweet perfume as two girls

aged about seventeen sauntered past, mohair sweaters bulging with promise, lips full and glistening red with lipstick. He had an instant hard-on and knew he'd found his score for the evening. The carnival had rich pickings as far as the city's hunting grounds went. He wasn't stupid and knew he had to get those chicks out of this place, before he struck. As I read more, he described the lure, then the capture and finally the execution. Memories flooded back to me as the words sharpened into vivid mind-movies. They were the same girls Charlie and I had witnessed being slashed to death by Pa and his hedge-trimmer, so many years ago. He described our presence at the murder scene and the reactions we gave to his act, with pride and sadistic humor.

Pa revealed himself to me in those journals, most of it I already knew from personal experience but I did learn some useful tips and tricks of the trade. For example, first rule of hunting—don't kill where you want to return. Apart from being downright foolhardy, Pa knew he'd ruin his chances of ever mining the same vein twice if he was too obvious. And the words continued, filling each page as his method duplicated itself time after time, in slow deliberate precision.

In the back of the journal were newspaper clippings, neatly folded and arranged in chronological order. Their presence in his journal left no doubt in my mind, that his corresponding words were testament to the amount of killings described in the clippings. The only difference was that the journal entries far outweighed the amount of murders listed in the articles. I knew Pa kept the furnace burning day and night when he was at home and I had first-hand experience with the basement and the kind of 'parties' that went on to the early hours of the morning.

Whenever Pa brought his 'other women' home, there would inevitably always be a sweet pungent odor emanating from the furnace room in the basement. It smelt like overcooked pork but I knew what it really was thanks to the war books I read, with the lurid descriptions of the smell of burning bodies emanating from the concentration camp ovens. The best thing about Pa's parties was that I had a ready-source of canvasses to choose from. Different colors, bra-sizes, hair color, pain tolerance …

34

Whoever made it out of the basement alive was mine to play with in the tunnels below. At first, I had fun with them on my own, but lately I had let Cain and Able, Charlie's Rottweiler dogs, return to their killer heritage and hunt down some tunnel rats for a bit of sport. I was bored and flat-lining on paranoiac phobias and neuroses—an unfortunate, but inescapable side effect of my acute psychopathology. My motivation levels were winding down with the end time in sight, for the completion of my latest installation.

As I continued to read the press clippings, I recognized descriptions of some of my own art amongst the third-rate journalism. Pa had been keeping up with news reports of other unsolved murders in the area. Whether he knew that Charlie and I had inherited his insatiable bloodlust I'll never know, but the loving way he had folded each clipping so symmetrically, betrayed an obvious respect for our work. Our crimes became more public as we left behind evidence of our creativity. Pa on the other hand, had always espoused the adage that 'no body, no evidence' was the best policy, hence the eternal inferno— burning twenty-four hours, seven days a week, in the basement.

The journals continued to outline Pa's sordid lifestyle and experiences that shaped his pitiful world. He spoke of the years of poverty and the events that led to a change of fortune. He wrote of his surprise at inheriting his father's run-down estate on Artaud Avenue in 1984. The elder Cunningham had apparently converted to Pentecostalism and had become imbued with the Christian spirit. As part of the redemptive process, he had gifted Errol the house in his last will and testament as a way of making amends for the abuse he'd so unmercifully dished out to his son as a child.

When the lawyer, who tracked Pa down to a seedy flophouse near the docks where we lived in a single room with no running water and mattresses on the floor, finally caught up with him, Pa was suspicious to say the least. The lawyer presented Pa with the deeds to the property and a brief reading of the legal requirements. After some more convincing, Pa could scarcely believe his luck. His father had retired to Fey County in the Midwest some years before and owned some substantial rural acreage that he had inherited as well.

The house on Artaud Avenue was not worth much as it was in a bad state of disrepair. Occupied by rats and winos, the house had not been properly tenanted for nearly five years and as such was not the generous gift it could have been if properly looked after. Errol was more than happy to have someplace to call his own and soon fixed it up enough so that his new wife and twin sons could live comfortably in its rundown first-floor rooms.

Errol detailed how he converted the massive property into a rooming house by sub-dividing the ground-floor rooms. He began to make a reasonable income by tenanting the place with local hookers and dockworkers. Within a year, he had built up a regular clientele and was bringing in more cash than he needed. He converted the massive basement into a den and built a large garage on the rear of the section where he kept his beloved Ford. Judging from the account of his and Ma's marriage it was about the only good fortune Errol and Vera ever had and after years of living in poverty. Pa and Ma believed their fortunes had changed for the better.

The journals also detailed Pa's career as a small-time hood, spending most of his adult life in and out of jail while Ma was described as a fulltime alcoholic. Suddenly, thanks to the inheritance, my lowlife parents became the owners of one of the finest old residences in Portvale's Eden Park district. However, I can testify to the fact that it wasn't long before the house, much like its occupants, became even more decayed and run-down than before.

After moving in to the large house on Artaud Avenue, the Cunninghams kept to themselves, preferring the company of people from outside of the neighborhood. Any sign of life usually occurred in the evening when noise could be heard from behind the tall fence. A parade of misfits and small-time hoods came and went, day and night. Despite what he wrote in his journals, Ma and Pa were a match made in hell. All the neighbors steered clear of them at all costs. Pa was a tall tattooed muscular man with a penchant for violence and criminal activities. Ma was a small thin ex-call girl whose size belied her explosive temperament. Like Pa, she was fond of the alcohol and chased its grim effects at any occasion.

Everybody in the neighborhood knew they were up to no good,

but as in most communities they were left well enough alone. The tenants never complained as they were always invited to the parties, some never left of course.

From A Sordid Life: The Life and Crimes of Errol Cunningham (London: Lowdown Press, 2003)

On one particularly bitter occasion, Errol walked out to leave his wife and their twin sons on their own for five years. Vera took to the bottle and was soon on the streets, selling her worn-out body for money. In August 1979, a year after he left the family home, Errol was sentenced to five years in prison for the robbery of a rural gas station. Samael Cunningham, Errol's father, died while Errol was in prison. A month before Errol's release, Cunningham Snr had prophetically (in light of Errol's own death) committed suicide on the rural property he owned in the mid-west. Errol was released early for good behavior and returned to Portvale in 1984. The home front was still a duplicitous minefield of bad memories and prevalent temptation. In no time at all he was back to his old ways.

Errol hit the road again, spending time with relatives scattered across the country and spending time at his deceased father's ranch. In July 1985 and on the loose again, he robbed a store and was apprehended the next day, drunk asleep behind the wheel of a stolen car. Sentenced to ten years in prison—by some stroke of luck he was paroled after serving barely two.

Shortly after his release in July 1987, the homing instinct took him back to Portvale once again, where he moved back into a flophouse with his wife Vera and their two teenage sons. Managing to stay out of trouble, it seemed as though he was trying to get his life together, until he was picked up for questioning regarding a string of murders that would later be known as the 'Dockside Ripper' homicides. Vera must have known about Errol's nocturnal habits, although with the state she used to get herself in, it is surprising that she would have noticed anything outside the mediocrity of her own drab and intoxicated existence.

Fortune smiled on Errol despite his reputation as a low-life criminal. A lawyer arrived on their doorstep one day to deliver some financially uplifting news to the Cunninghams. As the only heir to the Cunningham estate, Errol received a substantial inheritance including the rundown rooming house on Artaud Avenue and a substantial cash inheritance including a farmhouse on a 10-acre plot in Fey County. Upon receipt of the sizeable inheritance and the further income generated from the hostel, Errol effectively retired himself from honest employment.

The hostel had a dubious past and bad reputation that became increasingly notorious with the new owners and their bizarre criminal behaviour.

It wasn't just the stench of burning flesh, which neighbors reported. There were various complaints lodged which included tales of orgies, screams, and the use of power tools buzzing late into the night. However, in this grim part of town, the sound of screams was not uncommon.

The police would make routine checks but would usually leave with nothing to report. On many occasions, witnesses recalled seeing patrol officers talking with Errol as he handed over an envelope, presumably filled with hush money.

In late May 1997, after nearly a decade of staying out of trouble, Errol is brought in for questioning as the prime suspect in the 'Dockside Ripper' murder investigation. After intensive interrogation, he was set free to return home. The authorities had made it clear to Errol that they would not stop until they had charged him with the murders of over thirty Dockside Ripper victims.

With the constant surveillance and a lengthy prison term inevitable, Errol went to ground and the hostel was forced to officially shut its doors to the downtown drifters and down and outs.

Cunningham knew his days of freedom were numbered. Word of an application by the DA for a warrant to search the property reached Errol via the street grapevine. This seemed to be the catalyst for his suicide. With his death, he effectively managed to disengage any further investigation at the time into his involvement with the 'Dockside Ripper.' Mounting evidence and DNA matching recently undertaken, has identified Errol Cunningham as the prime suspect, for close to forty of the 'Dockside Ripper' killings. His son, Charlie, has also been questioned as a suspect in the more recent 'Portvale Slasher' killings but has managed to avoid conviction due to lack of DNA evidence linking him to the crime scenes. The possibility of a copycat killer, whose activity overlaps both sets of homicides and Charlie's period of incarceration, has further complicated investigations.

Errol Cunningham took his own life the day after he was released after intensive questioning about the Dockside Ripper homicides. Charlie's twin brother, Caleb, discovered his father's lifeless body in 1997 in the garage at Artaud Avenue, hunched over the steering wheel of his 1960 Ford Fairlaine, a hose from the exhaust pipe in the rear-window, the engine still rumbling quietly.

Next door to the run-down Cunningham house is an empty lot, on the other side, an equally decrepit row of clapboard houses and as a backdrop, abandoned factory buildings and the wharf cranes crowd the skyline. Down the road sits an old brick Methodist church, the notice-board outside is one of the few surfaces in the neighborhood free from graffiti, proclaiming with its own slogan that it offers pedestrians "Peace and Sanity in a Mad, Mad World."

Behind the church is a desecrated graveyard populated with head stones dating back to the 1800s. The churchyard affords no sanctity for the dead, from the determined youths who mark their territories with spray-cans like base animals and the junkies that fix-up amongst the broken head stones. This is the breeding ground of two of the most prolifically violent serial killers ever, convicted or suspected.

4

I remember a time when I naïvely thought I knew what happiness was. It is only upon reflection that I recognize the truth of what it is I really felt. For years, relief and happiness were synonymous to me. If there ever was an emotion such as happiness then the actual feeling of relief was the closest I ever came to it. I remember the relief I felt as a child one hot summer's afternoon, as we drove west in the old man's black Ford, howling across those long stretches of compacted dirt and asphalt that seem to be infinite, a cloud of dust billowing from the back of the car as we ploughed on deep into the desert pushing 140 kilometers an hour. We didn't travel often but this was a special occasion, we were going to Grandma's funeral and then to the reading of the will. Someone had died and that meant we were to benefit in some way or another.

Charlie and I sat solemnly in the back of the car, each with a well-thumbed comic book clasped in our young hands. Charlie's copy of *Eerie* showed a ghoulish corpse rising from the dead, one hand stretched from the dirt, while a gawping eye peered insanely out of the front cover at me.

I looked across the front seat at the back of the heads of my parents as I plucked my damp shirt off my sweating back, the leather seats hot as hell. Pa sat hunched over the steering wheel dragging on a cigarette and sucking back a beer every few minutes. His prominent brow betrayed a striking intelligence that unfortunately did not govern his sadistic nature. The glare from the sun shone off the hood of the Ford and glistened in his oily slick-backed hair. He flipped the empty beer bottle out of the driver's window, Charlie and I craned our necks to watch it explode into hundreds of glass shards as it broke against the road behind the car.

Ma gazed vacantly out the window at the desert as she smoked a cigarette, her bleached blonde hair blowing in the warm breeze as the car sped into nothingness, the sun blaring down. Charlie put his comic on the seat between us and sat upright, sucking on a cigarette, dragging that dirty old smoke down into his thirteen-year old lungs. I took a drag on mine and looked through the front window. Up ahead stood a grove of tall cactus plants on the side of the road, appearing out of the flat horizon of the desert like a mirage.

A siren burst from nowhere in a blur of black, white and chrome. Resplendent in flashing red and blue light, the squad car peeled past us, and then drew level with the driver's side window.

"Mother-fucker!" the old man hissed, as the cop waved us over to the side of the highway. I heard the click of the hammer as Pa cocked the revolver he had stashed under the driver's seat. The Ford growled to a halt in a spray of gravel as the cop pulled in behind us and stepped from his car.

"Errol? Errol, don't do anything crazy in front of the boys?' squawked Ma, half-heartedly.

"It's about time they learnt a thing or two," Pa said in a low dark voice as he looked back over his shoulder at Charlie and I, as we pretended to read our comics intently.

The trooper's midsection appeared in the driver's side window, gloved hand resting on the butt of his revolver holstered on his hip.

"We got us a fuckin' for real cowpoke here, boys," laughed Errol as he lit a smoke. Vera covered her eyes with her hand and shook her head.

"Let's see your driver's license, sir?" asked the cop, obviously pissed at Pa's last comment. Pa handed him his beat-up license and the officer leant down so his face was level with his as he compared the ID photo on the license with the head on Pa's shoulders.

"Last name, *Cunningham!*" said the cop with a laugh.

"Y'all from 'Happy Days' or sumthin'?" asked the pig, with a sneer on his mustachioed Stetson-capped face.

Vera started screaming hysterically and pounded her fists on the dashboard of the car. The cop looked over the top of his mirrored aviators and slowly stepped back from the car, withdrawing his pistol as he went.

Pa bet him to it and drilled a perfect hole in the left lens of the cop's sunglasses. The interior of the Ford echoed with the deafening blast from Pa's snub-nosed .44.

I looked at Charlie and he looked back at me, both of us had our hands over our ears. Before we could look away, Pa leapt from the car and began to drag the dead cop back towards the squad car. I watched as Pa leant over the cop's lifeless body, boot-knife in his hand. His slick black hair hung down over his face, bobbing as he worked the knife deep in the cop's eye socket. After what seemed like forever he held a glistening object up to the sunlight, wiped it on his shirt and stuffed the .44 slug in his jeans pocket, before throwing the dead cop in the front seat of the squad car.

Ma had stopped screaming and was now smoking another cigarette.

"Make yourself useful boys. Get outta the car and help your old man. You clear his trail good now, you hear. You do a decent job or you'll be walkin' back to Portvale!" she ordered.

Charlie and I busied ourselves with the business of disguising Pa's blood-soaked tracks. We kicked gravel and spread handfuls of sand and dirt across the bloody drag-marks where the body had been pulled along. I remember finding a long stick on the side of the road and using it like a broom to brush away any tire tracks remaining. Charlie said later that he was sure he'd hidden bloodied chunks of the cop's brains in the sand that day. We hurried back to the car as a cloud of black smoke billowed from the patrol car. Pa pumped the gas and the Ford hit the highway again pushing ninety and climbing. My heart banged loud as all hell.

Charlie and I looked back as the cop's car burst into a fireball in the receding distance, the blue sky in the background framing the whole surreal scene. Pa let out a holler and Ma began whooping up a storm as they counted the money they had stolen from the trooper's bloody wallet.

"Got me a damn fine pump-action, Vera. Gonna pull me some serious cash with this baby!" Pa smiled with glee, as he admired the matt-black barrel of the shotgun he'd taken from the cruiser.

"It sure looks good on you, sugar!" Ma exclaimed with a wink.

Pa pushed the accelerator hard to the floor and aimed the car into the dying desert sun until we hit the beginning of miles of fields and farmlands. I thought I felt happy then but it was actually relief, that emotion I spoke of earlier. I was relieved, or happy, that it was the cop dead back there and not Charlie or I. Happy that my old man was doin' the killing' and not someone else back at us. I thought I felt just happy to be breathing right there in the back of that hot dusty sedan, screaming towards my grandma's funeral. Pa was right—I had learnt a thing or two that day. I'd learnt a thing about killing and I sure had learnt a few things about my old man.

5

That was the first time I witnessed a killing, on *that* family trip when Pa wasted the pig just doing his goddam job. Pa had made Charlie and I clean up *his* mess. Blood, brains, and shit. But that wasn't to be the last time. There was the time in the basement, when Charlie and I held a plastic tarpaulin up as high as we could to keep the mess off the walls, as the old man, one arm in a plaster-cast thanks to Ray Truman's heavy handed police tactics, attacked two teenage girls with an electric hedge-trimmer. The girls were bound nude with barbwire to a life-size crucifix in the center of the room, one to the front and the other strapped to the back—both with duct-tape wrapped tight 'round their eyes.

Our prize for bringing them home to meet Pa was to watch their nubile young bare breasts, explode in a hail of gore and screams. I still remember the wet dark warm feeling of the blood as it splashed against our faces and hands as we tried to look away, our young stomachs churning with disgust and a strange kind of hunger, gnawing at the pit in our guts. I remember looking at Charlie and noticing he was visibly erect as he stood there staring, trembling with excitement and fear.

The sick fuck.

I would never stoop to be so obvious.

How tactless!

My curiosity got the better of me and I made the mistake of asking Pa why they had to die and, just before he knocked me unconscious, he said that they were a 'present for a pig.' Later on, I would find out for myself exactly who Ray Truman was and what he was capable of.

I wasn't that concerned about myself, but I worried about Charlie in those early years. I could tell that mentally he was somewhat unhinged from an early age. He was always morose and depressed and never really said much. Before he entered the oppressive world of incarceration, he suffered quietly in his room at home. Full of his own importance, his mind brimmed with a callous hatred for his fellow human beings. He didn't want to work, let alone attend school. Charlie had already been in trouble with the law on numerous occasions. Mainly getting picked up for theft and petty misdemeanors, but nonetheless crimes serious enough to land him in reform school for a few years.

I stayed out of his way at this stage. I had my own shit going on and we avoided talking with each other despite living in the same house. I was relieved when Pa eventually kicked my scrawny self out to the loft in the garage at fourteen years of age. At least I was out of the house. While Charlie was at home, we existed amicably enough together. We were twins after all and our common language was largely unspoken. One day he surprised me and woke me up in an obvious state of distress.

"Its bullshit!" he exclaimed vehemently.

I knew he was talking about the fact he didn't want to be told what to do with his life. That he was sick of living under the same roof as Pa. That he was tired of denying his true nature.

"It's all bullshit," he shouted angrily again, his hands clenched and unclenched into fists as he paced back and forth on the mezzanine landing.

His eyes were dancing around his head and I knew he was high again. I prompted him to tell me what was troubling him and once he started talking, the words just flowed from him like a river. I was surprised by his emotional outpouring and thought to myself that I was seeing the *real* Charlie for the first time. His vulnerability endeared him to me ultimately at that point for I knew I was the only one who could ever understand him and who he could trust.

From then on, we talked about everything and he started spending more time with me out in the loft to escape Pa's relentless abuse. With our new sense of camaraderie established, our deepest darkest secrets and psychological desires became conversation pieces. It was only later that I discovered that what I thought was truth and emotional honesty, had been Charlie's way of playing me for whatever purposes suited him.

Charlie reckoned that the only things he enjoyed about his life were lifting weights and masturbating. He loved the feeling he got when he lifted more weights than the day before. That tight feeling in the biceps and the gut, the lightness of the arms, the adrenalin rush and the feel of cold sweat running between his shoulder blades. A similar reason drove his love of masturbation and the fact that he didn't need to interact socially to satisfy his bodily needs. Or so he said.

I knew Charlie was doing his best to toughen up. For some reason he used to be the kind of guy who always had kids kicking dirt in his face and then when he was rubbing his eyes they would kick him in the balls. One of the main visual differences between Charlie and I was that he wore glasses—the big black-rimmed coke bottle lenses. Other kids flicked snot at him and ripped his glasses off his ears, then took great delight in grinding the battered bifocals into the ground, time after time. Luckily, despite being so-called identical twins, I had perfect eyesight so avoided wearing glasses unless I chose to do so to alter my character. After a while, he just stopped wearing them and put up with his poor eyesight

Fuck the specs and books!

He didn't need to read what some other cocksucker wrote.

And fuck school too—that was for pussies!

He started collecting knives and taking as much perverse pleasure in the suffering of as many living objects as he could destroy. Mainly birds and neighborhood cats fell prey to his stones and knives. He stole a set of weights from somewhere and started working out every day. Charlie started living by his own set of principles, much the same way that I had done years before.

Charlie began to bulk up. As his pimples got bigger, so too did his muscles. He swore he would get even with all the 'shitters' in the world. Soon he was punching well above his weight and none of the other kids made the mistake of teasing him about his weird behavior and specs anymore. No one was going to push Charlie around and tell him what to do. On his fifteenth birthday, he dropped out of school, slapped Ma's face, punched the kid's front teeth out next door and killed the cat nine different ways—all in the same afternoon.

When Pa came home, Charlie got the crap beaten out of him— first in the kitchen, then in his bedroom after the old bastard dragged him out from under his bed by his hair, kicking and screaming like a girl. The old man booted him down the stairs and right out into the middle of the street, slapping his head to the left and to the right until Charlie's face was a swollen mess and blood flowed freely from his nose and mouth.

Just to slam the point home, Pa stripped off Charlie's clothes, ripping at him like a wild animal, much to the chagrin of all the neighbors, winos and local kids who, by this time, lined the curb in unreserved amusement. Soon most of the tenants joined the crowd on the sidewalk to gape at the spectacle.

"This is no son of mine!" exclaimed Errol.

"He can live like the animal he is without my help!" he stated to the crowd, holding the boy's torn clothes above his head with a triumphant grin - obviously enjoying his moral heroism and the eyes of all upon him. Errol flexed his tattooed muscles and strutted up and down the pavement outside the rooming house, ceremoniously tossing his son's clothes into the littered street as he went.

Charlie was not enjoying himself as much as Pa—he cupped his hands over his exposed genitals and hobbled down the street, screaming in rage over his bruised shoulder—*"I'll kill you, you goddamn motherfucker. I'll kill you if it's the last fucking thing I do"*—tears streamed down his bruised face.

"You try it you little punk and it'll be the last thing you do," Errol yelled back at him, extending his powerful forearm and flipping his son the bird. The whole street cheered, whistled, clapped, and laughed as Charlie stumbled bare-assed down an alley and headed toward the sanctuary of the abandoned factories at the end of the avenue.

6

Charlie lived in a disused automotive factory on the outskirts of Eden Park for two weeks, bare-assed and filthy. He looked like a wild man and felt more alive than he ever had before. He slept on the cold factory floor on a bed of abandoned overalls he'd found in the locker room. He would fall asleep listening to the rats and other night creatures as they chattered in the dark. The full moon turned Charlie into a werewolf in his mind, he ran through the deserted industrial streets like a wild man. He often picked himself up off the ground with a bloody nose after running headfirst into a lamppost or chain mesh fence in the dark.

He howled at the moon, his bare body vibrating with the dark night's cool caress. He stood on the roof of the factory in the blue-white glow of the moonlight, overlooking the sleeping diseased suburb of his birth.

"FUCK YOU!!! FUCK YOU ALL!!!" he screamed down at the houses and the drunken bums and cars that cruised the avenue. He felt powerful in that moment, untouchable, like a wild animal. He tilted his head back and howled as he stroked himself, firing off round after round of spent fury, down into the polluted night below.

The next morning, sunlight broke through the broken windows and cracks in the factory walls. Charlie lay on his makeshift bed and watched the dust dancing in the slashes of sunlight spilling through the gaps. The interior of the factory was dark, cool and quiet. The only noises were the sounds of an occasional rat scurrying across the trash-strewn floors and the drip of water leaking from the rusty broken pipes stretching like arterial veins across the length of the high ceilings. Charlie had been holed up in the factory for thirteen days now and was firmly in the grip of a substantial bout of cabin fever. He heard sounds coming from outside. In the near distance, the sounds of kids at play echoed across the wasteland surrounding the abandoned building.

"I got you, shitface!"

"Nah you didn't, my fuckin' ol' lady can throw shit better than that!"

Squinting through a crack in the wall, he watched some boys from the neighborhood playing war amongst the dirt mounds and piles of industrial debris that surrounded the abandoned factory.

He felt strangely excited, his body trembled, he was sure he could smell blood. He felt like a panther preparing to strike, his muscles as tight as springs. He scoped the landscape and identified his targets. There were three of them, he chose the one closest to his size — not quite big enough, but *it* would do.

Charlie edged close to the broken side door, and stood ready, close enough to hear them breathe outside. He waited. The biggest kid backed his ass right up to the workshop door. He could hear it breathing now; Charlie's own heart had stopped beating. He could hear nothing else, just the in and out breath of the object directly in front of him.

Charlie hesitated briefly, thought of his father, then struck — smashing the chump on the back of the head with a rusted spanner he'd found in the old factory tool shop. The heavy spanner made a deep thudding noise as it connected with the back of the boy's skull. The hard shock ran up Charlie's arm, warm blood splashing on his cheeks and in his eyes. The kid dropped like a sack of stones to the ground. Charlie wiped his sweating forehead with the back of his filthy hand as he rested his bare foot on the quivering boy's neck. Charlie applied more pressure with his foot and the kid stopped shaking with a gasp, his eyes rolled up in his head, lips blue, skin ashen. His blood stopped flowing as his last breath left his body.

Charlie dragged him quickly inside the door and stripped him of his clothes, leaving the kid naked amongst the rubble on the factory floor. Charlie paused, noticing the teenager's flaccid member. He felt like cutting it off, because his own was half the size. Instead, he stuffed a handful of grimy rag in the unconscious boy's mouth and plugged up his nostrils with dirt. Picking up a cinder block, Cunningham proceeded to break eighty-percent of the bones in the boy's lifeless body. He then covered the kid carefully with more trash and broken packing cases before he crept off into the dark depths of the factory to change into his new clothes. They were a tight fit, but comfortably so.

In the pocket of his new pair of jeans, he found a switchblade. He thought about attacking the other two kids, still throwing cans and bottles at each other outside, but thought better of it. He hadn't quite worked out how he felt about his first kill. He'd remembered Pa killing in front of him on more than one occasion, but this time it sure felt different, but easy.

Charlie felt in the other pocket and found a crumpled twenty-dollar note. With this discovery he forget about the other brats playing out the back and ventured forth into the light of day, down the front steps of the old factory, heading down the Avenue toward the railway yard and the train platform. In the distance behind him, he could hear the other boys yelling for their pal, he smirked and increased his pace.

Charlie felt important for the first time in his life, like he could be somebody. He was splitting for the big city, that's where the action was. He remembered all the junkies, hookers and dope-fiends that he used to supply drinks to at his father's parties. They talked about 'up-town' like some holy Mecca—where all the best drugs, wine and women you could have, could be had.

Charlie thought to himself, *'If I can live for two weeks in that stinking factory butt-naked and fifteen years in this shitty motherfucking place, I can survive in the big city easy enough. First thing I'll do is get me a razor and shave this head of mine then I'm going uptown.'*

Or so he thought.

7

Charlie stopped at a water fountain on the platform of the old train station. He hurriedly washed his hands and face, trying to remove the evidence of his first murder. The blood was hard to get off and made his skin a strange translucent pink color. He could see his warped reflection in the chrome chicane of the spigot. He quite liked the strange but somehow powerful vision of himself. He held his hands up and admired their strength, and pinkness. He tried to feel normal, whatever the fuck that was, but his animal passion had been aroused. A strange glow in his loins made his head numb and his heart pound.

A pair of shapely legs, followed by a pair of trembling voluptuous breasts, bounced past. He gazed hungrily at the heart shaped ass that followed, wrapped in skin-tight denim, as it walked around a corner …

"Jesus fuckin' Christ," he said to himself. He had a hard-on fit to burst.

He rubbed his eyes and his crotch at the same time, surprised at the clarity of his vision. Maybe he didn't need those stupid glasses after all?

The smell of a burger-bar enticed him away from the train station. All he had been living on for two weeks were bottles of milk and anything he could steal when he crept into the suburbs on a midnight raid.

He saw some mousy-haired broad waiting at the counter, dressed in a black parka, smoking a cigarette and looking nervously over her shoulder at him. He could smell her fear and it charged him.

He bought a burger, eyeballing the greasy cook across the counter who just shook his baldhead and went back to flipping patties on the grill. Charlie spat on the ground, made a lurching motion towards the girl who pulled back in fright. He laughed out loud and swaggered off, munching ravenously on the burger he had picked off the counter.

'I bet that fat bastard grease-monkey took a dump and wiped his ass on the bread buns,' Charlie thought to himself, a disgusted

look on his face, as he chewed gristle and stale bread hungrily. The burger tasted good, but it made him feel strange—almost altered his vision. He felt himself slide toward a certain degree of normalcy again—he didn't like it. He wiped his hands on his new jeans and headed toward the train station. He didn't look back once, as he left Portvale on the 4.30pm express to the city.

"Fuck that place and everyone in it," he said to himself.

"I ain't ever goin' back!"

After an hour's travel Charlie began to see the vast sprawl of the city appear on the horizon, as the train clambered towards its destination. His heart beat fast. First thing he was going to do was pull some serious cash and he knew exactly how to get it.

After stepping off the train, Charlie made his way to the nearest drug store—a small shop underneath the noisy highway overpass.

Storefront covered in multicolored advertisements and graffiti.

Deep alley on south side. Possible out. Possible dump.

Garbage bins stacked high on left.

Check cars.

Check.

Check humanoids.

Check.

Check motherfucker with deadly intentions.

Check.

The smell of carbon monoxide and fried food assailed his senses—the streets were filthy with litter. He felt choked by it for a brief moment. *'It isn't much different than where I've come from,'* he thought angrily.

He entered the pharmacy. The bell over the door jangled. There was some old broad stooped behind the counter. She looked to be aged about sixty years old, wearing a blue dress under a white lab coat and glasses on under a gray mop of hair. She waved and said something to him.

Charlie didn't hear her. He heard the other voices. The voices that told him how to hunt, kill, and maim.

"Where's the fuckin' razors?" he muttered as he scoured the shelves filled with various packets, cans, boxes and bottles until he spotted the disposable shavers next to the sanitary pads on the bottom shelf.

"Have you hurt yourself, young man?" The old woman's feeble voice asked from behind him.

"Huh?" he replied, slightly confused at the question.

"There's blood all down the back of your shirt. What have you done to yourself? Have you been …?" Her voice trailed off as the shiny blade sprang from Charlie's clenched fist. Her eyes suddenly enlarged in the thick lenses of her spectacles, a startled look on her face.

"What do you think you're …?"

Her gut made a queer fizzing sound as he pulled the knife out, black blood pumped out, gushing from the wound in her belly and splashing on the mint green linoleum. He pushed the blade back in, a little higher this time, and felt her life trembling on the end of his blade as the warm blood soaked his hand. He pumped the blade a few times and heard her gasping voice whisper, *"Please … please …"*

With a final twist of the knife, he stepped away from her as the old girl clutched her stomach then looked at her blood soaked hands, a shocked look on her wrinkled face as she took a few tentative steps backwards. She produced her right forefinger and tried to plug up the holes in her stomach with it—poking and prodding in grim desperation.

She slipped suddenly in her own mess and staggered sharply backwards into a Hallmark card stand, knocking season's greetings and happy birthdays every which way as she fell on her backside heavily, crashing into a glass shelf stacked with pill bottles and cough medicine. Charlie heard her bones break like dry twigs. A huge crash and the bottles spun into the air, clattering everywhere as they fell.

She lay on her back amongst the debris, gasping, with one frail arm behind her old back, the other bloody hand extended horizontally at her side. Almost as if on their own accord, the fingers crept around on the floor amongst the pill bottles and blood like a crippled crab. Charlie aimed his boot and stepped down heavily, grinding it forcefully for good measure, grinning as he heard the thin fingers crack and crush underfoot. The old bitch passed out with a gurgle. He picked up a pill bottle and poked it in her toothless mouth, took a clothes peg from a packet off the shelf and clipped it on her wrinkled nose, despite having a strong suspicion that she was already dead.

Charlie flipped the sign on the door over to 'Closed,' and locked it as he turned out the light. He stood at the window for a while, watching the nameless faces wander pass, back and forth. The train rumbled by on the tracks overhead as it began to rain.

In the back of the store he decided instead of shaving his head he'd dye it black. Finding a suitable hair-dye on the shelves he doused his scalp with the black dye, streaks running down his face like mascara tears, making his blue eyes seem all the more intense. He took off his bloody shirt and swapped it for a checked flannel shirt he found on a $10 rack in the store, a bit big but what the hell. He ripped the sleeves off to expose his youthful muscles.

There was only one hundred and twenty five dollars and eighty-five cents in the cash register, but after a thorough inspection of the old girl's corpse, he found a key on a neck chain beneath her bloody blouse. Under the coffee table in the back room, he found a small trap door in the floor and sure enough, there was a small safe hidden inside.

"Shit it's my lucky day," Charlie said out loud.

"There's gotta be at least five fuckin' grand in here!!"

Laughing, he greedily filled an old briefcase he found in a cupboard with the bundles of used notes. He was about to leave the store when he saw the magazine rack. He chose the filthiest smut rag he could find and went out the back of the store to whack off. When he finished, he felt strangely relaxed. He took another look out the window and saw the rain pelting down harder than ever—he didn't feel like leaving. In fact, he decided to stay the night—the old girl wasn't going to give him any trouble after all. He sat down with his back against the wall next to the Pharmacist's corpse, as a pool of urine mixed with blood beneath her, spread towards him. Charlie considered her lifeless body for a long slow moment and began to feel aroused.

'I might even cuddle up to her and give her a bit of the old

Charlie magic,' he joked to himself. He rubbed his groin and then punched himself in the face. He sat there banging his clenched fist on his knee. Then his fingers scrambled on the floor between his legs and he picked up the stiletto switchblade. He stared at the corpse bug-eyed, and then launched himself on to his knees as he simultaneously plunged the long sharp blade repeatedly into the head of the lifeless woman. Over and over and over again.

Charlie caught his breath and lowered the knife to the floor between his legs, his stabbing hand fatigued with effort. His chest heaved with the exertion; adrenaline coursed through his veins like electricity. He licked blood from his lips and ran his slick wet fingers through his hair. He smiled as he felt the warm damp front of his jeans where his discharged DNA now mixed with her blood.

Still breathing heavy with the pleasure and the exertion, he looked hungrily at all the medicine bottles strewn across the floor. Picking one up, he opened it and marveled at all the brightly colored pills. Grabbing a cola out of the fridge in the kitchen, he took a mouthful of the cool beverage along with a few of the pills. Hoping to relieve the pounding headache that had been nagging him since Portvale.

He stumbled around the store, blindly pulling items from the shelves, leaving a trail of bloody footprints behind him. He started feeling very light, almost as though he were weightless. Must be the pills, he deduced. With that thought, he swallowed the rest of the bottle and tuned the store radio on to a local rock station as he faded into a pharmaceutical coma.

8

"**O**pen your fuckin' eyes you son of a bitch!"

The slap rocked Charlie awake. Red and white spots of color exploded in front of his eyes. He slowly focused, his head spinning madly. Amongst a swarm of white doves in slow motion flight, he made out black uniforms, flashing red lights, and the dark look of murder in the blue eyes of the big city cop who had him by the throat. Ray Truman held him at arm's length as if disgusted by the sight of him.

"What's your name, punk?" he demanded.

Charlie's mind swam in a drug-induced haze. He heard himself answering the cop, confessing his name.

"Charlie Cunningham. What's yours, pig?"

Another slap rocked his head back.

"I'll ask the questions dipshit!' spat the cop.

"What's your father's name?"

Charlie hesitated, confused that he was actually talking to this muscle-bound gorilla in a uniform, let alone answering his questions. He felt very outside of himself. Almost as if he was watching himself in a spy movie, being interrogated by some agent from the KGB.

"What is your father's name, punk?" Ray asked again with emphasis.

Once again, Charlie heard his own voice echo in the distance, as if down the end of a bad phone connection.

"Errol. Errol Cunningham."

Ray smiled to himself and grabbed a handful of Charlie's dyed black hair, slamming the back of the boy's head into the side of the blood-spattered shop counter. Everything went white and Charlie felt sick, his head throbbed and his vision went askew. His face felt numb against the cold linoleum of the shop floor. He watched the cop's black boots stomp away from him in slow motion, pill bottles and other products spinning across the bloody linoleum as he walked through them. Charlie's world descended into darkness once again.

Ray Truman was well known in Portvale as a hard ass cop. An ex

Golden Gloves boxing champion at eighteen who could've turned pro, he had the world at his feet when he first became a beat cop and introduced Portvale's local criminal fraternity to the long end of his nightstick. Now, twenty years later he had lost none of his edge, in fact he was more hardened than ever. The amount of death and violence he'd witnessed in his long career had turned his heart to stone. He stood six-two and one-hundred and ten kilos of hard muscle, slick-backed black hair flecked with the first signs of gray and a pair of cold blue eyes. He'd been sweeping Portvale's streets of scum for two decades and he wasn't about to let a screw-up family like the Cunninghams taint his turf with their white-trash ways.

Ray had dealt with the Cunningham family previously. He had done his research way back when he first heard of their activities, as had his father before him. The Cunninghams moved into the neighborhood in the late seventies and Errol soon made himself known to the local precinct cops. On more than one occasion, officers visited the Cunningham residence after reports of domestic assault. After its transformation into a rooming house, the visits became more frequent as the residents came under scrutiny as well as the owners.

When the Cunningham family moved in, Artaud Avenue had been a fairly tidy but run-down section of Portvale in a suburb called Eden Park. Reasonably modern state housing mixed with turn-of-the-century examples of once-grand houses, had invariably degenerated into a working-class slum like the rest of the city. The only businesses that seemed to thrive, were the corner bars and the dealers that stood outside them, pouring bindles of cheap heroin and crack into cars pulled up to the sidewalk. Hookers paraded their wares up and down the Avenue like zombies, their vacant eyes searching the car windows that crawled pass for their next trick. A largely itinerant population of drifters rented dismal rooms at the Cunningham property by day and staggered through the night, from street corner to street corner, hustling their next fix.

It wasn't long before Ray was called to the large run-down brick residence and he knew, before he even stepped inside the front door, that this family would be trouble. The place reeked of bad energy. The back yard was littered with various car parts and hadn't been cleaned up since they'd taken occupancy. The trash bins at the back door over-flowed and cats darted about as they scavenged for scraps and rodents.

Ray had been working street patrols for six months—he'd been to a few domestic incidents in the Portvale precinct and had a feel for what to expect. He'd never met a couple like Errol and Vera Cunningham before but had heard about their rooming house down at the precinct station. It had a bad reputation as a hangout for low life, junkies, pimps and whores.

When Ray and his partner entered the rooming house and climbed the stairs to the owner's quarters, most of the residents on the ground floor evacuated as quickly as the two officers had arrived.

Ray kicked in the apartment door and found Errol, belt in hand, standing over Vera in the kitchen. Her bloodstained blouse was ripped open from the back and her shoulders were covered in purple welts where Errol had obviously been lashing her with the business end of the leather belt. Both of them turned in surprise as Ray and his partner entered the kitchen, pistols drawn.

"Step away from the woman," Ray commanded.

Errol just stood there, white t-shirt streaked with his wife's blood, his muscular arms twitching, his black pupils drilling into Ray's eyes, searching for weakness. Finding none, he tossed the bloodied belt on the kitchen table and crossed the kitchen to the fridge to get a beer.

"Get the fuck out of my house," Errol growled at the cops.

"Yeah, get the fuck outta here you pigs," screeched Vera, peering through her long matted hair with a swollen eye as she stood up, holding her blouse together and wiping blood off her hands on her skirt.

"We got a report there was a woman in trouble," said Ray's partner.

"Well fuck off, there's nuthin' to see here," said Vera.

"Yeah why doncha take a hike, copper?" suggested Errol as he took a swig on his beer and slung his free arm round Vera's scrawny shoulders as she hobbled to her bare feet. Ray noticed she winced and shook his head.

"You want to press charges ...?" asked Ray

"I told you before ..." Vera started.

"Yeah I know, 'get the fuck outta here,' right?" said Ray

"You got it pig. Take a hike!"

Ray holstered his revolver and turned to exit the squalid apartment.

"But ..." his young partner started to protest.

"Just leave it," Ray said, as they made their way back down the dimly lit stairway and out to the squad car. He lit a smoke and instructed his partner to wait with the car. The recruit shrugged and lit a smoke as Ray stuck his prominent jaw out, turned and headed down the side of the old house toward the back door once again.

Truman's nightstick caught Errol in the solar plexus, dropping him breathless to his knees. Vera grabbed a knife out of the over-flowing sink and rushed at Ray who promptly side-stepped and caught her across the back of her matted skull with a slap, driving her headlong into the wall. Ray turned to Errol who was attempting to rise to his feet and swung the police club overhead in a wide arc, straight across the back of Errol's exposed calf muscle.

"Fuckin' pig ..." Errol gasped as he choked back the pain, hands locked around his throbbing leg.

"Now that's no way to speak to your superior, Errol!" Ray joked, grabbing a handful of Errol's greasy black locks and yanking his head back so he was looking directly in his face. Errol struggled, trying to push the cop away but Ray just bought the club down across his flailing hands, a broad grin on his face as he did so.

"Look at me you fuck!" Ray spat, anger blazing in his eyes as he unclipped his holster and leveled his service revolver at Errol's sweating temple.

"If I hear another goddam peep out of you, you'll regret it. Ok?"

Errol moaned and weakly tried to spit in Ray's smiling face.

"You sure are one dumb fuck ain't ya?" Ray stopped smiling and forced Errol face down on the filthy floor, twisting his arms behind his back as he snapped handcuffs tightly on his bruised wrists. Ray gripped the chain that joined the cuffs and hauled Errol to his feet, simultaneously breaking Cunningham's wrist …

"*Fuuuuucccckk yoooouuu piggggg …*" Errol howled in pain, before he lapsed into unconsciousness.

9

Ray learnt more than one valuable lesson the day he met the Cunninghams. The most important being, if you're going to teach your perp a lesson, you have to read the genius in the hatred that drives you to unleash violence on a helpless man. In other words, if you are going to try and fool the law, hiding behind a badge, do not go to battle against people potentially smarter than your good self.

It wasn't Errol who was smarter than Ray, not by a long shot, but some smart-ass lawyer fresh out of Harvard, who took one look at Errol's broken wrist and an eyewitness statement and a wad of cash from Vera Cunningham, and that was all he needed to get Errol out on the street again.

Errol was in the can for only half a day before he was released without bail. Ray, however, would wind up on a two week suspension for 'use of unnecessary force' and a pending assault charge. Little did Ray know, but that mistake would cost two hookers their short lives in Errol's basement the night he was released, despite having a broken wrist.

Ray himself was first on the scene when the mutilated remains of the dead hookers were found in a dumpster behind the police precinct. The report came in anonymously and was directed to his attention. At first Truman didn't put two and two together, everyone thought it was a drug deal gone bad or a pimp dishing out some rough justice to his bitches. It was only after more bodies were found that Truman realized the two hookers were the first in a long string of unsolved murders that would haunt him for years to come.

It was only with the passage of time and obsessive investigative work that eventually lead Ray to place Errol Cunningham at the top of his list of suspects. Despite his suspicions, Truman lacked conclusive evidence to get Cunningham off the streets. As his suspicions grew, he realized that the death of the first two hookers coincided exactly with Errol's release date from custody, after Ray had arrested him and broken the dirt-bag's wrist. He knew Errol was laughing at him. Taunting him.

One thing Ray did know for sure was that he wouldn't make the same mistake twice. Scum like Errol Cunningham shouldn't walk the streets. When Ray was a boy, his own father who had served as a police officer, warned him about the Cunninghams. Truman Senior painted a picture of the devil stalking the mean streets of Portvale, of all things evil, a family called 'The Cunninghams' and now Ray was battling the next generation—continuing the Truman crusade.

Cunningham could wait. Ray never forgot and he was damn sure that piece of shit would either die in jail or breathe his last breath while looking into Ray's eyes. He wanted to be the last thing that Cunningham saw before he wiped him off the streets of Portvale, forever.

After his suspension, Truman knew he would have to play it safe with any investigation concerning the Cunningham family. He had read the historic case files and it was obvious that Errol had someone on the inside with their back against the wall. There was too much immunity for the family; too many occasions where warrants were requested and subsequently denied. There was talk in the locker room and on the street that photos of some high-ups were in the wrong hands and were withheld only in exchange for protection and silence. The story goes that Errol had hired a private investigator to monitor the DA and a handful of the judges who worked the Portvale criminal referrals in the Municipal courthouse. His endeavours had paid off when the PI snapped pictures of at least two of the judges and the DA in separate compromising situations with local call-girls.

Apparently, the photos of the judges and the DA in the company of sex workers had not been enough for Errol, despite the fact that all of the officials were married and had good reason to conceal their nocturnal activities. He pursued them relentlessly with the intensity of a federal shakedown, until he hit pay dirt. With video footage of each individual in various compromising and unmistakeable acts, which included footage of graphic acts of BDSM and paedophilia, Errol had the means to blackmail his way out of any legal situation in Portvale he might find himself in.

After Truman made detective he himself had numerous requests for search warrants denied on grounds of insufficient evidence, despite having obvious enough reasons to search the Cunningham premises. This was proof enough for Ray there must've been truth in the rumours, to allow the Cunningham's this certain carte blanche over the years. So Truman did what he could do but frequently bent the rules with necessity and grim determination. He planted eyes and ears inside the rooming house while it was still in operation as a business. Five informants had resided at the Artaud Avenue property and had reported on happenings there.

Most of the feedback suggested that Errol engaged in wild sex parties in the basement of the large building. Parades of misfits and hookers entered the building and the screams of raucous sex and drunken arguments filled the nights. It was not so much what these drug-riddled junkies and crack bums said to Ray, down dark alleys in the morning hours, in exchange for immunity from prosecution. It was what happened to them after they talked that confirmed Truman's suspicions.

Of the five informants he used, not one returned alive from the rooming house to walk the Portvale streets again. Two overdosed and the other three disappeared without a trace. Ray was the only one who missed them. It seemed he was the only one who believed the Cunninghams were a sick bunch of perverted killers. Hookers were murdered every day in Portvale and across every major city in the world—who gave a fuck? Who cared if these dregs of society were removed from the face of the earth? Deep down, Ray did. None of his colleagues at the precinct house knew Ray's mother had raised him on her own after his father disappeared and that she'd used whatever means necessary to put food on the table.

Over the years, Ray had infrequently used the local services of the more upmarket hookers to satisfy his own needs. He'd even had a girlfriend for six months when he was younger who sold herself for cash. So Ray knew what they went through and he cared, he fucking cared a lot. He wanted those Cunningham sickos to pay for what they had done to the local down-and-outs. He wanted them to pay dearly for their arrogant criminality. Most of all he wanted them to pay, for having the audacity to think they could shit in his backyard without any retribution or penalty.

Errol had his own plans for Ray. He sat at the kitchen table nursing a bottle of vodka and his broken wrist as he imagined Ray's family and what they might look like dead. He had heard his Pa talk about the Truman family in the past and that Ray's father had been a cop in his Pa's day. Errol knew that Ray had a beef with him and he wanted to find out why. He'd been careful with his fun and games but he also knew he was guilty of liking the fear he imparted to those around him. He knew that he had a reputation on the street. Errol knew exactly what kind of beast he was himself and he knew that was public knowledge. He just didn't give a fuck. But he didn't know Ray Truman from shit. Errol put the boys on the street that night to go and talk with the pimps and dealers down on Dockside Avenue. If anyone knew anything about that pig Ray Truman, the boys would find out. And find out they did.

The boys discovered was that Ray's father had been investigating Errol's father in relation to a string of murders, when he had mysteriously disappeared. With this new information it suddenly became all too apparent why Truman was hot for Cunningham blood. It also revealed that the Cunningham family bloodlust had its origins deep in the past. Charlie and Caleb quietly gave the news to Errol who took it to the basement with him. The boys watched him go, his fists clenching spasmodically as he descended the steps into the dark. Both boys' brains churned with the new knowledge regarding the blood-related origins of their own dark natures.

From all accounts, Ray Truman hit the streets hard when he was a young recruit. He'd served his rookie years in some of the toughest districts of the city before ending up in Portvale, earning a well-deserved reputation as a hard-man who couldn't be fucked with. He didn't take bribes, he didn't bow down to the mob or suck up to the gang-bangers on the west-side, he didn't step back from a fight and he certainly didn't care for the likes of the Cunninghams. He'd come from a family of cops in the mid-west. Seeking more of a challenge than country policing, Ray's father had packed up his family and moved to the south-side borough of Kings, just north of Eden Park. Truman prided himself on his blue-collar background but he had his inevitable share of run-ins with the law growing up and running the mean-streets of a gang-plagued neighborhood. He could've gone bad, but he had the good fortune of being mentored by a local hard-ass cop turned boxing coach named O'Malley, who ran a youth club for juvenile delinquents.

Soon, O'Malley had Truman punching way above his weight and he began winning fight-night trophies and cash awards, which he took home to his Mother. Truman won a national Golden-gloves prize for his age and weight class the day after his sixteenth birthday. He could've turned pro but instead won a scholarship to a military academy, graduating with honors three years later and enlisting with the city PD cadet program.

Truman's old man had been a cop all his life but had disappeared in the summer of '72 when Ray was a tender fifteen years old. After the disappearance of his father, Ray lived with his domineering mother who tended to treat her only son harshly but with affection. His father's disappearance affected his mother badly and as the bills mounted up she turned to the bottle and the streets, turning tricks to pay the rent and feed her son and her growing dependence on alcohol and drugs. As the years rolled by and still no word of his father's whereabouts, Ray responded to her smothering ways by throwing himself into activities outside of the house but always continued to support her until her death in 1986. She was the apparent victim of an unsolved hit-and-run accident on a pedestrian crossing in broad daylight. Ray suffered hard for the loss of his mother and grew bitter, blaming one of his many arrests for her death. Some of Ray's colleagues began to suspect that he was suffering from paranoia.

Despite his personality, he had carved his way through the ranks, excelling in his work with one of the highest arrest records in the district. The only blemish on his otherwise impeccable work history was the disciplinary hearing related to Errol Cunningham's broken wrist and the counter assault charge that was subsequently overturned, when the charges against Cunningham were dismissed. This indiscretion troubled Ray and fanned the flames of a burning hatred in his heart for the Cunningham family. Coupled with the bad history between his father and Errol's own, Ray's hate manifested itself in a seething rage that soon developed into full-blown obsession.

II
It's All Relative

There will be time, there will be time
To prepare a face to meet the faces that you meet;
There will be time to murder and create ...

T.S. Eliot, 'the Love Song of J Alfred Prufrock'

Cruel with guilt, and daring with despair,
the midnight murderer bursts the faithless bar;
invades the sacred hour of silent rest and leaves, unseen,
a dagger in your breast.

Samuel Johnson (1709-1784).

10

When Charlie appeared before the court, resplendent with shaved eyebrows and head, his legal aid attorney pleaded that the psychiatric evaluation was evidence enough of her client's diminished responsibility. Charlie had just shaved his skull with a contraband item he had also been charged with being in possession of. Someone had mixed up the police report and had stated that Charlie was under the influence of narcotics before the attack. These things, combined with Charlie's bizarre courtroom appearance, his lawyer's continual pleas of mitigating psychological circumstances and dysfunctional family life, rolled the judge over for a twenty-year stretch. Charlie got off lightly as the usual term of imprisonment for murder one was a mandatory life sentence.

They didn't snag him for the factory job and a few other unforgettable events of necessity. Charlie smiled and felt somewhat sanctified at his perceived deception. This is where his idea of 'the Eternal Now' kicked in, becoming a central ethos to his personal version of a pilgrim's life.

The fact that the judge had received the best sex of his life with his secretary in the cleaning closet, two hours before court opened for trial, probably helped things a long a bit that day as well. He was in a damn charitable mood that day when he handed down a twenty-year term to my brother.

Charlie, he didn't give a damn.

Three years of the sentence were to be served in one of the country's toughest psychiatric facilities for young offenders. Charlie laughed as the judge read the sentence to the court. Not really hearing the rest of his sentence, he began rolling his eyes wildly and proclaiming in his most prophetic voice, his fists shaking with his handcuffs, that he "would see them all one day in hell." As the remand guards led him from the courtroom, Charlie swore he heard the judge say, "Get that crazy bastard out of my sight!"

Some of the worst young murderers, rapists, child molesters, and violent offenders were housed alongside Charlie, until he was transferred into the general adult population of a medium-security prison called Breakhouse Bay Penitentiary, situated on a nearby island in the harbor. One of his transfer conditions was that he attended regular counseling sessions and mandatory doses of psychiatric medication administered accordingly. Charlie saw this as an opportunity, not only to improve himself, but to gain early parole. Some days he battled with this thought, unable to kick-start his conscience and unsure as to whether he actually wanted to be released.

He didn't mind being inside. He didn't have to work, didn't need to talk to anyone. If he just did what the pigs expected of him, he was left alone. After a couple of years, the screws didn't even bother giving him his monthly shot of anti-psychotics. He was glad when they stopped that. He began to lose weight and slowly slipped back into a vivid world governed solely by his imagination. The counseling sessions had slipped by the wayside a year before. Charlie had managed to convince the doctors of his sanity and the evolution of his conscience. I, on the other hand, still had a hard time convincing the people around me that I was sane. I was spinning off on colors and killer clowns from outer-fucking-space along with a morbid obsession with all things death-related. I guess I had a death wish like my brother.

To celebrate his first month off the sedatives, Charlie shaved his head and eyebrows close to the bone in the fashion of his first court appearance. We both had shaved heads and were the same height, but there the similarities ceased in my mind. As his madness consumed him, it was like watching a birth in a sense. Out of the madness and violence that was my brother's life, a monster emerged. Except this monster was my brother and now *I* was even wary of him—his eyes were like black obsidian. I could see no whites to his eyes. I was having my own mental-health issues with regular hallucinations and 'color flashes,' seeing colors of every description and yet I still couldn't see any white in those eyes of his, only hate and the reptilian look of a cold-blooded predator determined to survive and kill at any cost.

Mind you, I had the same look in my eyes on dark nights in front of the cracked bathroom mirror. However, Charlie had physically changed to the point that we would no longer be easily mistaken for twin brothers. Ever since he began his stretch, he'd made full use of the gym facilities at both institutions. He had bulked up in the joint from all the weights he'd been lifting. He was physically quite a lot bigger than me now. He had muscles in his shit, but not in the same way as those posers at the downtown gym. Shit, he'd be killing *them* soon enough when he was released. I wouldn't like to fuck with him. He was a well-oiled killer, lubed and ready to go at the drop of a hat.

His muscles weren't the only thing he'd been working out. Charlie had started to develop some disturbing ideas that reflected his depressive psychotic state, more so than usual since he had been locked away. During one of my infrequent visits, we somehow got around to the topic of Capital Punishment. I asked my brother through the bulletproof glass screen, "Aren't you worried about the death penalty, bro?" He just turned to me and said emphatically, "Death means nothing to someone who wants to die."

He started to look anxious and began mumbling incoherently. His eyes rolled in his head and the veins on his arms stood out as he strained against his shackles. I knew he was having one of his 'attacks' and watched with the interest of an observer as his symptoms revealed the sickness of his mind.

He raised himself from his seat as if to leave but instead stood there in his black prison t-shirt, orange jumpsuit rolled halfway down and tied round his waist, shaved head cocked to one side, the smooth flesh of his scarred face glistening under the fluorescent lights, his manacled tattooed arms flexing with muscle hard as granite. A Chinese dragon curled around his right wrist, the claws digging deep into Charlie's arm, inked blood run down his forearm to a skull on his wrist. I noticed he had the same on his other limb.

"How the fuck are ya?" he said suddenly, as if greeting me for the first time. His demeanor had changed slightly and he seemed as if he was back to his old self again as he bent forward and seated himself once again, behind the glass partition.

I only had to talk to him to know that Charlie was in the grips of a very deep and dark psychosis. His mind was wandering off in tangents, reflected in the way his speech danced from one subject to the next. All the while, his eyes darted around the confines of the visitors' room as if searching for an escape. I didn't have the heart to tell the guard standing behind Charlie, that his life was possibly in danger of being snuffed out at any moment. I didn't want to give him the impression that I actually gave a fuck whether or not my brother ripped him a new asshole or not. I studied Charlie carefully as he seemed to zone out again. I watched the rise and fall of his chest as his breathing relaxed after a moment and he settled back into his chair as he appeared to gather his thoughts and talk clearly again.

I asked Charlie about his routine and what he did with his days. He gave me a history of what he did inside. He told me about how, in his formative years of corrective training, he had worked himself into an almost religious daily routine of exercise that consisted of endless sit-ups, push-ups, and shadow boxing in his cell and weights when he was allowed out in the yard. Within the first year he bulked up, soon he had muscles in his shit. No one fucked with Charlie and he continued this exercise regime up to the last time I ever saw him.

A few had tried to mess with him in the past however. One inmate particularly—'Terror,' a hulking two hundred and forty pound meat axe with a shaved pink skull, black pig eyes and a hair-lip—complete with a crudely tattooed swastika on his forehead and body odor that was smelt before he was seen. As soon as Charlie hit general population, the creep started to target him.

Terror tried to talk Charlie into joining the 'Skins.' His small mind figured that because Charlie looked like a skinhead, that he was one or wanted to be one. He didn't realize that Charlie had two completely different reasons for going topless. One—he hated his brown hair and hair dye was at a premium in the can, and two—he didn't like hair in his eyes when he was fighting.

Terror would heave his bulk past Charlie and shout "Heil Hitler!" His fat tattooed pink arm outstretched before him in a Nazi salute. Charlie would just stare vacantly at him, visibly disdainful. Terror would slouch off muttering under his breath as his crew cast oily glares at Charlie as they scurried off to the block latrines, or wherever it was rats like them hung out.

11

One inevitable day in the lunch hall, as Charlie ate his daily slop at one of the long tables, Terror and three of his moronic devotees parked themselves down right next to him. They all grinned inanely and chuckled like hyenas.

"Are you too good for your white brothers, bitch?" asked Terror, leaning forward in expectation of an answer or a scared retreat. Charlie just kept eating, shoveling his food in with the plastic spoon provided, despite the stinking breath of the fat pig crowding his vision in front of him.

"I asked you a fuckin' question, you punk-ass faggot. You a Jew nigger lover or somethin', huh?" Terror asked again, leaning back and grinning at his baldhead pals. Charlie looked up, bored with the scenario confronting him.

"I don't discriminate. I hate everyone—especially you, you fat brainless piece of shit," said Charlie, before returning to his lunch. Terror's eyes bulged. His face grew ten shades of red, his cheeks puffed ...

"Fuckin' kill him," he screamed.

Fabian, the anorexic skinhead to Charlie's immediate right smiled a toothless ugly smile and flashed something shiny across the side of Charlie's face. Warm blood spurted across the table in an arc ...

"I got him Terror!!" squealed Fabian with glee, dancing around the table with the razor blade still gripped between his thumb and forefinger. Charlie put his fingers to the gaping wound that extended from his forehead to his jaw-line. He sized up his opponents across the table, focusing his gaze on Terror, as he methodically licked the blood off his fingers. Charlie reached across in one swift motion, grabbed Terror by the shirtfront and pulled the obese skinhead towards him sharply, simultaneously driving his plastic dinner spoon into Terror's left eye socket with all his strength. The place exploded in a flurry of blood and violence.

Eight guards finally beat and wrestled Charlie to the hole where he remained in solitary confinement until he was sentenced for his latest violent acts. The warden decided he'd had enough of Charlie and the prison committee decided to ship him out to the Saint Michael Hospital for the Criminally Insane. Luckily, the 'hospital' was in Kings, a middle-class suburb situated just before the North Shore Bridge, so visiting wasn't a problem. When he was first admitted, I couldn't see him for a while as they immediately doped him with sedatives and anti-psychotics for the first two months of his new sentence. Meanwhile, back in the prison where Charlie had come from, Terror became known as 'Cyclops' and soon became a muscle-bound Muslim's bitch. Fabian spent the rest of his sentence in the prison infirmary on a life support machine that eventually had to be switched off for 'humane reasons.'

With the help of the orderlies at the institution and their loose-lipped gossip about Charlie's condition, word spread and he soon earned a new nick-name—'Scar.' The first six months alone in his cell weren't easy and Charlie retreated to the boundaries of his sanity. He sang nursery rhymes he didn't even know he knew. He scratched great furrows into his skin with his ragged fingernails and paced the narrow confines of his cell bare-assed. The staff said he looked more like an insane leopard, his muscular body covered in bloody scabs. It would take three of the strongest guards to secure Charlie's limbs while the doctor administered a syringe full of sedatives and anti-psychotic medication. When this failed to placate his behavior he was given Electro-shock Therapy, strapped to his bed, a leather belt in his mouth, and electrodes on his temples as the doctor wound the dial until Charlie's body arced and bounced on the bed.

After a while, they stopped the ECT treatment and resumed his medication. They still kept him confined to his cell where he would bathe and eat his food and as the drugs did their work, he seemed to grow calmer and his behavior slowly normalized. Once over his initial reaction to the twenty-four-hour confines of his small cell, he adapted quickly to his surroundings and managed to teach himself a new way of thinking. He spent the remainder of his time in solitary, learning to read properly with the help of the hospital optometrist who provided him with his first pair of contact lenses—fully state-funded and free of charge of course. He was even able to choose the color he wanted. He chose black of course, just like his idol Richard Ramirez.

The doctors decided to let him mix with the other patients and inmates after six months of intensive psychiatric treatment. Charlie used his new freedom to explore the library and get his thoughts together. Soon he had read all of the magazines in the library and after another year had managed to read all the modern classics by authors such as James Joyce, Kafka, Chekov, Camus, and Hemingway to name a few. He thought most of them were full of shit. A bunch of pussies.

He thought that Dostoyevsky stood out from the others as someone who read as though he knew what he was talking about, especially when it came to murder. Charlie began to have enough confidence in his own abilities to begin a daily journal, subsequently a whole new world opened up for him. He began keeping a diary to record his thoughts and to make sense of the world he inhabited. Essentially, Charlie had all the ingredients for a new philosophy, which would dictate the path he would follow once released.

12

After his morning routine of one hundred and fifty press-ups and an equal number of sit-ups, Charlie would sit naked on his bunk—his hands trembling with anticipation and physical exertion—while he reread *Crime and Punishment* from where he had left off the previous night. He identified with the character of Raskolnikov but thought that he was essentially a weak individual. He knew that he himself was superior, in that he didn't have the same problem with his conscience that Raskolnikov's character did.

Charlie liked the instinctual driven nature of Raskolnikov and felt that he learned a lot about avoiding capture, thanks to Dostoyevsky's thorough analysis of the crime of murder committed by his protagonist. Charlie swore the author must have killed before to write with such intimate knowledge of the emotions befitting such a crime. The clarity of experience shone like light on the bloody hands of the killer.

Charlie did not however have the same clarity of vision when recalling his own crimes. Partly due to the strong medication and because of a well-developed lack of conscience, to him they were nothing more than inconveniences or mistakes, whilst others had been premeditated attempts to secure good shelter, food and ready access to the best free gym in the state.

A conscience was something he had yet to acquire. Even if possible, it was not something Charlie was willing to encourage while being a guest of the state (a conscience that is). Regret or guilt were emotions he could not afford to have in the joint.

After Charlie had settled into the routine of his new life at Saint Michaels' and had earned his visiting privileges, I began to visit occasionally. I noticed the change in him as the months went by, as he began to confide in me his philosophies about life. He told me what it was like to be locked up 24/7 and how most of his trials and tribulations in solitary confinement were in coming to terms with who he had become.

Most of the issues he had were with himself—the rest were with Pa. Ma seemed to remain inconsequential to him, at least consciously. In fact, he didn't even seem to consider any aspect of her existence—the mere thought of being born turned his stomach inside out. He tried not to think about it, but when the library ran dry and all that was left was the detritus, his imagination numbed itself in a trance-like daze or spun off in kaleidoscopic tangents.

The concept of birth both repulsed and intrigued him, as did death. Sometimes he thought death would be a welcome reprieve from the pointlessness of everything, if not for any other reason than to stem the flow of his thoughts and the perpetual odor of ammonia and urine.

Charlie's main problem was his narcissistic worldview. Considering his existence to date had consisted of a series of violent tragedies—by anyone else's standards, existentialism was a philosophical viewpoint that would have been best left uncovered by Charlie.

Charlie had come to terms with his existence much as I had with mine. The major difference was that I had the ability to explore my world from a more unfettered viewpoint. I had freedom of movement in my world and the possibility of social connections and interactions. I could satisfy my desires whenever I chose. He of course had no hope of any type of relationship with a woman, unless he managed to seduce a psychiatrist or a visitor. The obvious differences in our lives had become apparent to the point that a feeling of being split from each other ensued. While I knew that we would always have a special connection as twin siblings, my realization that Charlie was a different animal from myself forced me to sever my emotional bonds with him.

Knowing that Charlie's world had separated itself from my own, I stepped into my own reality with a newfound independence. I started to consider the possibility that a proper relationship with a living, breathing female, might not be beyond my grasp. I had met someone in the neighborhood but there was no way in hell I would tell Charlie about that while he was inside.

III
Love Lies Bleeding

*"Murder is born of love,
and love attains the greatest intensity in murder"*

Octave Mirbeau

13

She moved in to the house across the road a year ago. I found it hard not to notice her: she was hot. Damn hot! She had a great body and a tough attitude that she wore with obvious pride. She snapped me looking at her from the top window of our house. The other kids on the street called our house 'the Dead Zone' but she didn't seem to mind that I lived there. In fact, after making eye contact with each other she began to spend more time out the front of her house, so I could see her in her cut-off denims and tight t-shirts.

As I came and went from the house, I would catch her checking me out, but just stare blankly back at her with dead eyes. I don't know what she saw in me, I wore old jeans and black t-shirts most of the time along with a shaved skull. She looked like she'd been around but looked sweet nonetheless. I began to think about her often and knew her appearance belied a beauty that she held deep inside. From the first time that I really saw her, I wanted her.

With her short denim skirts and constant smoking of her stolen cigarettes in the front yard, I knew she was trying to catch my eye. She would pretend I wasn't there but would cast sly glances as I walked by or crossed the avenue. By this time, I had become obsessed with Lucille and knew I had to talk to her. When I thought of her during the day, my visions would alternate between saintly images of her resplendent in the bright light of a divine innocence, to staccato snapshots of her naked corpse in various stages of dismemberment.

I seized the opportunity the next time I saw her sitting on the porch. I crossed the road and walked in front of Lucille's house to get a better look at her. We looked at each other briefly, her sitting on the steps smoking a cigarette, me walking past trying to look casual. I paused, considering whether to approach her but I knew that I didn't need to. She was interested and I knew that it was only a short matter of time before she would come to me.

Lucille thought about me often from that point. She needed to think for a while about what my obvious interest held for her. She knew I was as interested as she was, but she also knew she had issues that would conspire against her in any normal relationship she might wish to pursue. Luckily, she knew little of my own issues or she might just have run in the opposite direction, if she knew what was good for her.

She told me later that her crack-whore mother warned her to stay away from me.

"Fucking skinheads. They're all the same those losers!" she spat at her daughter.

"You stay away from him. He's a fucking jailbird—just like his old man and his brother!" When her mother ordered her to stay away, Lucille knew she had to meet me even if only to spite her whore of a mother.

She sat smoking a cigarette on the porch steps. Lucille took a drag and continued to dream about Caleb through the fresh blue smoke. The veranda peeled dull blue paint in the heat. The remains of the sun felt good and warm on her skin, her white t-shirt flapped languidly in the late afternoon breeze. At the end of her ragged jeans her small bare feet breathed freely in the cool air, feeling the worn grain of the wooden step. She flipped the cap on her steel lighter, tapping her feet on the top step to a silent beat, a Ramones tune playing in her head. She caressed the lighter. The flame, as if from her fingers, danced in the whispering air.

Lucille stared into the flame. White spots burst around the flickering light. She ran her fingers across the flame, the heat numbing the pads of her fingers as they played in the fire. She thought about Caleb until she tired of her own weak sentiments. She knew that the attraction had been merely taboo at first. He was everything her mother hated in a man, he had rebel written all over him but there was something else that made Lucille think about him a lot lately. More than mere fancy, somehow there was a dark mystery attached to Caleb Cunningham, a deep melancholy that echoed her own sad life. She wanted to know if his secrets were as bad as hers.

Lucille tired of her thoughts as the flame from her lighter began to consume her senses. She yawned and tugged her sneakers on, lighting another cigarette as she measured the sun's slow descent towards the horizon. The night called to Lucille as she entered the house and made her way upstairs to her bedroom.

She stood in front of her cracked bedroom mirror, zipped up her black nylon parka and pulled a red baseball cap low over her pretty eyes. Her clothes were camouflage as much as protection against the cold of the coming night. Dogs began to bark across the neighborhood and the noise of the vehicles passing outside seemed to grow louder as darkness settled on Eden Park. Turning the light off, she looked out her bedroom window, as a bus slid past, half-lit against the twilight—the passengers inside sat rigid, faces forward, vacant eyes—floating along like dead leaves on a breeze until home again.

Sitting on the corner of her single bed, Lucille lit another smoke. The light from the flame glowed orange white in her stony gaze, as she watched the smoke drift out her bedroom window. She spat out the window, closed it and checked her pockets before closing her bedroom door behind her and switching on the yellow hall light.

The house stank of meat and grease—flies broke away from the walls and dirty dishes in the sink as she entered the small kitchenette off the hallway at the bottom of the stairs. She opened the fridge— last beer left. A white spark then darkness, the bulb blew—she fumbled in the empty rank fridge for the beverage and left the house. The screen door snapped at her heels as she sucked down a mouthful of beer and headed on into the musky night, slamming the chain-link gate behind her.

She thought about her father for a brief minute, he wouldn't be home again—lost somewhere in the desert between then and now. Her mother might be home tonight, if she didn't score; at least she didn't bring her tricks home anymore. She figured the old bitch had probably realized it was easier to let them do her in the alley behind the bar—less of a walk to get the next drink from another trick.

'Fuck 'em both,' she thought in disgust.

Lucille wanted them both very dead.

She was tempted to burn the house to the ground but instead, she swallowed her rage and walked into the night, just like she usually did when she needed to cool down.

Outside the burger-bar on Main Street, moths beat themselves to death on the popping fluorescent lights under the street cover. The burger tasted good. Lucille's thin stomach moaned with gratitude as she licked her fingers. Another smoke. Walking again. Damn, she needed some cash. She'd just spent her last loose change. A plane rumbled overhead—ominous, its undercarriage low and visible, wings blinking red and green against the black night sky, then gone. She lit another smoke with the butt of the last and kept walking, images flashing faster in her brain. Her mother, her haggard face white and wrinkled blood-red lips, charcoal dead eyes, bleached blond dry hair, soulless posture. A grainy photographic image of her father, black and white, long beard, shaved head, jailhouse tattoos, straddled on a clapped out motorcycle. Fire. Always fire licking the edges of everything—the houses the moon, cars, windows, trees, fences, people ...

A few blocks more and she found what she was looking for. It was perfect. People moved inside the white house. A family scene. Steaming dinner on the table. All smiles and throwback head laughter. Man cuts the meat. Mother hair buns, blue apron, dishing out the sliced pink roast. Plump blond children squeal, banging the table with fisted knives and forks ...

Lucille stood hypnotized, rooted to the spot. Her face dissected in the reflection of the quarter windowpane. It was like these people were from another world. She didn't even know people like this lived in Portvale, let alone Eden Park. She didn't know how long she stood there, watching, trembling—mind blank. Her calloused thumb obsessively flicked the flint on her lighter. The woman appeared in the window, a laugh on her red lips, head turned, looking back over shoulder, as she drew the curtains across her large apron encased breasts.

Lucille snapped out of her trance. It was like she woke up, but was outside of herself. There was no color. It was like being in one of those old black and white movies that were on TV late at night. She watched herself walk around the corner of the west wall and stand before the half open bedroom window, the linen curtain slowly flapping in the breeze against the white window sill. She closed her eyes and dreamed a dream, flicking her cigarette lighter obsessively as flames danced in her brain.

Lucille kicked the gate open and walked up the steps to the dark porch. Her mother wasn't home as usual. She sat on the top step and looked across the road at the Cunningham place but there were no signs of life. She looked up the avenue from where she had just come. She caught her breath as a cat suddenly howled for sex over the neighbor's fence. She laughed to herself and turned her attention back toward the dark avenue as a car slid its way up the empty street, cruising for whores.

In the distance, a siren started to peel itself out of the black night. Lucille lit a smoke and took a drag, holding the cigarette up and watching the red ember glow as it took to the thin cigarette paper—her other hand cupped the damp urge in her torn jeans. She thought about Caleb.

An orange glow broke out in the distance, about a kilometer north, above the black silhouettes of the houses and industrial buildings on the horizon. White smoke flowered from the horizontal half-moon of the fire, tapering up, drifting slowly into the black still night.

Lucille's eyes glazed as she flicked the smoldering cigarette butt into the dead flowers next to the porch. Her breath quickening as her hand worked against herself—the siren now multiplied, screaming. Tumbling red lights danced frenetically towards the fire. Blazing cinders spread like small red stars high into the warm night sky. Yellow smoke billowed into the blackness, hanging heavy in the sky, framed between the porch banisters.

All Lucille heard was her heart beating, blood pumping like a drum in her head. She thought of Caleb and smiled, wondering what he was doing, whether he had seen the fire. She thought of the flames again, rising from the house where she had lit the curtains as they flapped lazily in the breeze, just before she came.

14

The day after Lucille set the fire I was going about my business as usual, tidying the house and doing chores upstairs, when I looked down from the window and saw her standing at the front fence. I watched her for a minute as she paced up and down smoking the last of her cigarette, she flicked the butt into the street and adjusted her bra-straps beneath her t-shirt, unaware that I was staring down at her. Without really comprehending what I was doing, I found myself hurrying down the stairs and outside via the back door and down the side of the house. I knew before I reached the gate that Lucille was standing on the other side waiting for me. I opened the gate and there she was, her blue eyes burning into mine, her full lips moist and hungry, she hesitated for a brief second and stepped towards me.

We melted into each other, standing there at the entrance to the house, embraced in a kiss full of passionate lust. I shut the gate with my boot and pulled her inside and towards the garage. My mind ticked over with each passing second. It was obvious she wanted me as much as I wanted her. I led her to the rear of the garage and we went inside. I thought about the pictures on my walls and it suddenly occurred to me that I would probably have to kill her. Nonetheless, I wanted her bad enough to not care about whether my room would shock her. As it turned out, she thought the loft was 'cool' and we 'made love' many times that night. My left hand gripped the handle of my Buck knife underneath the pillow as we furiously expressed our desire for each other until we collapsed, exhausted, yet satisfied for completely different reasons.

As we lay next to each other in bed that night, she asked me if I had seen the fire. I replied that I hadn't and as she started to tell me about her firebug tendencies, I knew I had made a mistake. Not because she was an arsonist; shit, I was a killer. I was more pissed off at letting my heart direct my actions; more specifically, in getting involved with anyone who could potentially be a threat to my grand plans. I couldn't trust anyone with my dark secrets and as she poured out years of tormented angst, I began to feel a slight distaste for her pitiful existence. I began to feel split in two from that point on—the allure of her sweet young body was great, as was my urge to kill her. As we lay next to each other I envisaged my hands wrapped around her smooth neck, squeezing hard, her eyes bulging with surprise, so close I could see the small blood vessels burst in her retinas.

But as she began to talk, I found myself surprised by my interest in her words. I found myself willingly being led by someone else's life and felt like I was standing on the edge of a gaping crevice in the ground. My skin felt taut as if stretched as she described her family life and what she thought made her want to light fires. I felt myself teetering on the brink of dark unfamiliar territory and I knew she completely trusted me, as I knew that was the same emotion I felt as well. I wanted to trust her on some level. 'Trust,' that was the word that kept coming to mind, as I tried to analyze my response to human emotion on some sort of logical grounds. I couldn't quite grasp the concept I had invented for myself, on any level.

And so it began, this new feeling unlike any other that I had ever experienced. I knew it wasn't 'love' but something more akin to 'like.' I had never had a 'real' girlfriend before Lucille and I knew that any relationship I entered into would be fraught with problems. I thought about the literature I had read about people like me and began to realize that I was not necessarily cut from the same cloth. In that first hot flash of desire I came as close to a sense of normalcy as I imagined it. Other players co-existed with their wives and children, pretending that their outer image was who they were, because they could act. I didn't want to pretend I was something I wasn't. I didn't want a partner, in love or crime. But I did have regrets at that point. I regretted that I couldn't turn back time and take back all the things I'd done, so that I could live without the feral paranoia that choked my brain and perhaps live a life like all the other poor slobs polluting the suburbs. Sure, I had regrets but I had learned to live with them thanks largely due to a little think called a 'lack of conscience.' Lucille would do as a nice distraction and allow me to see how good my own acting skills were but I knew our brief union could only end in one of two ways. That is, with her alive, or dead.

We only lasted a month but it was real and it scared the hell out of me. My bravado wavered when I found my heart for the first time. The feeling confused the hell out of me as I mistook it for a fit of conscience. Of which I have told you—I do not get! It was the biggest crazy human emotion of all time ... Anyway, I told you—I don't like it and it has to stop. But still a month passed and we saw each other every couple of days. I think for both of us that was something of a world record. It was like we needed a day to recover from the day before, spent with each other. A weird suspicious love, I felt—but love, nonetheless. I knew I would have to reveal my other sides to her as she had already shot a few "who are you?" questions at me.

Despite my abhorrent slip of emotion, I had to get her out of my life and the truth was possibly the best available option. The truth was I didn't have to wait much longer as my state-of-mind decided that it was all too much and needed a shut-down. The first sign that something was not right was when I became aware of my paranoia regarding Lucille, as I considered her potential as a perfect underground federal narc. Shifts in time and space were next and the black shadows of the day became all the more blacker. Things came forth from the shadows. Evil, bad things and they screamed at me until I found myself in the dark light of the garage with a razor in one hand, my genitals in the other, and Lucille waiting for me in bed in the loft above. I fought with myself and managed to harness my urge, centering it in my heaving chest. I slowed my breath and swallowed my exhalations until my head spun. I took a couple of breaths and staggered back up the steps to the loft, pausing briefly before I stumbled through the loft-door and ended our relationship. A brilliantly insane plan, totally organic.

I felt my senses corrode with each gasping breath, as my ribs seemed to shrink in my chest, crushing my lungs and heart, forcing me to gasp sharply. I glimpsed the slight look of disgust apparent in her startled face, as I doubled onto the floor, my knees drawn up to my elbows as I curled naked on the floor, gasping for oxygen as my anxiety attack tilted me on the verge of explosive insanity.

I got to my knees and pulled a switchblade out of the pocket of my jeans, ejected the steel and ran its razor sharp edge across my open palm. Dark blood spilled from the incision and cascaded slowly to the ground, as if in slow motion. I smeared the blood from my cut palm across my mouth and tasted the warm salty flavor of my own life fluids.

The sickly aroma and taste refocused my mind and I picked my clothes off the chair in the corner of the loft with my clean hand and strode down the loft stairs, naked and smeared with blood, into the fluorescent glare of the workshop. I picked a rag up off the workbench and wiped my face with its grimy surface. I cleaned as much of the wet blood from my body as I could before tugging my clothes back on. I looked at the 16-inch chainsaw sitting on the shelf above the bench, the teeth of the saw slick with polished steel. I stretched the bones in my neck, titling my head as far to the left as possible, then to the right.

I looked at the blade of the saw and saw her naked form in the polished metal surface, framed behind me on the bottom steps leading to the loft. I felt fully in control of my power at this point. I once again felt like I could punch holes in the clouds, so to speak.

"I'm going for a walk and I want you to leave now."

Lucille went from slightly coy, to slightly fucked off in a quick second.

"What have I done?" she whined.

"You need to leave now," I reaffirmed.

Lucille cupped her hands across her naked breasts, as her sense of betrayal propelled her back up the steps to the loft to retrieve her clothing and to curse the short time she had spent with me.

I lit a cigarette, lighter clutched in a shaky fist. Just to hasten her exit more quickly, I flipped the starter switch on the powerful 40cc chainsaw engine and inhaled the rich aroma of burnt petroleum and ground metal. The machine roared to life and throbbed in its cradle on the shelf. I was tempted to set it free of its confines but didn't, instead I reached out and depressed the accelerator trigger on the handle as Lucille fled across the garage, stumbling blindly to the side garage doorway, her eyes wide, mouth open, face mortified with terror and then she disappeared into the night.

Living across the avenue from each other, it was inevitable that would run into each other from time to time. I nodded 'hello' when I saw her again but hardened considerably after that point in time, as I wished Lucille to be out my life. She looked like she wanted to talk to me, her pretty eyes sad with unanswered questions, at other times filled with hurt anger. As soon as she had fled that night, I tried my hardest to think nothing of her, to wipe any trace of her from my heart. Later on, I would come to see her like some strange blip on the failing radar of my memory. My illness let me down on several important occasions, this being one of them. Besides, we'd received word from Saint Michaels' that Charlie was soon to be discharged. Despite having an obviously dysfunctional family, no-one stood between me and my brother at that point in time.

No bitch.

No lover.

No muse.

No nothing.

In fact, I felt strongly that only death could ever separate my brother and I. Death and insanity runs deep in the blood. And so I said goodbye to Lucille.

15

When Charlie was released from the Sanitarium, drastic changes began to occur on a daily basis. Despite my best efforts at removing the memory of Lucille from my heart and brain, I had found myself thinking about her far too often. I wondered what could have been and imagined her in my life, but I knew that to see her again while Charlie was around would be a big mistake. I knew he would want my undivided attention when he was released and he had already warned me about getting close with anyone. It wasn't that I was scared of Charlie, I certainly knew what he was capable of, it was more a question of feeling obligated to my twin brother and the inclusion of me in his plans. Besides, the way I'd treated her the night she fled my house, I doubted that she'd really be interested in ever having a relationship with me.

I decided to play it cool and focus on spending time with Charlie. Life was getting slightly more complicated than I wanted it to be, with his plans and my own activities, outside my infatuation with Lucille. I was confused and unsure as to why I even felt the way I did about her and felt that avoiding her would be for the best.

Within a few days, I distanced myself sufficiently from Lucille, allowing me to reassess the recent events that had intruded upon my life, including my brief relationship with her. It was strange to feel so aware of the compartmentalization of my feelings for Lucille, almost as though I had a piece of carpet on the floor of my mind where I could sweep her memory under and hide her away for a while. Charlie didn't seem to notice any change in me. His big plans seemed to cancel out anything else on the periphery of his life.

Despite my feelings of obligation towards my brother as kin, I knew he was a stranger to me and that he had always been no more than that. I knew that Lucille and I would be nothing other than a brief flirtation, a weird twisted rendezvous without truth. If she knew or even suspected what I was or what I did, it would be a potential tragedy. So, I pushed her to the back of my mind, switched off my libido, engaged my brain, and went to work.

Charlie and I worked hard to fortify the decaying ramparts of our family castle. We both knew it had secrets that needed to be kept enclosed. To be buried deeply. Charlie's plans were winding up and a lot of hell was about to be unleashed on our small part of the universe. Number Seven Artaud Avenue was the epicenter of a coming storm of fear and pain and we needed to keep the perimeter secure.

Charlie was hungry for blood.

At the time, Portvale was in the midst of a major police investigation into the disappearance of local prostitutes. No one asked about where he'd been or why he'd come home. He just appeared unexpectedly on the doorstep. The 'prodigal son' was how Ma described him. Charlie wouldn't speak of what he'd been doing during those absent years.

My twin brother was completely different to how I remembered him. He was sinewy with muscle and his once-bright eyes were black with dead hate. His skin was pale, ghostly almost, but covered in ink. His chiseled features betrayed no emotion. He knew Pa was dead, but he didn't mention it and no one thought to talk to him about it when he walked in the front door unannounced like a spirit from the beyond. Ma just shrugged and gave him a half-hearted absent-minded slap on his back and walked off looking for her smokes with a huff and a chuckle. Charlie settled himself into a spare room in the main house.

Charlie is pissed at the tenants and soon starts his stand-over tactics, giving me some idea of how he survived all those years in the 'big house.' Within one month of his return home, every tenant had vacated his or her dingy room or just disappeared. Ma was past caring for herself, let alone a rambling old property with more rooms than windows. I couldn't have cared less about the place as long as I had somewhere to sleep but I went along with Charlie's plan to secure the perimeter.

With a certain amount of relish, Charlie and I ripped the signage off the front of the building and permanently sealed the entrance of the rooming house by running the iron fence directly across the front of the building, securing the main entrance. The whole place was now ours to do with what we would.

I had held down a job for the last three months working at a local pallet-making factory and had been paying Ma steady rent money. Soon Charlie was out earning and with the additional rent coming in, Ma had more than enough to cover her meager needs and since the place had long been freehold, there was no mortgage to get in the way of our newfound privacy. She didn't seem to notice the lack of tenants downstairs or seem to care.

I read in the daily newspapers, reports about a number of bodies that had been found burnt beyond recognition in a vacant industrial lot on the North Shore. Police had discovered the charred remains of more than seven bodies in a 40-gallon drum. It seemed even the 'good' side of town had its own set of problems to deal with. Meanwhile, mine were just beginning to evolve.

The rear concrete yard was riddled with weeds growing between the cracks. The old gray iron roof was covered in crow shit. The demonic bastards would sit up there all day sometimes, their beady eyes glued to our every move, their cock-sure heads twitching this way and that as they observed every movement. Charlie swore that if they worked for the feds, criminals would be redundant. I agreed.

Even though we couldn't keep the dirty old crows out, the first thing we did when Charlie got out was to make sure the perimeter of the house was secure. The two-meter high iron fence that ran the length of the perimeter was reinforced from the inside with diagonal bracing, and along the top of the fence were six-inch sharpened nails, secured with lengths of strap metal, facing skyward. These measures, combined with the surveillance provided by the crows, kept any neighborhood spies at bay and any potential 'issues' from escaping. Our neighbors either didn't give a fuck or were too stoned to care about the penitentiary nature of the place.

When we started constructing our revolutionary plans, we knew we needed a secure base for our operations. Charlie had his own ideas about why he needed such a place but I had my own agenda, which I preferred to keep to myself. After securing the perimeter, the next thing we did was to trespass-proof the garage and secure the 'home front' so to speak. Only Charlie and I had keys—six keys each for six separate locks. That garage would contain and generate many haunting memories in the time ahead. We also installed a heavy-duty trundle gate, which made both quick access and exit a breeze. Soon, Charlie had it wired up for electronic remote control.

The best thing about the property was that in the northwest corner at the rear of the yard, was an access trap to the Portvale storm-water system. The circular iron cover had a convenient handle that required considerable force to lift it in order to access the set of ladder-steps, down into the cavernous underground below. Charlie began to use the tunnels sporadically but he had his own method of operation, preferring the use of a vehicle to trawl the city for his fun. I on the other hand made full use of this underground warren to access the whole city. With the aid of a powerful torch and a detailed map of the underground tunnel system I found in Pa's papers, the city was mine to do with, what I would.

Every night I would return home from my journeys underground, emerging from the tunnel like a miner after traveling miles of concrete pipes—sometimes laden down with more than I could carry. I even bought myself a proper LED miner's light that secured around the skull with an elastic band to give hands-free mobility. This made getting around the tunnels a breeze. As I got more sophisticated and taught myself how to use computers, I ordered many new things online that would help me with my projects. One of the most useful tools I purchased for my subterranean adventures was a set of night-vision goggles or NVGs. It proved an essential part of my 'night-kit' and made me feel like superman with x-ray specs.

Despite all its advantages, I was growing tired of living in the house. It had been home once, but it was also a prison. A prison of bad memories and scream-filled nights—the smell of fear, wet and heavy with blood and bad dreams filled my senses. I had grown accustomed to my own company and now that Charlie had returned, I couldn't help but feel that my personal space was being severely threatened. Besides, it was still Ma's place and as long as she was alive then the bad memories and the suffocation would persist. I started to spend more time below ground than above.

Charlie's return home had been abrupt. His release date came around soon enough, but nothing prepared me for the disruption to my usual patterns due to his erratic behavior. I would never know where he was, one day he would be home the next he would disappear for indeterminate periods. When he was home, Pa's old Ford still parked in the garage after all these years, was a committed obsession for Charlie. He tried to fire it up but the engine had long since seized. That's how I ended up getting to know my brother again after all those lost years. He wanted another pair of hands to hoist that old shitbox motor out of the car and I couldn't think of a reason not to help him. I ended up becoming closer to my brother than I ever imagined.

We both tried hard to get the car going. The thing was fucked but we still spent the weekends pulling it apart and putting it together to no apparent avail—half the engine parts strewn across the garage floor. After a month, I gave up and left Charlie to it. I had more important things to do with my time. Apart from his plans of revolution, Pa's car is the only other thing Charlie is focused on. I knew he was restoring the car as a sort of homage to Pa. Charlie and Pa were more similar to each other than I could have imagined. He even resembled Pa. His deep-set dark eyes were filled with an innate evil, just like Pa.

Soon Charlie had Pa's car fired up as if it had never stopped running. All I can think about is how that pile of junk had been in the garage ever since the night Pa stuck a garden hose through the window and sung himself to sleep, listening to his old Chet Baker cassettes, blue exhaust smoke charging his spent lungs with Black Death.

Ever since that night, no one had driven the Ford, until now.

The day after Pa's death, things changed drastically for me. Things would never be the same and now that Charlie was home and had wheels, things would never be the same for a lot of people.

Him and his fucking plans!

Entry for Illustrated Crime Library 'Compendium of Killers' (NY: King Billy Publishing, 2008)

According to court transcripts and psychiatric reports, Charlie Cunningham was abused by his parents and bullied by his peers at a young age, as was his identical twin Caleb. When he started attending school, the violence he experienced at home followed him into the classrooms. Charlie was constantly fighting with the other boys and girls and was perpetually reprimanded by school authorities.

From an early age, he worked on cars at home and for a local garage after school. At age fifteen, he quit school and absconded after being publicly humiliated and beaten by his father in the street outside the family home. Emotionally, Cunningham was battling an intense hatred toward people in general. He was a fully-fledged misanthrope from an early age with a very grim existential world-view.

Cunningham was a competent burglar and had a penchant for breaking into homes and apartments where young women lived alone. He would quite often steal money and under-garments and when charged with the slaying of a dispensary owner, it was discovered that he had amassed over 200 pairs of women's panties found stashed in an abandoned factory he used as a makeshift shelter. It was a particularly brutal and callous killing and displayed hallmark signs of sadistic tendencies and a penchant for symbolic displays of violence. He was also suspected, but never charged due to lack of evidence, of the murder of a young boy found badly mutilated and discovered at the same disused factory he used as a shelter.

Cunningham was tried and found guilty of 'culpable homicide' due to 'diminished capability.'

He was sent to the South Lakes Industrial School for Boys until he turned 18 years old whereby he was considered an adult, fit to serve the remainder of his ten-year sentence in the adult prison population of Breakhouse Penitentiary, situated on a virtually inescapable island 25 kilometers offshore, south of Portvale. It was during the court proceedings that Cunningham first heard himself described as a psychopathic killer by the prosecution lawyer.

The first half of Cunningham's Reform school sentence was spent in a subdued drug-induced state in almost solitary isolation. Upon his release into the general population of the reformatory, the young Cunningham was attacked and gang-raped by older boys on a regular occurrence. He spent the rest of his time lifting weights and trying unsuccessfully to escape from the reformatory.

After one such rape by a group of hoods that ran his wing, he stole a knife from the galley, slit the throat of the gang-leader, and beat each member of the clique brutally, putting one of the youths in the infirmary in a near-vegetative state. After this attack, he was brought before the court and sent to the adult prison, Breakhouse Penitentiary, but only received another four years on his sentence. By this time, Charlie Cunningham had significantly increased both his physical stature and his status as a 'hard man' and was left alone.

During his time at Breakhouse, he was involved in several violent incidents. One serious confrontation resulted in the loss of a prisoner's eye and the death of another inmate who had stabbed Cunningham with a homemade 'shiv.' Cunningham had the good fortune to avoid further jail-time being added to his sentence but had to serve the remainder of his time confined to solitary.

Despite his newfound reputation as a 'hard man,' he still repeatedly attempted to escape which resulted in physical fights with guards. Finally, Cunningham had a severe psychotic breakdown and became catatonic for a period that resulted in his transfer to nearby state mental hospital, Saint Michael hospital for the Criminally Insane.

After finishing the remainder of his full sentence at the Asylum, Doctors found him sane enough for release back into the community.

It was only a short period of time after his release before Charlie Cunningham was again the focus of police scrutiny. Within months of his release, a string of violent homicides across the Portvale region began to occur—these murders were eventually dubbed the 'Portvale Slasher' killings. Cunningham was brought in for questioning, on at least three occasions, in an attempt to help authorities with their inquiries. Each time, he was released without charge, but remained the primary suspect in the continuing investigation.

16

With plenty of practice, I soon perfected my art. The key to my continuing success was to remain anonymous, using the dark to my advantage, using the city's warren of subterranean tunnels and selecting my canvasses with care. In the beginning, I was looking for throwaways for my first project. That particular installation needed six packages to prepare the seventh, the seventh being the one that would go into the world and announce my presence. I committed my first to eternal life well before my eighteenth birthday. Now with practice, what I reveal is what I have chosen. For every one found, six remain hidden, until I choose otherwise. With over ten official so-called 'Portvale Slasher' discoveries, you do the math.

Apparently, the authorities were blind to who was behind the murders. Shit, they still hadn't realised that I was using the drain tunnels to travel to and from the crime scenes. It was such a common denominator amongst all the crime scenes that it was overlooked, repeatedly.

It was sort of like not seeing the wood for the trees.

Of course, it could be possible that they just didn't give a good goddamn about my work. Some folks just don't appreciate true art, or trash walking the streets.

So I would hunt in the day, searching the city maps I'd inherited from Pa, looking for the location I needed. I would find the exit point first; no exit point, no location. The manhole would be located in an alley or behind an industrial building near a main road. It was simple enough to steal a vehicle or catch a city bus to the neighbourhood and approach the space from every possible angle, walking across the manhole cover until I felt it through my sneakers. I could see the old map in my head and it was usually accurate. Sometimes, a manhole would have been sealed-over to make way for a building or a roadway, but usually access wasn't far from the original site.

It was a fail-proof system. With the map and my reconnaissance missions, I would have a kill-site within a day. I would indelibly trace my escape and entry point on my mind-map. The neighbourhood would have to fit certain criteria. My subjects had to pass the entrance to the alley, vacant lot, or building, near the tunnel-mouth. And there were always no shortage of subjects, especially as the afternoon succumbed to the night. The freaks come out at night. I had a sturdy set of plans that would give me more power, than I had ever possessed before.

Meanwhile, my mediocre 'other' life continued.

Things happened.

I lost my job at a local pallet factory shoving shit around until sundown. No big deal. The boss caught me out the back with the nail-gun, firing six-inch nails at beer cans perched on the fence behind the workshop. This job had lasted three and a half months, which was quite a while for me. There were plenty of bum jobs around the docks so it didn't bother me that much. Besides I had money, a job for me was something to do during the day rather than a means to an end.

Charlie disappeared again.

This time he was gone for three months.

Ma began a new campaign of domestic terror while he was absent, haranguing me with every step I took outside of the garage. She must have been watching, waiting for me as I came and went. I could tell that her dementia was back with a vengeance. She was talking to herself and her behavior was becoming worse each day.

Being home during the daytime made me a prime target for her obsessive boredom. It got to the point where she would take a broomstick and hammer it against the side of the garage. Shrieking with her cracked hag's voice:

"*CALEB!!!* I want you off my property, you good for nothing bum. You're just like your useless father"

On and on it went.

I lay on the bed with a pillow jammed against both ears.

The old bitch had spun out.

She'd finally lost her sanity.

Her eyesight was going as well. Quite often, when she wasn't harassing me, she thought I was Charlie. I used to play along with it. She would invite me inside for a cup of tea, clear some junk off a kitchen chair and set a filthy glass cup in front of me with what looked like dishwater in it. Faint echoes of sun tried to grasp for a hold on the kitchen bench, the grease covered windows thick with grime, built up over years of neglect.

Cobwebs brushed my head as I walked in.

She'd sit me down.

I would pretend to drink the poison she served me.

"That Caleb or whatever you call him is good for nothing, Charlie. I want him off my property," she would declare earnestly.

I'd play along.

"You know it's not your property, Ma. The old man left it to Caleb in the will."

"Don't you love your old Ma?" she would croak, through a cloud of cigarette smoke and crocodile tears.

"Caleb's good, Ma," I'd reply.

"He does a lot around the place, puts out the trash and pays fifty bucks a week board."

She could never argue with that. Fifty dollars kept her in cask wine for at least three days. So it would go on. I would try to tell her that I was actually Caleb and she wouldn't believe me. The more I talked to her the more I wanted to kill her. I am sure Charlie's plans didn't include this. He said she was useful. 'Cover' is what he called her. After all, who would expect that the Liberators of the Free World lived in a derelict garage out the back of an equally derelict house that the local kids called the 'dead zone?'

Despite his absence, Charlie still managed to exert his subversive influence over my life while he was away. Wherever that may have been.

He had left me a list of things to do, obviously thinking I had nothing better or more important to do with my time. The note he left on my bed simply read as follows:

```
To get:

1. 20 x 2 liter Ammonia/bleach
2. 10 x 25kg garden-variety fertilizer
(green pellets)
3. 10 x 40 gallon oil drums (empty)
```

```
4. 300kg sawdust
5. 1 x cell phone
6. 160 gallons of gasoline

To do:
1. Dig 2 x 2 meter space in south wall
corner of garage
2. Clear garage of any extraneous objects
other than tarpaulins, sheets, workbench,
tools, Ford.
3. Keep mother happy
4. Steal $10,000
```

Well it was quite a list, it went on but I won't bore you with the finer details. Just about everything on the list was a go—the only thing I had reservations about accomplishing was 'keeping mother happy.'

Thinking logically, which sometimes happened—I decided to steal the ten-grand first. I didn't really want to steal the other items so figured I may as well steal enough money to just go and purchase them, saving myself a lot of time and trouble.

I had a plan of my own I had been working on a while and, as usual, I needed to prioritize in order to achieve goals.

Four blocks away was a superette. In fact, it was the only store within a two-kilometer distance—conveniently providing the suburb with the only lotteries and liquor outlet in that area. I knew someone who knew someone who worked there, who had said: "The money is all there man. The money's all fucking there! They don't bank any of it—can you believe it? I overheard the wife saying they're gonna take the cash and blow town with a big 'fuck you' to the IRS!"

Charlie was with me at the time,

"How much is there?" he asked nonchalantly, passing the young kid a big fat joint. The kid took a toke on Charlie's skunky homegrown weed.

"At least twenty-five grand, man—they get me to bag it up at night. There's heaps," he said, coughing on the smoke.

Charlie took the joint back from the kid and gave him a fifty.

"Don't say a thing," Charlie said to the kid.

"Don't say a thing, OK?" His coal black eyes boring into the stoned boy's soul as the kid nodded in furious agreement.

"Once a narc - always a narc. Don't ever be a narc, Caleb," he told me as we walked away.

Anyway, so I knew the goods were there for the taking. In the garage, up on the mezzanine floor of the loft, I lifted a floorboard. Wrapped in oily rags—five bundles, each one containing a weapon. I checked the magazine of the army issue .45 and confirmed it full. Charlie came home with it tucked down his pants after a night playing pool with an off-duty army officer.

"I talked nicely to him and he let me have it," Charlie said.

I tucked it down the back of my own trousers, lit a joint and then slipped on a pair of latex surgical gloves—the kind you buy from the chemist for fifty cents a pair. I took a drag, pulled on a blonde curly wig and hunched my shoulders into my backpack. I looked the part of a homeless surf-bum.

I locked the garage door and closed the fence gate behind me, stepping out into the night.

The air was soft and cool on my skin.

The moon bulbous in its white brilliance.

The sky blue-black.

I pulled on my hoodie and slipped on some fake spectacles to complete my look as I walked briskly due-west toward the store. Each step I took increasing with speed along with my adrenaline levels.

17

The guy was face down on the floor behind the counter, his head covered by a white and red-checked dishcloth. His wife lay next to him, spread out like some androgynous Christ, but considerably more well fed. The guy moaned so I gave him a sharp kick in his ample gut and his breath escaped quickly with a gasp. I pressed the barrel of the .45 against the bloody cloth covering his head and whispered in his ear.

"Where the fuck is the cash?"

He sucked his breath in with a sob and tried to tell me there was no money other than what was in the cash register.

"I know you have a safe. Tell me where it is and I'll let your wife live you fucking maggot!!!"

I rolled him onto his back and removed the cloth blindfold from his swollen face. He stared in fright at me with his one good eye and started sobbing uncontrollably.

"That is all we have. That is all we have. Please take it and leave us. *Pleaaaassssssee ...*"

I grabbed a handful of his unconscious wife's hair and a ballpoint pen off the counter. I straddled her fat body and unceremoniously positioned the tip of the pen in her right eardrum as I held the barrel of my .45 and leveled the butt of the handgrip against the pen.

"Tell me where it is or she's dead," I whispered.

The guy started blindly pointing to a trapdoor under the bottom shelf.

I kicked some cans off the shelf onto the yellow linoleum and opened the door. From the shadows, I pulled a gray duffel bag.

The guy on the floor was wailing now, repeatedly telling me that I had the cash and that I should now leave. I walked back towards him and he scurried like a crab into the corner where he curled into a fetal position and wrapped his arms across his head. I walked across to where his wife still lay unconscious on the floor, the pen still positioned in her ear. I leveled my automatic at him and told him to look at me. One bloodied eye peered from behind his bruised arm and I noticed a spreading pool of urine beneath him. He started to say *'no, no, no, no, no ...'* as I drew back my boot and drove the pen deep into his wife's brain.

"I hate liars," I said, before I shot him three times.

After recovering the spent cartridges from the floor and the bullets from the dead shopkeeper, I smashed some bottles of vodka on the counter.

With the duffel bag over my shoulder, I lit a smoke as I left the shop, flicking the burning match across the room into the flammable liquid now covering the floor.

A massive *'Whuuuummpp'* rattled the door behind me.

I turned around and felt the heat on my face as the front windows burst out with the explosion.

I took a drag on my cigarette and walked away.

I quickly strode along the littered banks of an aqueduct running quick with slick black water. The darkness swallowed me up. I took the wig off and the glasses and put them in the duffel bag. I had to remove the automatic from the front of my trousers as the hot barrel was starting to scald me. I placed it in the bag and continued walking briskly south for ten to fifteen minutes, listening to the sirens behind me.

I broke into a light run until I reached the spot I needed.

I found the drain entrance tucked behind an electrical conduit and hefted the heavy iron cover free before dropping down inside.

I turned my mag-lite on, making my way down the circular storm drain, water lapping at my sodden sneakers. The light cast off the slick dark water, the occasional rat muddling its way to the edge of the light in front of me. The sound of water sloshing around my shoes echoed off the damp hollow walls.

I found my bearings quickly. First, turn right, then left. Straight ahead past seven arbitrary tunnels of death—Rue de la Mort, then left again and right into a narrower pipe. After what seemed an eternity I came upon the rusted iron doorway hunched in the graffiti-covered wall. I felt under the covered handle, found the padlock and inserted my key. It snapped open with a few twists of the key and I made a mental note to bring a tube of grease down with me next time and give it a lube. The heavy door opened with a deathly creak as

I made my way into the next chamber. I closed the heavy door and padlocked it behind me.

Scrambling up the service ladder, my torch flickering and casting ghostly shadows on the tunnel walls, I pushed with my damp shoulder against the underside of the hinged drain cover. With a final exerted heave against the heavy iron cover, I lifted it upwards and slid it to one side and peered out into the cold night.

The moon shone down on the house. From the corner of the yard I looked both ways, making sure there was no one in sight before I hoisted myself above ground level. I closed the heavy drain cover gently and covered it with a rusty sheet of corrugated iron and a couple of old tires before making my way quietly across the enclosure to the garage door.

After stashing the handgun and money under the floorboards in the loft, I quickly shaved the five-day growth I had cultivated on my face and changed my clothes completely. I took a bag of fine pepper pre-purchased from the supermarket the day before and went back outside, sprinkling the pepper around the drain cover, and where I would have walked earlier. I looked at my watch—two-thirty in the morning, the moon high in the night sky, my breath blowing clouds of fog in front of me. It was quiet tonight, a few horns blared in the distance and I could hear the sound of the bars and the drunks fighting on Artaud Avenue in the distance. I could also hear the sirens four blocks away.

I ventured outside through the side entrance and let the pepper spill where I walked, the sound of a car crawling up a side-street street propelled me quickly back toward the fence. I had just closed the gate behind me when a strong beam of light cut through the cracks in the fence, probing the shadows of the street. I pressed my back against the gate, slipping the bolt quietly closed over my shoulder.

I could hear the crackle of the police radio as the squad car cruised past, my heart thumped intensely in my chest. I clasped my nose between my thumb and forefinger, stifling a sneeze bought on by the pepper. Hopefully, it would have the same effect if they happened to run tracker dogs past the house.

The squad car went past again.

I waited, my heart pounding with adrenaline, listening, until the sound of the motor died in the distance.

The morning light woke me up, sun spilling through the oblong skylight. I lit a smoke, scratched my scalp, and yawned simultaneously. I picked the gray duffel bag up and shook it vigorously—a wadded pink sock fell onto the white crumpled bed sheets, along with the automatic and disguise. I picked up the sock, surprised at its weight. I peeled the sock back, wads of grimy cash crawled like centipedes across my vision. I sat down on the mattress and started counting.

Thirty six thousand, seven hundred and sixty two dollars.

I had hit the mother lode. It counted like a whole life's savings.

I peeled four tens off the wad and put the rest in a plastic bag under the floorboards. I lit a fire in the bin outside and threw in the hoodie, wig, socks and shoes, watching them as they began to smolder then burst into flames. As I watched the evidence of my crime go up in smoke, I knew that no fire could burn out the satisfaction I was feeling at that moment.

A week later I had dug the hole in the corner of the garage in accordance with Caleb's 'to do' list, finding several antiquated soda bottles and a rusty pocketknife in the process. I had also bought most of the other supplies on the list and placed them in the false wall in the back of the garage. The only things missing from Charlie's list were the drums, sawdust, gasoline and fertilizer.

The garage was spotless.

Shit, I even polished that old shitbox Ford.

I spent a little bit of the cash—went to the track, bought some good gear and some company for a few intoxicated nights. I made sure I spread that money around carefully, always wearing my cap and tinted prescription glasses. I saved the news clipping about the armo. In bold typeface it read:

'Man and wife dead in 24/7 lottery shop blaze.'

The story went on to say how the husband and wife shopkeepers were burnt alive in a suspicious fire at their work premises. It went on to say the police were investigating what looked like a bungled robbery. Of course, no ammunition was found; the spent slugs were well and truly at the bottom of a nearby viaduct. It had taken me a few minutes to extract them from the bleeding corpses of the shopkeeper. The holes dug made excellent repositories for the fuel that would later help incinerate their corpses.

Aside from the thirty-six thousand seven hundred and sixty-two dollars procured from 'Operation Superette', I had also stocked up on cigarettes, bourbon, and ten boxes of .45 ammunition which was about all the duffel bag could carry. One boring Monday evening, I proceeded to down the bottle of bourbon, smoking cigarette after disgusting cigarette, just wishing for lung cancer. A late night news report had a small piece on the superette slayings, basically informing anyone who might be interested that the pigs were no wiser now than when they began their inept investigation.

The bourbon quickly took effect and soon I was good and drunk. I switched off the TV and slithered down the loft stairs and outside into the evening air. The sunset was red sky streaked with black clouds. The streetlights burned a dull yellow—moths doing their death dance in their glow. I could see a bastard crow up on the TV antennae, watching my every move.

18

Charlie eventually returned and it wasn't long before we were engaged in more great discussions late at night in the loft—the sound of mice skating across the oil-covered concrete floor of the garage, tinkering in the toolbox, amongst the beer cans. We discussed 'World Destruction,' ways and wherefores and added names to the 'hit list'—essentially a chalkboard with names listed in order of 'hate ratings,' ten being lowest, one highest.

The President had been at the top of the chart for six months now, but we were slowly coming to the conclusion that he would better serve our purposes if he were a live moron, rather than a dead martyr.

Our means to harness and release a campaign of mass destruction upon the world was looking bleak to say the least and he, the President, seemed to be doing a good job of destroying the planet without any help from Charlie and myself. The more we talked, the more I started to get an idea of what it was that Charlie had planned.

It went something like this. We were to begin our campaign on a local front, an UAP (Urban Attack Program). All electrical generators or sub-stations, as the city-council marked them, were to be destroyed with a view to taking out the main power source for the neighborhood.

This, of course, would have major repercussions.

He called it the 'Earthquake Effect,' or 'EE.' One small tremor releases a larger seismic occurrence followed by mass chaos, anarchy, and eventually, world destruction.

Charlie put it in perspective by reassuring me, to never underestimate the power of stupid people let loose in large groups.

"It would take care of itself, like an avalanche," he said, earnestly.

"Einstein even suggested that the difference between stupidity and genius was that genius had limits!"

He further eased my concerns, by pointing out the undeniable truth that humanity was teetering on the brink of catastrophe. And by bringing about the initial action required to get the whole thing rolling, this was in itself something tantamount to a public service. Almost like the mouse pulling the thorn out of the lion's paw. Eventually of course, the thorn would fall out, someone else would pull it out, or it would dissolve in the milky pus of its own wound. But by pulling out the thorn, without fear of repercussion, the mouse placated the angry lion and saved the spread of any infection and eventual death.

Charlie further suggested that rather than worrying about punishment or any unforeseen circumstance or problems, we should be thinking of the service we were doing for humanity and indeed the earth as well. Due to our efforts, we would effectively be saving the planet from itself.

After all, civilization was in a state of slow extinction. Apathy, indifference, and disillusionment, had been injected into the psychic consciousness of most of its discontents long ago. It needed someone free of fear like us to wake the world up.

"Make fear your friend and then direct it toward your foes. Basic transference, that's all it is, Caleb," Charlie would say emphatically.

This initial phase was known as 'creative destruction.'

It sort of made sense and to tell you the truth, any excuse for a bit of mayhem was excuse enough for me at that time.

His underlying precept for a 'war at home' was that the fundamental basis of western civilization was built on a power system of greed and moral righteousness, which only really catered for the needs of the few, who incidentally happened to be the ones in charge.

Charlie's revolutionary sights were set on targets of authority. As he would reiterate: "A patriot must always be ready to defend his country against its government."

Charlie would continue with his diatribe for hours. He would educate me on the subject of politics, revolution, psychology, and the 'pointless pursuit of liberty.' Usually, I would switch off and let him think I was listening to what he was talking so passionately about.

However, I was intrigued by the prospect of some adventure in my otherwise meaningless existence. The idea of blowing up various inanimate objects owned by local government amused me to the point where I volunteered to detonate Charlie's explosives in the first electrical sub-station I could find. I wanted to blow up the one down on the corner of our street.

He quickly dampened my naïve enthusiasm, pointing out the rash stupidity of 'shitting in your own backyard.'

Instead, we took a long bus-trip across town one smoggy evening, the yellow streetlights glowing sickly in the twilight haze. The bus stopped in the middle of the Heights district, a series of sprawling subdivisions populated by the upper percentile of the city's urban dwellers. Large pastel houses with harsh geometric architecture and stucco exteriors—millions of dollars' worth of unimaginative boxes that would look twenty years old in ten years' time.

We walked into the night, down suburban streets far removed from the filthy industrial borough where we lived. Tree-lined avenues and small cul-de-sacs with neatly manicured lawns and tall fences were silent and spotless. The wide streets were landscaped and pristine, it was like walking through streets in a foreign country.

We found the substation.

The pipe bomb wedged nicely underneath the metal cover.

With the aid of a tree branch, I managed to ease it underneath to the center—the fuse being long enough to light from the outside edge.

A thought struck Charlie and I at the same time: *'How quick would the fuse burn?'* We were in unfamiliar territory and did not have any escape routes planned.

"Think smart" he said forcefully.

"Think fuckin' smart! We don't and we are dead. Alright, boyo?"

He told me to wait in the bushes in a small park at the end of the grove.

I lit a smoke and pulled my jacket tighter against the cold frost. Charlie disappeared. The soft lights of the houses glowed yellow against the black night. I finished my smoke just as Charlie came jogging around the corner. Breathless, he motioned me to light the fuse.

I lit another cigarette and touched the glowing ember to the fuse. It sputtered and sparked, finally catching to a quick burn. He grabbed my shoulder and turned me into a run, his head thrown back, eyes glistening insanely, laughing like a maniac.

We tumbled around the corner and Charlie shoved me toward a black BMW. We jumped in and he had the pig up to fifty kilometers an hour before we heard the explosion, a row of streetlights going off in a shower of sparks behind us as we sped off into the black night.

Forty minutes later we were in the loft, our hearts still beating like Japanese drums, rolling on the cluttered floor like insane hyenas. We pulled ourselves together long enough to tune in to the Dick Smith police scanner.

The reports were coming in thick and fast.

The coppers and fire service had the whole block cordoned off.

No reports of a search for subjects.

No mention of a black BMW leaving the scene.

No news about two skinny white guys with no hair letting off homemade pipe bombs.

The power had gone off across the whole Heights subdivision. Ten blocks of million-dollar homes and not a backup power generator amongst them. Fifteen minutes after the first reports about the substation explosion, we learned the authorities were treating it as a malfunction.

'Council's problem on Monday,' the sergeant in charge fed back to the station. A report came through about a burnt out Black BMW Sports Series sedan still ablaze in a vacant lot on the outskirts of town, not three blocks from our place.

"It's no good," said Charlie. "What's the point in doing it if nobody else knows we did it? We need a new plan. We need a new fuckin' plan."

His eyes were black marbles.

He was ready to murder.

I was completely exhausted.

19

Despite Charlie's attempts at prioritizing his own big plans, I decided that my own plans needed equal attention and so I proceeded to carry on as normal when he wasn't at home. Charlie had vanished again and the sub-station explosion was an inconsequential memory, so I hit the streets and resumed my hunt from where I had left off. After hours of walking, I grew tired and headed home, returning from my non-eventful scouting mission via the subterranean tunnels. All I managed to turn up was a lucky drunk outside a liquor store, fresh-flushed with cash and a recent purchase of Johnnie Walker Whisky, half the bottle of which I drank before I reached home. I relieved myself against the back fence and noticed the lights weren't on in the main house. The old bitch must be out. I tried the back door but it was locked. I found the key under the mat where it always was and let myself in.

I made my way up the dimly lit stairway to the top floor and stumbled through the littered hallway in the dark, suddenly unsure as to why I was in the house. Food was my first inclination. I measured my bearings and made my way in the half-light into the lounge to get to the kitchen entrance. The buzz of flies alerted me to the stale aroma of the withered corpse sitting hunched in the darkness. I flicked my lighter and there she was, bent forward in the easy chair, a cigarette butt still stuck between her withered fingers. The smell was sickly—a dark deep pervading waft of lingering death and stale urine. She still looked pissed off. It was Ma, Vera Cunningham the great undead. Now dead, for all eternity.

I was unsure what to do. I flicked the light on, rolled up a discarded newspaper from a nearby stack, and pushed her shoulder with the end of it. I heard a grating sound like bone-on-bone and her head tilted to one side, her old yellow stained skin pulled tight over false teeth, cheeks drawn, eye-sockets deeply encrusted. Two empty prescription pill bottles lay next to her on the floor. She was definitely dead.

"She's definitely dead, old boy," said an unmistakable voice behind me. Charlie stepped from the shadows of the kitchen doorway.

"What the fuck …?" I stammered, taken aback at his sudden appearance.

"We've got a problem, Caleb," he said in a solemn voice, his black pupils large and uncompromising.

I didn't care about any 'problem,' all I wanted to do was scream at him— *'Where the hell have you been?'* I knew it was pointless. He wouldn't have told me anyway. His business was his business only.

"We need to clean this place up. Let's get some sleep for now, we've got a lot of work ahead of us."

He put his bony hand on my shoulder, a toothy grin spread across his ghoulish face.

"You been drinkin' again, eh?" he asked, as he smiled a knowing smile and led me through the debris of Ma's living quarters, down the stairs and out into the sobering cold night towards the garage. All the while, what seemed like a million questions surged through my brain: *'When had he got out of prison? Was he real? What are we going to do with Ma?'*

I woke up with a headache that reverberated around inside my skull.

Charlie was nowhere to be seen. Had I dreamt he had returned?

No, there was one of his cigarette butts stubbed out on the floor. He was home again.

Ma was dead.

Ma was dead.

Ma was dead …

I pulled on a t-shirt and jeans and tumbled down the loft stairs into the harsh morning light with a full bladder. The previous evening seemed like a dream—I stood against the fence and drained myself of the night's excesses. A box full of newspapers landed on the cracked concrete in the middle of the yard with a dull thud behind me, then another. An old nicotine-stained lampshade followed. I looked up. Charlie was in the open window of Ma's bedroom, ceremoniously hurling things from the second floor.

"Come up and give me some help," he called as he threw an armful of moth-eaten clothes down onto the pile of debris in the yard.

I made my way up the worn stairs; the place stunk of cat piss and dry farts. It always gave me a chill when I climbed those stairs, I never knew what I was going to find at the top of them.

"In here," Charlie called.

Ma's room smelt like death—like earwax, or what a Mortician's room full of damp cadavers might smell like.

"Help me with this," he said, dragging a huge leather suitcase from under the bed.

I grabbed one side and we hoisted it on top of the bed. Charlie pulled a switchblade out of his back pocket, flicking the blade open in one swift motion. Within seconds he had it opened—

"More fucking newspapers" he said in disgust.

I took the first one out.

"Hey look at this, Charlie—the astronauts have landed on the moon."

I turned to show him the yellowed picture depicting Neil Armstrong proudly holding a flag on what was apparently the surface of the moon.

"Screw the moon, Caleb. Look at this," said Charlie, pointing at the remaining contents of the open suitcase. Wads of cash filled the suitcase. Dirty bundles of tens, twenties, fifties …

He picked up a handful of notes and began counting.

"Shit, there must be fifty grand here at least. Take this." He shoved a roll of notes at me and stuffed one in each of his own jean pockets.

"You keep cleaning this trash up. Watch out for any more stashes. I'm just going to make sure this is put somewhere safe." He dragged the suitcase out the door into the littered hallway.

Thump, thump, thump … as he made his way down the stairs.

I counted the roll of cash, nearly five hundred dollars. This was turning into an interesting week. I could feel something in the air. Some strong energy force was hovering around us—something was building up. Charlie seemed different somehow, more resolute, more intense. I could feel myself changing too, becoming more single-minded, more insular. Things that might have bothered me no longer mattered, I busied myself with the task at hand. The room was cleared of all but an old cigarette-burnt dresser and a stained mattress and bed-base. I looked out the window down into the yard at the piles of refuse piled high on the courtyard below.

Charlie was nowhere to be seen.

I thought about the money and how useful it would have been if I'd known about it earlier. The crafty old bitch had obviously been saving it up for a while. What we were going to do with her was beyond me now and, after all, she was Charlie's mother as well. It could be his problem. He could decide what to do with her lifeless carcass. Part of me wished I felt more for Ma than I did. Part of my consciousness cried out for the mother I wished I'd lost, but the rest of me was glad she was dead. I remembered the savage beatings she gave me as a child and the torturous regime of a domineering matriarch. I knew her influence would never leave me; that she had twisted me into a monster of her making. Combined with Pa's genes and his own set of murderous exemplars, I knew what I was and what I would be. With Ma now following Pa to hell, I felt released. I felt as though I now had a black glistening pair of wings, capable of lifting me to the dark realms of limitless space.

That evening, back out in the garage while watching the late news, Charlie materialized again. Like a ghost, he appeared at the top of the steps on the mezzanine.

"I'm moving in to Ma's room," he said.

I started to say something but thought better of it. Sure enough, Charlie answered my question as though he'd read my mind.

"We have to carry on like nothing has happened. We'll get rid of the body tomorrow night. Nothing has changed, the plans are still the same."

"What are we gonna do with the money?" I asked.

"You leave that to me. With that money and your stash we can move our schedule forward three months."

"How did you know I ..."

"I know everything, Caleb. I am God. I can see everything you do—every thought you think."

I couldn't find any words. I tried to think of nothing, afraid he was looking into my thoughts at that very moment.

"As I was saying, we're ahead of schedule. Tomorrow we're moving the Ford out onto the street."

"Why do you want it on the street?" I asked, curious as to his motives.

"What better place for it?" Charlie said with a sneer, his eyes blacker than ever.

Tomorrow came around soon enough. Charlie woke me up from a sleep full of nightmares, banging on the side of the garage. The sun was starting to push its way through the cracks in the blinds. Sleepily, I tugged some clothes on and helped Charlie open the main gates and get the garage doors open. The Ford looked like some inanimate rock in the middle of the garage, but soon enough we had strained and pushed that old pile of trash outside the front gate.

"Tomorrow I'm skippin' town, I'll be going' away for a few weeks" Charlie announced as he locked the front gate behind us, wiping sweat from his pale skull with a grease-covered forearm. I lit a smoke and gave one to him.

"But what about ...?" I started.

"Tonight we get rid of Ma. I'll see you at sunset."

20

While waiting for night to arrive, I had nothing to do that day so to kill time I locked up, rode the subway into the city and went shopping downtown.

It began raining bleakly.

Beyond the skyscrapers, the sky was a foreboding dull gray, heavy with cloud and the promise of a storm.

I went to the downtown markets, bought a new leather jacket, some expensive cigars and a new pair of black boots. After shopping, I went to the movies. It was some old re-run, part of a b-grade horror festival. The movie was called *Driller-Killer*. A scene, where some poor bastard was crucified, between two alley walls with a drill-bit through each hand, was particularly engrossing. Another scene showed the killer painting a mad picture of a staring bison's burning red eye, nostrils flared. Murderous. The guy kills a rabbit and uses the blood to finish his painting. Pure mad genius.

I grabbed a burger after the flick and jumped a bus home. I thought about the movie all the way home and decided I wanted to become an artist. I looked out the window seeing myself half-reflected in the dirty glass. I looked like Charlie except with better color. The rain had stopped, replaced with an opaque fog that blanketed the city. The fog always came from the southeast side, from Portvale and the docks, from where I lived. It seemed to follow me whenever I ventured forth out of the dockside suburb.

Back in Portvale walking down the avenue toward the house in my new boots, finishing a nice fat cigar, I noticed the yellow glow of a light in the upstairs window. The twilight cast dark shadows across the street as the day drew to a finish. The Ford was gone from where we parked it. I presumed it had been towed. I unlocked the gate and crossed the yard, stepping on a rolled-up rug amongst the other piles of debris on the ground.

Charlie was standing on the porch in the shadows smoking a cigarette.

"Good movie?"

"Yeah," I replied, wondering how the fuck he knew I had been at the cinema.

"I'm a bit worried about you boyo! Caleb ... am I living with a bonafide killer?"

He spat on the ground and looked up at me as if it was really something he wanted to know

I didn't say a word. Shit, I didn't know—as I said, I hadn't been feeling myself lately. I had no idea why the fuck he was asking me this question. I was beginning to suspect that he could actually read my thoughts. I suddenly felt suspended in time, almost removed from everything. In fact, I felt very detached, almost like I was looking in as an observer of myself.

I forced myself to snap out of my thoughts and speak in an even tone.

"Let's get rid of Ma. I've got a lot of my own things to do, Charlie," I said impatiently.

"We wait until midnight," he continued. "Come and have a look at this."

He motioned me to follow him toward the garage, the sun now going down in the distance. As I followed him, I imagined a sledgehammer flattening the back of his skull. Inside the garage where the Ford had been, ten symmetrically placed forty-gallon oil-drums sat. Beside them were stacked about twenty, twenty-five kilogram bags of fertilizer of some sort and equal quantities of sawdust.

"I've got a job for you, Caleb. After we get rid of Ma we're going to fill every one of these drums." He seemed maniacal, his black eyes burned and his hands twitched uncontrollably.

"Any questions?" he asked. His eyes bored into me like giant drill-bits. Daring me to question his authority.

Fuck, he looked like Pa.

"No, Charlie," I said. "It's all about as clear as day."

He locked the garage door, grabbing a full jerry can on the way out. We headed toward the house in the near dark. I was about to step over the rolled-up rug at the foot of the back steps when Charlie told me to 'grab an end.'

Ma sure was light—I think the rug weighed more than she did. We took her to the corner of the yard and Charlie began to clear the debris I had placed over the drain cover. Charlie hoisted the heavy iron lid off the top of the entrance with one muscled arm and went down the stepladder first.

"Throw her down, Caleb."

"But won't she fall?" I asked.

"She's dead. She won't feel it."

I stood over the cavernous drain, trying to feed the lumpy rug into the opening. The rug went limp suddenly and I heard a sickening thud below.

"Leave the rug up there—I want it for my room," said Charlie.

We carried her between us, the jerry can on her stomach, Ma swinging between us, nightshirt in the water. Charlie led us deeper in to the warren-like catacombs that stitched themselves together under acres of industrial and residential neighborhoods. I didn't know that he knew about the tunnels. Judging from his effortless sense of direction, it seemed that he knew their layout as well as I did.

I was shocked when we passed the entrance to my own 'lair,' an alcove set back in the tunnel wall. In the darkness, it was impossible to see the small rusted service entrance, set back in the rough-cast concrete. The thick steel door led to a large abandoned room the size of a two-car garage. Inside, the walls were lined with disused electrical conductors, twelve on each side of the room; their antiquated metal containers decayed with rust, the dark green paint that once covered their exteriors, peeled like flaking skin.

At one end of the dark chamber was a concrete platform, just big enough for a human body to rest, much like a slab in an old mortuary. It was in this room, under the light of flickering candles that sat upon the conductors, that most of my art was practiced, far from prying eyes and possible intruders.

As we kept walking through the damp tunnel, I couldn't help but think that Charlie somehow knew about my lair.

"In here," he mumbled, leading me into a narrow culvert that led to a chamber, the mag-lite clenched between his teeth illuminated a concrete platform that looked like a slab in a tomb. Dark rust colored marks stained the surface. Charlie had used this space before. Somehow, I had never noticed it previously, despite having passed the entrance many times before.

We hoisted the body onto the damp slab. Rats scattered into the black water. The torch glowed eerily in the dark space, our voices whispered as the echoes of our sodden footfalls resounded through the drain tunnels.

"Move back," said Charlie, "unless you want to be barbeque."

He gave me the torch and started splashing gasoline on Ma's broken corpse. One of her arms was now at right angles to her body, her leg bent underneath her. The side of her withered head, flattened by the impact of the fall down the drain entrance—a glazed eyeball protruded from her shattered cheek.

The fuel made her look as though she was covered in a glistening placenta. Sort of like she had been hatched recently, like some malformed stillborn. The smell of the petrol made my head spin, my stomach queasy.

"Step back," said Charlie, motioning me back the way we came in. He took a rag from his pocket and stuffed it in the top of the jerry can.

"Get ready to run, boy," he warned.

Charlie lit the rag and flames leapt from the top of the gas-can. He held it at arm's length and bought it back in a swinging arc, the flames licked his hand. Charlie seemingly impervious to the pain as always, a yellow-toothed smile across his skeletal face. He threw the flaming canister in a tumbling lob toward Ma's twisted corpse.

The flash of the blast blinded me for a minute as the fireball engulfed the concrete room, singeing the hair from my eyebrows. I fell backwards, more with surprise than the force of the explosion. The dirty water covered my face and vision for a second and all I could see was the red flash of fire, followed by a dazzling white array of dots dancing before my eyes.

I scrambled to my feet.

Soaked to the skin.

Breathing hard.

Spitting storm water.

Ma lay burning on the concrete platform like an effigy in a funeral pyre. The flames danced above her withered form; black billowing smoke filled the enclosed space. The stench was sickening. I turned and started to make my way back the way I had come. Disorientated. Shaken.

'Where was Charlie? Where the fuck was he?'

I thought I heard a faint hollow laugh, echo down the tunnel. The light was fading behind me as I stumbled helplessly deeper into those suburban catacombs. Black smoke drifted around me, its twirling tendrils reached their foul fingers into my lungs and blacked out the waning light until I could see nothing.

I called for Charlie again but there was no reply.

My hands were cold and damp on the concrete walls.

The freezing water was up to my knees. No light anywhere.

My heart banged in my chest like a piston.

Adrenaline coursed through my veins but still I felt nothing but the cold. I called for Charlie again, choking on a mouthful of corpse smoke. I listened, the pounding of my heart clearly audible. Not another sound, just the echo of my voice and a faint rumble of water in the pipes. I started to panic, I knew there was an automatic water release every two hours, apparently to back off pressure and keep the pipes clean.

How long had I been stumbling around in the dark?

I had to get out. I could feel my panic levels increasing with every sodden footstep. I felt through my pockets and discovered my lighter. I wished I had brought my night-vision goggles. After a couple of attempts, it flickered into life. I was in a long tunnel covered in graffiti that I didn't recognize. I may as well have been in a different country. Maybe it was the fact that we had just incinerated ma, or maybe I had been more affected by the blast than I earlier thought. All I knew was that my ears were ringing, my sense of direction was impaired, and for the first time underground, I felt fear. The smoke was starting to thin but I noticed it seemed to be trailing away past me down the tunnel into the dark. I was completely disorientated.

There must be airflow in the same direction.

I briefly thought about trying to find my lair but I felt quite sick, the petrol fumes and the smell of Ma's burning flesh made me hungry for fresh air. I splashed after the fleeting wafts of smoke like a hunchback, holding my lighter as far out in front of me as possible, fingers burning. Not caring about the pain, just wanting to escape.

I managed to trace the passage of the smoke around a few turns until I saw a circle of faint light ahead of me. I headed toward it as the lighter sputtered and pinged, exploding in my numb hand, a shard of plastic embedded itself deep in my palm. I kept moving, arms wrapped around my quivering hunched self. The moon grew bigger with each cramped step. I looked over my shoulder and got another mouthful of Ma.

I burst from the drain mouth, dropping facedown into a concrete viaduct. Fortunately, I only fell a short distance onto a pile of damp trash beneath the tunnel mouth. The true moon above cast a faint blue light over everything, the viaduct stretched for miles each way, wide enough to race a couple of eighteen wheelers side-by-side. I brushed myself off and scrambled up the block embankment.

I caught my breath, coughed some smoke out of my spent lungs, took my soaked tee shirt off, wrung it out and put it on again. It was fucking freezing. I couldn't tell where I was. It could have been anywhere in this suburban shit-hole.

I jumped a fence, praying there were no dogs waiting to rip me limb-from-limb on the other side. A clothesline afforded me the privilege of some considerably drier clothes—a sweatshirt and pair of track pants. After changing my sodden clothes, I moved quickly down the side path of the clapboard house and closed the front gate of the property quietly behind me. I tried to look as casual as I could as I strolled to the corner of the street in the moonlight. Maple Crescent. I was only three blocks from home.

When I returned to the garage I grabbed some fresh clothing and made my way to the main house. I took a very hot shower and changed into some dry clothes. I still couldn't get the smell of toasted flesh out of my inflamed nostrils. I lit a smoke and walked through the empty house, checking each barren room as I went—Charlie was nowhere to be found. *Was he still underground in the maze of storm-*

water drains where I had last seen him? I left the house and walked across to the corner of the rear section to check the drain-cover.

Fuck him, I thought.

I hope he's dead like Ma.

The heavy iron drain cover was as we had left it. I covered up the drain entrance in the corner of the yard and sat on the porch steps of the garage. My hand shook violently as I inhaled on my cigarette. I had never thought like that before about Charlie. Shit, I didn't want to believe he'd left me to die in the drains but I'm sure I heard him laughing as I cried out.

I flicked my cigarette and once again walked across the yard to the house, once inside I climbed the stairs back up to the top floor. It looked completely different now that Ma's things had been cleared out. It was still filthy and smelt like death and the strange feelings I'd always had in the house, remained ever-present. I opened the door to Charlie's new bedroom and stretched out on what used to be Ma's bed. It was surprisingly comfortable despite the concave bow in the center. Despite my unease about being inside the house, I soon fell into a deep sleep, the smell of burning flesh still acrid in the back of my throat.

Strange dreams of things were brewing.

As it turned out, Charlie didn't turn up and I caught pneumonia. For three days and three nights, I lay in Ma's bed sweating, shivering, vomiting, and not eating until I could take it anymore. I don't know how I managed to get to a phone and then down the stairs, but pretty soon a cab turned up and drove me straight to the after-hours Doctor's surgery. The on-duty doctor promptly referred me to the hospital where I stayed for a week, pumped up on drugs and pretty night nurses. Clean sheets were a luxury. The food wasn't that great but I didn't need to make it myself. Soon I was discharged, feeling pretty good and about ten kilograms lighter. I arrived home and discovered Charlie had still not returned. I thought about the empty drums waiting to be filled with death in the garage and decided they could wait. I thought about Ma and savored the moment, as I pushed her memory to the back of my consciousness.

IV
A Stranger To Myself

*People begin to see that something more goes to the composition of
a fine murder than two blockheads to kill and be killed - a knife - a
purse - and a dark lane. Design, gentlemen, grouping, light and
shade, poetry, sentiment, are now deemed indispensable to attempts
of this nature.*

Thomas de Quincey (1827)

*Murder in the murderer is no such ruinous thought
as poets and romancers will have it;
it does not unsettle him, or fright him from his ordinary notice of
trifles; it is an act quite easy to be contemplated.*

Ralph Waldo Emerson

I unlocked the garage door and found a note on the floor. It read:

```
Caleb

So you are still alive - you have passed
initiation 101. You are now an official
'STORM TROOPER OF DEATH,' otherwise known
as a 'Liberator Of The Free World,' or
whatever you want to call yourself. As I
told you, I am away on business for two
weeks. You have three things to do:
     1. Mix ingredients as directed (see
instructions on your filthy bed)
     2. Buy large van under false company
name 'Renfield's Pest Exterminators'
     3. Don't kill anyone.

C.


P.S. Make sure our guest in the garage is
quiet and fed once a day - key is on your
bed alongside instructions for Renfield's
Pest Exterminators new product range.

P.P.S. Be careful what you wish for.
```

I crumpled the note and put it in the pocket of my jeans, taking the steps up to the loft two at a time. Sure enough, there was the key on top of the other note. *What the hell was the key for? What fucking guest?* I looked over the edge of the mezzanine balcony; down below I noticed nothing out of the ordinary—save for where I had dug the square hole in the corner of the south wall. Where the hole used to be, a solid looking workbench now stood. I picked up the key and instructions and proceeded downstairs.

I noticed under the workbench sawdust strewn all over what would have appeared to be the floor to any unsuspecting visitor. I tried to move the bench but it felt fixed to the floor. Now anyone else might have assumed this, but since I dug a two-by-two meter hole there, I knew that Charlie would have wanted it dug for some reason. I gave it another shove and felt it give sideways.

I thought I could hear something, like a muffled scream. I shoved a broom under the bench and swept aside most of the sawdust. Sure enough, the table looked to be secured to a two-meter squared slab of plywood. And there it was—a large galvanized pad bolt with a security padlock fixed tight.

I unlocked the padlock and slipped the bolt back. Faint thumps and scratching could be heard below the bulky entrance. The bench would not budge. I tried to lift it and felt the weight shift; it seemed to be hinged like a trap door. I gave one final push and the bench tilted to the left, revealing the black confines of the hole I had dug. In the shadowed space below me, I saw two big scared eyes blinking back at me. For a moment, I thought I was looking at Lucille. *Everything shifted to slow mo.*

It was her.

It was her.

It was ….

She was about twenty years old and reasonably attractive. Her long straight blond hair covered in grime and cobwebs, her white blouse held together by clawed fingers. She was very pale and thin; in fact, she could have passed for Lucille's sister if she had one. She was making incoherent mumbling noises and shaking visibly. I asked her name—she looked up at me and started sobbing, *"Where am I? Who are you? Why are you doing this to me?"*

I slammed the workbench back down on top of her and slid the bolt home hard.

Why am I doing this to her?

Fuck Charlie, he had left her there. She was his responsibility.

I remembered the note: 'Feed our guest.' She had looked rather emaciated. Judging from her thin figure and the length of time I had spent in hospital, I would surmise she had been locked up in the garage for approximately three solid days. I went back to the main house and took a packet of biscuits and a couple of tins of sardines from the kitchen back out to the garage.

"I'm going to give you some food so stop crying and settle down," I shouted at the plywood trap door.

I slipped the bolt back and threw the food in for her, closing the trap door quickly again. While she would no doubt be consuming her meal ravenously, I decided to mix the ingredients for the explosive devices as per Charlie's devilish recipe.

At four am that morning, I completed my task. The ten drums were filled each nearly three-quarters full with the fertilizer and sawdust. I removed the rag from around my face, breathed, and yawned at the same time. I went upstairs to the loft and slept until noon the next day, got up and caught the bus to the supermarket.

I still had a few hundred dollars left from the money Charlie had given me. Before I left for the supermarket I looked in the stash hole under the floorboards in the loft and found another five thousand with a note tucked in the rubber band: *'For van only—get receipt'*

The rest of the cash had gone and so had the weapons. I still had a small revolver hidden in a wall cavity behind a poster of a masked Michael Myers from the *Halloween* films.

I thought about the girl cowering in the dark hole in the floor of the garage …

I thought about Charlie's continual demands.

Hatred was beginning to build inside me as I continued thinking about all the perceived injustices I had to endure. I locked up and headed out the side-gate, making my way to the bus stop on the corner of Artaud and Dockway, picturing exploding heads and streets of blood all the way to the supermarket.

As the bus neared its destination, I contemplated returning and burning the house down, but thought better of it, as that would only attract unwanted attention. Knowing my luck, I would be the one who bore the brunt of any legal repercussions regarding Charlie's plans. I was still thinking of ways to get Charlie to pay for his demands and lack of respect when the bus pulled up outside the North Shore shopping mall.

The mall was massive, about the length of two or three football fields. After half-an-hour of navigating between anaesthetized shoppers and obscure directional signs, I found the food-court and chose a seat with my back to a wall next to an overgrown palm tree in a ridiculously small terracotta pot.

I ate a burger and washed it down with some flat soda. Everywhere young nubile women pranced back and forth like mutant gazelles at a watering hole, tight sweaters and jeans—preening and displaying themselves. I imagined an armalite automatic in each hand spraying the mall with death—bodies heaped lifelessly, strewn across the blood covered floor like discarded litter. Shit, one of those explosive devices I had made up for Charlie would be perfect in here I thought. I felt strange, very remote and the sounds came too slow—distant.

I saw what I thought was Charlie's skull floating amongst the throng of shoppers. I blinked. He was gone.

I lit a smoke and went to stand up. A skull hovered eye height in front of me—dismembered, floating.

"Sit the fuck down," it said in a rasping, guttural voice.

I gasped, choking back a cry of disbelief.

The apparition floated in front of me—gaping black holes where its eyes should be, rotting black lips peeled back exposing teeth yellow and broken, all set amongst chalk-gray bone.

"You have a purpose, Caleb," it hissed at me.

"Charlie is your partner. You both are the world's last hope. You are the liberators of the free earth."

My head was spinning.

Could anyone else see this thing in front of me?

"I want you to go home and liberate the woman in the ground. Free her Caleb. GO!"

I stood up, my heart racing. A strange feeling of duplicitous déjà vu washed over me in waves. The skull reminded me of Charlie, yet what it was telling me to do was the antithesis of what Charlie would want. He was more calculating, more direct in the focus of his hate.

'*Fuck the System*,' Charlie would scream at the sky.

He wouldn't care about a mall full of moronic consumer robots. I had to admit that the idea of leveling a place heaving with mindless idiots had a definite appeal. It would send a message directly to the sick heart of society. It would strike fear in the dumb throngs of the masses, even if just for a second it might trigger one or two to follow suit.

My t-shirt was sticking to my back with perspiration—adrenaline pumped through my veins as my brain ran looped movie-scenes of random violence. Despite the orders from the apparition, I had no real desire to set something free, especially someone as pretty as she was. I tried to delay leaving as I grabbed random items of food from the shelves in the supermarket, filling up a trolley as the apparition's words rang in my ears, knowing that I was sure to expect some repercussions for any disobedience. I made my way to the checkout and paid for two bags of groceries without knowing what I had actually bought. I was totally nerve-wrought and distracted.

Outside the supermarket entrance, still inside the mall, my shaking hands lit a cigarette. I looked over my shoulder for the ominous skull as I made for the exit. I nearly fell over a pram being pushed by a pregnant girl who looked no older than seventeen. I looked back once more before bursting through the exit into the car park, but Charlie or whoever it was had disappeared.

I watched myself from above spin on my heels in the crowded car park. The bright afternoon sun cast black shadows across the asphalt, as I looked down on my form below, looking south then east then north then west in slow motion black and white.

I arrived home, semi-convinced of the validity of what I had seen. *Was it a ghost?*

A hallucination?

It seemed so real.

I didn't want to go against Charlie, yet what if *it* was real?

What if freeing that woman was part of a greater plan?

I decided to check on her and then decide what to do. I opened the hatch—she sat hunched in a dark corner in a puddle of her own urine, apparently sleeping. God, I couldn't get over how much like Lucille she looked. Mind you, I saw Lucille everywhere. I dared not cross the road and speak directly to her yet every woman with the same color hair and figure and height ... became Lucille.

The skin on the back of the woman's neck was exposed, the curve of her shoulders revealed her lower back where her sweater had pulled up. Skin so smooth, despite the conditions of her accommodation.

It had been a long time since a woman was remotely interested in me and here one was. Not necessarily interested in me but attractive, supple—captive. Nobody knew she was here and Charlie was probably going to kill her anyway. My vision was singular.

An urge built up inside me, seeking release.

I lay down on the floor and leant into the hole to grab her. She sensed my approach and squealed, blinking crazily as her exhausted eyes adjusted to the fluorescent lights in the garage. She shrunk further into the black shadows of the corner, instinctively anticipating my reach. I leant further toward her, one hand behind me grasping the leg of the workbench, the other extended in her direction—fingers flexing.

Her big dark eyes looked over her shoulder, her cheek pressed against the rough cavity wall, a mixture of fear and anger apparent.

Suddenly she lashed out at me and I felt a warm flood splatter my cheek. I clutched my face where she had struck me with the sharp edge of the sardine tin lid. Blood coursed from the open wound, spilling in big black drops on the dirty floor below.

I stood up enraged and slammed the hatch cover down on top of her with a thud. I could hear her muffled curses and fists hit the heavy plywood trap door. I rushed up the stairs, blood gushing from the deep gash in my cheek. I fumbled behind the poster, finding my revolver. I checked it was fully loaded as I followed my own trail of blood back downstairs.

Without hesitation, I fired eight rounds in quick succession into the plywood covering the pit. I heard a strangled cry, then nothing— my ears ringing from the sounds of the shots in the enclosed space of the garage.

After a moment, I gathered myself together, yawning to ease the numbness in my ears. I bent down; blood still splashing on the floor from my wound, and lifted the trapdoor again. She sat hunched where she was when I slammed the lid down on her before, a perfect black hole in the top of her head. She didn't move. She was fucked. I lowered myself into the pit and took my Buck knife from the sheath on my belt; a minute later, I held her dripping head in my hands. I bagged it and dismembered the rest of her lifeless body.

Everything shifted to slow motion again.

I closed the trapdoor and made my way back upstairs to the loft, slowly, feeling very faint and unsteady on my feet.

I could smell sardine oil—my mouth was full of salty blood.

I placed the head wrapped in the plastic bag on the top of the TV in the corner of my room.

I tried to lie down on my bed but the room spun. Nausea and claustrophobia united to drive me back down the stairs and across the courtyard. I stumbled to the main house and up the stairs to the bathroom. I looked in the mirror and everything seemed to elongate in the background.

My cheekbone was exposed. My white t-shirt was saturated with coagulating blood. I found Ma's sewing kit in the kitchen drawer and stitched my face up quite neatly in front of the cracked mirror in the bathroom, the blood drying quickly on the stitched wound.

I couldn't hear a thing.

Everything went white as I dropped to the floor.

I woke up the next morning on the bathroom floor. The side of my face was swollen like a red balloon. I could only see out of one eye and my gums ached where the sharp tin had cut through the cheek into the soft upper gum. I was lucky not to have lost an eye. The stitches seemed to be holding ok. I took a half empty bottle of brandy from under the kitchen sink and drank the remains quickly. My senses adequately numbed, I made my way back downstairs and out to the garage to the loft where I fell into a deep sleep on my bed.

Three days later, I had gathered sufficient reserves of strength and stupidity to venture out beyond the confines of the garage. It was more to do with the smell of the decomposing head, still perched on the TV in the corner of the room; I probably would have stayed in bed another day if it were not for the pungent aroma. I ventured underground, processed the head as usual, and placed it on the installation altar to dry.

My vision was still a bit blurry but the infection in the wound on my face had subsided and I could now see out of both eyes. After a decent breakfast, I scoured the classifieds in the *Portvale Daily News* and managed to track down and eventually purchase a large white Ford Econoline van for four thousand dollars. It was perfect despite being twenty years old; it ran well and had no windows in the rear apart from the back doors. I managed to get the guy who sold it to me to change the amount on the receipt to five thousand dollars purchase price—a thousand bucks profit. Not bad for a few hours' work.

I registered the van under a false company name and it was good to go. I took the van on a tour of the neighborhood. It drove like a dream and was certainly big enough to house Charlie's latest project.

That night I stripped and dragged the remains of the dismembered corpse out of the garage, wrapped in an old bed sheet, and transported her onto the northbound freeway across the harbor bridge to the north-shore and the outskirts of town.

I found a quiet tree-lined lane that ended at a park with a trail big enough for a vehicle to get through. The wooded lane led to an off road area that ran down to the river's edge.

I drove the van down the bumpy track and parked the van in the dark cul-de-sac at the end of the lane.

I could see the park lights through the trees.

The night was quiet enough to make out the sound of river water tumbling gently past. I hoisted the dead girl's torso onto my shoulder in a fireman's lift and with shovel in hand made my way to the edge of the river. As I walked through the trees, I could see the glow of the city lights in the distance across the expansive flow of water. I dropped her body to the ground in the middle of a small grassy clearing.

I lit a cigarette and checked out the river. Downstream, I could see the hazy lights of cars drifting across the black silhouette of the hulking bridge that connected the North Shore to the freeway and downtown areas. I finished my smoke and quickly proceeded to dig a shallow grave beneath the overhanging bough of a willow tree. The earth was soft and damp. She was as white as snow and cold to touch, as I lay her down to rest in the fresh dark soil.

I walked back to the van and gathered her remaining limbs together, wrapped in the bloodied sheet, and hoisted them over my shoulder like Saint Nick with a bag of presents. After depositing the rest of her remains in the ground, I picked up the shovel and began to pitch the dirt over her. As an afterthought, I struck the fingers from her hands with the blade of the shovel and gathered them up before throwing them out towards the middle of the river. Without her head and fingerprints, she would take a while to identify if her grave was found. No soul, no life, an empty husk—where roots would grow and worms would feast.

I patted the earth down with the shovel and scattered leaves and debris in a uniform pattern across the grave. No swimming for this girl, she was a mistake and I did not want her found in a hurry. Charlie's mind-fucked plan would bring severe heat down on us if the body was found. She would become a political conspiracy screaming to be solved for years to come. Dead and buried, she would remain another missing daddy's girl. A cold case on ice.

The soft drizzle of rain drifted across the windscreen as I pulled back out into a lit up residential side street. I headed into town, turning the stereo on—CCR's *Bad Moon Rising* was playing. I lit a smoke and felt alive for the first time in ages. My face still throbbed with a tight nagging pain. I could feel the stitches starting to tighten as the skin grew over them. I thought about the girl and thought about Lucille, the hunger had returned. I needed to find her again. The driving rain now pelted the windscreen ferociously.

I headed back across the harbor bridge and took a cruise down the strip checking out the popping neon lights, bums propped up in doorways with brown bags, working girls busting out selling their wares, pimps ducking in and out of the pedestrians. Cruising through the strip and south to the lower eastside, I steered the van home. The suburban sprawl dragged back from the heart of the city like debris from a bomb-blast. Rundown suburbs dense with apartment blocks and mini city-blocks, bars and whorehouses stretched for miles in all directions. Long dirty streets — smoke stacks from factories spewing out luminous clouds of shit, the yellow glow of streetlights bouncing off the billowing smoke. The popping blue lights of storefronts, deserted. You get the picture, snap back to reality!

Through the rain, start spotting the occasional drunk as I roll on closer to the docks. One guy, trying to pick himself up on one stiff arm, pissed as hell in brown corduroy. I slow down to a cruise to check him out — no cars in front or behind. He looks up at me with his dirty scarred face all puffed up, one eye glistening black under a flicking neon sign advertising cigarettes — a blood moustache. Not much of a challenge—let alone a human worthy of the respect of a quick clean kill. Just a waste really!

Closer to home now, across twin tracks, some Chemical Brothers cranked on the stereo, the sub-woofer thumping under the seat. I drove onto another strip lined with garish fluorescent storefronts and strip-joints of hell burning before my eyes.

Three or four chicks with fuck-me boots on and short skirts stagger on high heels trying to look consumable, one chick with white tits hung out looking like they're dipped in flour. She looks at the van rolling past with dead eyes. A guy with slick backed dirty blond hair, slides out of a doorway and studies her, gives her a shot of booze and a hit on a joint, holding her by the shoulders as if propping up a store mannequin. He motions to me as if showing me a row of watches inside his jacket, his big stubbled grin with a cigarette perched between his yellow teeth, bead black eyes sparkling as he rolls his pelvis slowly, pulling his clenched fists back against his hips like an insane trailer-park Elvis impersonator ... I drive on, he gives me the bird.

I crawl to a stop at the curb and put the van in reverse. Back up quickly, to the pimp and his bitch.

He clapped his ring-encrusted hands and slid up to the passenger's window, running a hand through his grease-locked hair.

"Hey man, thought you was someone else, sorry 'bout that shit." He leaned in towards the van window, his pupils visibly dilated in the night light.

"How much?" I ask.

"Twenty for a vacuum an' fitty fo' a full flush. Cash"

"How much for her and for you to watch?" I ask, flicking through a wad of twenties in my wallet so he could see plain enough.

He raises his arched eyebrows looking at the cash and considers it for a minute, spitting on the pavement beside the van.

"One fitty and no funny shit a'ight?"

"Jump in. The bitch goes in the back."

I head due east and cut across the back of the South-East Portvale industrial zone. Old oil tankers stand hulked in the fog, moored to the decaying wharf, rust running like blood from their ghostly exteriors. Abandoned factories sat like desecrated tombs ringed with barbwire fences. I hit the boulevard that runs onto the coastal highway, through a few tagged-on suburbs hanging on to the remnants of the industrial work that lingers in the area. Through junkyards and empty lots piled with twisted steel and trash. Past barren garages and burnt out stolen cars. I found a vacant lot and park behind a blackened shipping container.

I turn on some *Slayer* and instruct the pimp to get in the back. He starts to freak when he notices the passenger's interior door handle is missing. I lean forward quickly and try to club him in the head with the butt of my .45 automatic. It glances off the side of his face with a faint splash of blood. He makes a play for me so I put a slug in his forehead—the roar of the blast almost deafens me in the enclosed space of the van. The back of the pimp's head explodes in a spray of gray-matter and black blood as he collapses in a broken mess, slumped over the back of the passenger's seat. I give him a shove and he slithers over the seat like a limp dead eel, slick with blood.

The bitch is in a panic, fumbling with the overhead light in the back of the van, making short sobbing gasping noises like she's having an asthma attack. I look over my shoulder quickly as I turn the van's ignition off. The yellow light suddenly flickers and comes to life, illuminates the scene in the back of the van in vivid detail. Bloody scratch marks on the white steel rear doors. Blood and flesh from the pimp covers the whore, hunched up screaming, her head bent low in the back of the van as she tries to stand, and then slips in the thick dark blood pooling around her stilettos. Her half naked body is slick with blood as she tries to stand again, using the pimp's dead body to steady herself as the van sways with her movement. Her hands extend out towards me, shaking hysterically as I holster my piece and turn the stereo up.

I unsheathe my Buck knife and flick off the light as I make my way over the front seat into the back of the van. She gives up screaming when I knock her unconscious with the butt of the knife handle. I flick the light back on for a second and look down at her, spread out against the once-white floor of the van, like a white swastika in a red pool of blood. I push the dead pimp to the back of the van and lay a tarp on the floor, rolling the whore on her back on top of it. I remove my clothes, fold them neatly, place them on the driver's seat, and flick the light off as she morphs into Lucille and *Slayer* launches into 'Dead Skin Mask.'

24

I changed clothes from the bag I kept behind the seat and drove a few blocks. I burnt the soiled clothes, caked with blood from the pimp and his whore, in a 40-gallon drum I found in a vacant lot. I took the van through a carwash a couple of blocks from home, a 24-hour 'wash all-nite' on Lower Dockside Avenue. No cameras. Separate stalls and a drain that ran-off directly into the Lower East Side Viaduct and straight into the river that flowed into the harbor. I caught a reflection of my face in the side window of the van and felt shocked, as I sprayed the tires with the water-hose.

I looked like a monster, a freakish version of myself. A suburban elephant man. With my new scar and fresh kill eyes, I look more like Charlie than ever before. After an hour of cleaning the interior of the van, I head home. Tired, sore, yet strangely satisfied and empty at the same time. I thought about the decapitated bodies of the pimp and his whore and went through a quick mental checklist, making sure I hadn't left any damning evidence behind. I had the head of the whore in a bag behind the front seat and by now the bodies were on their way out to sea on the strong harbor currents.

In desperate need of some serious sedation, I swing by the drive-thru bottle shop for a forty-ounce of Jack Daniels and a packet of smokes.

The next week rolled by, punctuated with fitful sleep and restless days. I spent two days cleaning the rest of the trash out of the house, smoked the last of my stash and generally just fucked around killing time waiting for Charlie. I started hanging around inside the house more, exploring corners and bad memories. Trying the house out for size like a bad suit, slowly getting a feel for it. Considering one of the larger rooms upstairs for my own living quarters. Thinking about Charlie.

What if he didn't return?

What if he was dead?

What was I supposed to do with the house and all that shit in the garage?

I kept myself busy painting the hole in the garage floor fire-engine-red—two by two square meters of blood—the red room. There was no trace of the girl ever being there now. I kept the drums covered with a tarpaulin. The smell of the fertilizer kept me awake the first couple of nights: an odorous allergic smell, cancerous in its own right. Finally, I started to think about what it would be like without Charlie around.

Happier? Probably.

Without Ma around anymore, doing a demolition job on Charlie wouldn't be a problem. However, there was the slight problem of my deep-seated mistrust of him. He could turn me to stone just by the way he looked at me. He would know I was coming for him anyway. I used to suspect he had the ability to read minds. My experience with Charlie had provided me with ample evidence of this ability.

Maybe I could skip town?

Take the van and the cash I had left and just hit the road.

Maybe pick up a few hitchhikers on the way for fun?

I wandered the ground floor of the empty house while I waited and planned my future. My thoughts were interrupted by the sound of a horn at the front gate. I took the steps upstairs three at a time.

From my vantage point I could look down on the street, sure enough a large black automobile sat idling in front of the driveway gate. I felt a twinge of anxiety in my chest—who could it be? It didn't look like the cops and we never had any visitors usually. Shit! Even the meter man didn't set foot in our property. Charlie had rung the electricity company and told them we had a ferocious pit-bull that would more than likely rip any meter men limb from limb, if they happened to set foot inside our gate.

I nervously lit a smoke and headed outside. The sun was sitting high in the blue sky, the warmth from the sun apparent on the back of my shaved head. I noticed the crow on the roof again, sitting directly above the window where I had been looking down from previously. I slid open the spyhole in the fence and went to look through at the car outside. A black staring eye gazed back at me from the other side.

"Open the fuckin' gate will ya, killer?" said the inimitable voice of Charlie.

I thought I detected a weakness in his voice, something not quite as confident, not so self-assured. I opened the gates, my plans temporarily put aside due to the unexpected arrival of my lord and nemesis.

The car he was driving looked brand new. The throbbing thump of a perfectly tuned V8 engine—metallic black lacquered finish—chrome mags and wide-wall tires slung low—tinted black windows with chrome trim.

However, it was an older model than I would have expected.

It was Pa's car, completely restored and modified. I could hear some old rockabilly trash playing on the tape deck. Charlie had one pale hand resting on the chrome chain steering-wheel, his eyes boring into me as he cruised past into the yard, parking in front of the garage and turning the motor off. Charlie got out clutching his stomach.

"What's wrong?" I asked

"You keep killing people," he said, as he walked past me toward the side door of the garage.

I walked behind him obediently.

He took off his leather jacket and lit a smoke, rummaging in his pockets for his keys. He was wearing a black t-shirt and jeans. For an instant, I thought I saw what looked like light shining through the thin material of his t-shirted midriff—a perfect hole about the size of a small dinner plate. I blinked my eyes and he disappeared into the garage.

I closed the door behind me as I entered the garage.

Charlie was conspicuously absent.

I turned the light on. Pa's car was parked next to the van—the van was parked next to the drums—everything seemed to be in order. I felt something cold and metal press against my temple. Charlie emerged from the dark space under the stairs, holding a chrome-plated .45 level with my brow.

"Why'd you do it?" he spat at me.

"What? What?" I stammered.

"The fucking girl, you idiot! The girl—why'd you kill her?"

I slowly turned my head and showed Charlie the deep scar across my face.

"She did this to me," I said.

"And what were you doing? I suppose you thought you could entertain her while I was away, huh?"

I said nothing.

Charlie reached into his backpack on the floor and threw a newspaper at me.

"Read it," he said.

The front-page headline screamed:

`'Mayor's    daughter    missing.    Police    fear kidnapping.'`

A photo underneath, of an attractive young woman, bought her image back to me like an actress in an old b-grade horror movie.

Lucille's face flashed in front of me.

I heard her pitiful pleas and screams.

My scar ached.

"We have to move our dates forward," Charlie said emphatically.

"I had big plans for her. Now we'll have to go back to the drawing board."

I didn't ask what part of his master plan she was supposed to be. I was over his grandiose schemes to bring the country to its knees. He seemed less tangible to me—less real like everything. I thought of the girl, aware of my even heartbeat. I thought of her head now perched upon one of the makeshift altars in my lair.

I remembered the flash of tin as she hacked at my face.

The calm precision of my actions.

The click of the hammer as it struck home.

The deadly bark of the pistol.

The kick of the recoil.

The whirr of the chamber as it revolved with the release of the trigger. The warmth of the revolver as it hung by my side in my steady hand. The acrid scent of spent gunpowder, hazy blue in the air around me.

The feel of the bone in her neck beneath my blade.

Charlie struck me across the back of my skull. For a brief second, I thought I saw fear in his eyes as I pitched forward into unconsciousness.

I woke up on the floor of the garage with a splitting headache. The back of my head was thick with a mass of dried blood. Judging by the lack of light coming through the painted windows, it must have been dusk. I felt slightly nauseous. I wasn't sure whether it was due to the blow or the fact that Charlie had actually hit me. I got to my feet and gingerly made my way upstairs to the loft and changed clothes—camouflage pants, boots, and a black parka.

I tucked a balaclava into my pocket and put my pistol in a backpack.

Anger was beginning to fill my confused and sore brain. Images of Charlie in various stages of dissection flashed through my mind. I wanted to cross the yard to the main house, open the door, climb the stairs and put a bullet in his fucking head. But I didn't, instead I slipped out the front gate and made my way to the bus stop, counting out my footsteps in an attempt to deflate the anger simmering in my brain. The pain in my head was deep and heavy like a migraine; no amount of painkillers could rid me of the dull ache that throbbed behind my eyeballs. I felt like smashing my head against a brick wall to relieve the tension. Instead, I forced it into a small space at the back of my mind as if pushing a tidal wave into a small box. The bus arrived.

Ideas began to evolve.

Combined with regular doses of alcoholic and narcotic sedation, inevitable consequences are sure to arise.

25

"**T**ake it. Take it. You go now. Please. No. No. No ..." the frightened woman screamed from behind the counter, her hands held up before her in surrender. Her husband hunched down next to her, his hands clenched over his head, forehead resting on the shop floor.

"Don't shoot sir. Don't shoot," she begged.

My .38 Smith and Wesson was pointed directly between her bespectacled eyes. The few customers in the liquor-store were spread-eagled on the shop floor in the aisles, whimpering like dogs.

"Open the safe," I demanded, my voice slightly muffled because of the balaclava.

"Can't open. Can't open," she sobbed. "No key, mister" she implored.

I could see the thin leather strap around her neck. Reaching across the counter, I quickly tugged it free from her scrawny neck. Sure enough, a key hung from it.

"Good night," I said and then shot her in the forehead.

For a second, the silence was immaculate, then a woman on the floor in front of the counter screamed. I shot her in the top of her head, the back of her skull exploded in a shower of gore as the .38 hollow-point exited. A male customer sprang to his feet and made for the entrance, knocking over a stack of cask wine in his haste to escape. The display shelf upended and the guy sprawled in a heap against a shelf, he tried to get on his feet again, scrabbling across the floor on all fours like a crippled crab.

I caught him with a shot in the right shoulder blade.

He went head first through the plate-glass door, the door chime rang crazily with the full force of the blow. Another female customer hiding behind a whisky display case began screaming uncontrollably. I stepped into the aisle and saw her curled in a fetal position on the floor—the fingers of both hands in her mouth as if she were eating them. I advanced towards her and placed the muzzle of the .38 against her sweating temple.

I could feel the shudders of her sobs.

The shock of the blast spun her into a display of cheap chardonnay. The bottles crashed to the linoleum, casting strange abstract trails of blood across the gray floor as they rolled their separate ways.

The tinny sound of a radio played in the back of the store.

I could hear the rasping breath of the male customer, lying slumped across the shattered entrance doorway. His shattered back gaped with a glistening wound pumping blood. Each shuddering gasp tinkled the door chime above him, as he slowly died.

I felt the lump on the back of my head where Charlie had knocked me unconscious with his .45. My vision blurred for a brief second as I swallowed back the pain and focused on my mission again.

I found the safe out the back under a coffee table. There was only about nine hundred cash inside. I stuffed the crumpled bills into my backpack along with three bottles of expensive scotch and a handful of cigars. I took a purse and a wallet from the inanimate corpses lying on the floor. I tore a blouse off one of the female corpses and used it to fill the neck of a forty-ounce bottle of vodka. I lit the thin bloodstained material and tossed the bottle toward the rows of spirits stacked against the rear wall of the store. Fire erupted instantly as the spirits ignited. In my haste, as I leapt over the dead body in the doorway, I nearly scalped myself on the broken glass still hanging from the top of the door frame.

A brief second later, the interior of the liquor store swelled with boiling flame and burst the front windows outward in a hail of glass and fire. The blast from the explosion knocked me off my feet. I picked myself up and stumbled backwards into the cool night.

I hurried across the road toward a large unlit concrete car park building. I looked back over my shoulder as I ran, the liquor store was now completely engulfed in flames, a huge smoke ring drifted up into the blackness above.

Minutes later, I heard the inevitable sound of sirens approaching in the distance.

My heart pounded madly.

I started to panic as I fled through the car park.

I had done nothing to prepare for this job.

Pure misdirected rage was the reason for my decision to rob the store. I was starting to slip, letting my anger over-ride my logic and consequently making stupid mistakes. Catching the bus from my neighborhood and exiting one block from the store was a good example. No planning. Completely random choice. I had seen a group of shops in the distance and signaled the driver to let me off at the next stop. At the store, I hadn't worn a disguise other than the balaclava—no change of clothes and most of the gear I had on was now sprayed with blood, the sleeve of my parka was torn from the jagged glass in the door. I hadn't even recovered the cartridge casings or the spent rounds.

I ran out the other side of the car park building and ducked down an alleyway, pulling the balaclava and parka off as I headed into unfamiliar terrain. Things were going wrong, my hands were shaking. I hadn't felt this much fear for a long time. And oh how the fucking adrenaline surged through my veins, up my legs, through my stomach, up my spine, into my brain! I kept my eyes peeled for a manhole cover that would take me underground. Instead, all I could find was a large waste bin. I discarded the bloodstained parka and caught my breath for a minute as I tried to think of what to do next.

The sirens circled closer, nearly upon me.

Three squad cars, lights flashing, briefly lit up the alley with blue and red strobes as they passed by at high speed. Minutes later, an ambulance and a fire engine chased after them.

I crouched behind the waste bin, shaking like a leaf.

I thought I would pass out, the adrenaline was so intense. I turned my camo pants inside out, the black lining disguising their previous appearance. I considered ditching the pistol, but held on to it for fear I might need to shoot my way out of a confrontation with the pigs.

I drew a deep breath and stood up, listening carefully.

I stepped out from behind the waste bin.

A burst of high-beam headlights blinded me. I quickly stepped back into the shadows behind the dumpster. The guttural throb of a V8 revved then idled, revved then idled. I ducked back behind the bin and checked the chambers of my revolver—all fucking empty. I fumbled through my bag and drew out my claw-hammer as I crouched, waiting. The long black bonnet of the Ford slid past then stopped. The passenger door directly in front of me. I waited breathless, my heart banging in my chest. The car-door swung open.

"Get in," Charlie instructed from inside the car.

I rubbed my eyes. Sure enough, it was Charlie, hunched over the chromed chain steering wheel. His back looked strange, like someone had taken a large ice-cream scoop and removed a portion of his shoulder and upper back with it. The green glow of the dashboard cast a sickly glow on Charlie's gaunt face. His teeth were black—glistening. His eyes were deep-set, his head a flesh-less skull. He looked like a ghostly old man.

"Get the fuck in, chump," he ordered.

I considered killing him where he sat, thinking of the lump on the back of my head. Instead, I threw my backpack in and jumped in after it.

In a few quick minutes, Charlie pulled over to the curb after safely taking the back routes away from the chaotic scene left behind us.

"You better drive, Caleb. I don't feel so good," he said.

He got out of the vehicle looking hunched. I could see in the streetlight the empty hollow in his stomach. I could see the rise and fall of his every breath—a slight flattening of his t-shirt in the hollow as he exhaled. I looked at Charlie as we changed seats and was shocked to see how sick and old he looked—a smoke hanging from his thin mouth, flexing his fist like a junkie preparing for a fix. My desire for revenge abated as I considered the obvious poor health of my brother. I slid the Ford into gear and headed down the alley toward the boulevard.

I drove steadily, not wanting to attract attention as I glanced over at Charlie in the passenger seat. I rubbed my eyes, unsure of what I was witnessing—his arm was fading in the half-light. First, his fingers seemed to retract, then his hand darkened, almost pixilated, then his forearm dissipated until it seemed to stop at his shoulder. The short sleeve of his t-shirt was flaccid. Empty.

"What's wrong? What's happening to you?" I asked. Shocked.

"You're killing me Caleb—you're killing me." He replied quietly, his voice that of the infirmed.

I looked straight ahead, lit a smoke and took a pull from the bottle of scotch in my backpack. I glanced back towards where Charlie should have been sitting—the seatbelt hung loose in the passenger's seat.

I nearly swerved off the road.

I gripped the steering wheel tighter to control my trembling hands.

My mouth was bone dry and the back of my head throbbed from where Charlie had cracked me with the butt of his .45. I looked at my wild eyes in the rear-view mirror and realized I was in the middle of some kind of psychotic episode, slightly beyond my control. I kept driving, staring straight ahead, my hands firmly clasped on the steering wheel.

Soon familiar landmarks and shop signs flashed past.

The steady purr of the motor.

I turned the stereo on—an old jazz station played blues.

I turned the dial—nothing, just that crazy old music. The hair on my arms bristled as a chill crept over me, condensation ballooned in front of me as I breathed—the car was an icebox.

I shivered and put my foot hard on the accelerator, heading towards home as quick as I could. I looked in the rearview to make sure I wasn't being followed and choked back a scream. Pa stared back at me with glazed dead eyes, his rotting flesh flaked from his skull and his bloated blue tongue lolled obscenely from the corner of his open mouth.

"Kill 'em all son," he whispered, with a terrible gasping breath. *"Kill 'em all."*

From Portvale Daily News (archive).

Pamela Raj, 57, was found lying on the floor of a superette in the East Dockside housing projects district. Her husband Sanjiv Raj, 59, was barely recognizable, his body burnt beyond recognition. Forensics had to peel his melted corpse off his wife's dead back. It looked as though he had tried to protect his spouse in his last moments from the ravages of fire, by draping himself across her unconscious form.

Both lived in a unit above the store and had no criminal priors or known enemies. Both had been badly beaten and their hands bound before being burnt alive. Witnesses reported a suspicious looking man in the area before the killings who was wearing sunglasses at night and what was obviously a wig or toupee. Various descriptions provided enough details for a police artist to make a sketch, which was published in various newspapers and posters fixed to lampposts and bus stops. Despite the efforts of precinct police and the media, no one has come forward to identify the mysterious man in the sketch. A similar attack occurred three months ago but police have yet to confirm whether they are related or not.

26

Icouldn't sleep for days, thinking about the vision of my dead father, speaking to me from the grave, or rather, from the back of his old Ford. I thought about Charlie disappearing on me all the time and shuddered with disbelief. Weird shit was happening to me that I couldn't explain, that was beyond logical belief. Fear gripped me for the first time in a long while and I worried that I was going insane. I had to regain my focus and get back on track with my life before it spiraled completely out of control. I needed to finish what I had to do here in Portvale, including carrying out Charlie's plans. He wants me to help him set the world on fire. He says, "It is better to die standing up for a cause, than to live on your knees like a dog."

He can shut your mind down with a sentence.

I have started copying his words into an old notebook. These words he calls: 'moments of truth,' or 'essential clarities.'

I like to call them, 'expressions of the eternal now.'

I never used to think much about what he said. In fact, I would try to block his repetitive words out of my mind, but then the words started slipping through, making sense increasingly.

Charlie used to say something completely random at any given moment, like "satisfaction is the death of desire; therefore we must kill desire by the satisfying act of destroying that which it is we desire."

It wasn't so much what he said, it was more like how and when he said it that struck home. When Charlie was around, I had no problem with the girls. Cops and bartenders on the other hand, were less convinced of his prosaic prowess, or mine for that matter.

I was worried about Charlie though. When he was around, he wouldn't shut up about his plans and was looking like shit. Since he'd got out, he'd lost weight and was tweaking again. He had a penchant for crystal meth or 'Ice' and would stay strung-out for days on end. His insomnia kept him awake as much as the crank and I couldn't remember the last time I had seen him eat a decent meal. He was strung out and I could've cut the tension between us with a knife. My visions, or whatever they were, led me to believe that Charlie's days were numbered. I could smell the thick stench of death on him. Like earwax or hot blood, the rancid aura hung about him like a bad perfume.

Sometimes I get so sick of Charlie's nihilistic rhetoric. I tell him he should have been a preacher. Instead, he's a thirty-four year-old high school dropout, ex-con, knocking up pipe bombs and homemade plastic explosives in the garage out back.

The plans Charlie has for me are secret—very secret. Yet, his plans become more transparent with each day until I almost know what he is thinking. He is changing, while his plans remain constant. Fixed. Set in concrete, like a narc at the bottom of a river.

With each passing day, he looks more ragged in his loose blue jeans and black t-shirt, his skin pale and drawn across his cheekbones. The once toned muscle he flexed with pride had been replaced with skin and bones. Everyday his eyes sink deeper in his shaved skull, the pupils glistening like polished coals. He is fast becoming the poster boy for Anorexics Anonymous.

As friends sometimes do, I had shaved my head like my brother's, although he had gone one better (as always) and got rid of his eyebrows. His bony head now resembled a polished skull.

His metamorphosis was complete.

I started to spend most of my time out of the sun, just hanging out in the loft, only venturing out at night. Consequently, I had taken on the ghoulish pallor of an embalmer's mannequin. It was now quite easy for anyone who chose to do so, to recognize Charlie and me as identical twins.

Charlie had disappeared again. I hadn't seen him since he picked me up in the Ford a week ago. Out on another of his 'missions,' I supposed. I hung around the house for a couple of days waiting for him to show. Instead, a mysterious package appeared on my bed one cold afternoon, tied in brown paper with red string. I was a bit dubious about opening it at first—it could've been a bomb.

A few shots of whisky and a fat spliff conquered my fear.

I ripped the paper free to discover Charlie's black backpack.

All the firearms were there along with the money. Combined with my recent swag, I had nearly forty-five thousand cash. Money was inconsequential to me now. It was just paper—dirty money. Blood money.

I wanted to burn it all and shoot up the night.

Instead, I stacked the cash into neat piles and bundled it up with rubber bands. After transferring the money into a plastic bag, I tucked it inside an empty paint can and buried it in a hole behind the garage.

There had been a note in the backpack which I read as I lay in bed that night. The note from Charlie said he was tired. He felt sick. His plans had all gone horribly wrong. He no longer wanted to 'give Al Qaeda a run for its money'—whatever that meant!

He just wanted to die in peace.

He was afraid of me.

I was sure he knew about Lucille and our indiscretion.

He didn't want to be around me anymore.

He wanted me to have the house and dismantle the explosive devices.

"Why not," he suggested, "use the van and start a business somewhere down south."

I could sell the house. I'd already changed the legal documents into my name after Ma died. Just sell the house and along with the cash I already had, I would have a nice fat lump sum to see me through a few long years of leisure. Part of me still ached for adventure. The adrenaline charge from a job fuelled my imagination and soul, more than any slide-glide down easy street.

A deep rage still burned deep within me.

Fuck Charlie! I was done with him.

I had to get him out of my head.

V
The Death of Love

A work of art is a dream of murder, which is realized by an act.

Sartre, Saint Genet

A murderer is regarded by the conventional world as something almost monstrous, but a murderer to himself is only an ordinary man. It is only if the murderer is a good man that he can be regarded as monstrous.

Graham Greene

I'm beyond giving a fuck about anything. The blood and fear have made me sick. I'm nauseous twenty-four seven. My mind is spinning. My gut churns and my skin is enflamed beyond repair. Black circles ring my haunted eyes—soul-less, dead.

I can't recognize myself anymore.

The man at the store talks to me as I place change on the counter for a bottle of Bourbon. His voice sounds slow mo, like the roar of the surf under a dark jetty. His face explodes in a mass of crimson and gray.

Reintegrates.

Explodes.

Reintegrates.

Explodes ...

Disintegrates.

I look away and get the fuck out of there, puking into the gutter outside the liquor store as the lights and sounds merge and roll into slick black night. I stumble blindly down an alley, smack-bang into the middle of a gang-banging crack party.

I try to run, head exploding, lights swirling, color flashes enraging me with my sickness. I swing my piece wildly as I look for an opening to escape. A baseball bat lays me flat, face first— the back of my head erupts in a flood of sticky warmth. I hear the voices cussing me out as each boot finds its mark against my ribs, head, stomach, back. Darkness closes in and I smell sweet relief as the concrete bears me up under their onslaught. I feel the cold steel muzzle of a snub-nosed .38 thrust roughly against my temple.

"Let's cap this crazy mutha-fucker, man?"

"Nah man, let that nigga be. He's already gone, dogg. Don't waste yo' fuckin' caps in his white ass."

"We outta here G. let's roll."

Footsteps.

Bottles smashing.

Pain flows in waves.

Whiteness.

Blackness.

Death?

It seems like days before I come to. Lost in a sea of unconsciousness and fever I was oblivious to having been rescued by the lovely Lucille. Like an angel gifted with providence, she found me there, all beat-up and in bad shape. I was lucky to be alive and she did everything she could to save my sick ass that night. She hailed a cab, took me home to her empty house, dressed my wounds and poured vodka between my parched lips until I opened my eyes again.

I thought I was back in a hospital ward again. The smell of white spirits reminded me of the cleaning fluid at the institution. A pretty woman, an angel, leaned over me with a cold compress. It was her and I didn't feel comfortable at all. It had been a while since I had seen her and now I was a fucked up mess. For all I knew, she probably watched my sorry ass get kicked all around that alley by those homeboys.

I felt weaker than I ever had and swore no one would ever get the jump on me again. Never. Three days later when I had regained my strength, I sat her down and told her. I very nearly got used to feeling wanted by someone or something other than my own ego. I had to get away and that's why I said what I said to Lucille. I told her Charlie must never know about us and she agreed. But I already knew that Charlie knew about us. He knew, because he could read my fucking mind.

I stumbled over a thousand regrets as I turned away from her for the final time. It was the last time I would see Lucille alive again. She was dead already and she didn't know it. I flicked a switch in my heart that would never be used again. She was dead to me now, despite all she had done for me. It was as much for her own protection as it was for mine. As I closed the front door to Lucille's house I paused on her door-step a minute to light a cigarette. I looked up and saw Charlie, staring down from Ma's old bedroom, his face a mask of seething rage.

I managed to avoid Charlie but later that night, asleep in the loft, I had a series of vivid dreams—lucid visions of a world gone horribly wrong. The first dream I recalled began with an image of me in bed sleeping. The dream progressed quickly to me waking, in my dream, to a dull thudding noise similar to a heart-beat. *The noise was coming from the garage.* I made my way downstairs as if I was floating. The thud, thud, thud noise, was coming from the hatch door in the floor.

Thud.

Thud.

Thud.

A sickly yellow light fills my dream. I turn the light on, my heart pounding in time to the sickening thuds. I lift the table, along with the trapdoor underneath. Charlie grins from ear to ear from the black shadows below. Where his eyes had once been, now two gaping bloody black holes. His teeth are yellow and broken and his breath rattles in his throat. In his pale invertebrate arms, he holds the rigid body of the mayor's daughter. She is unrecognizable other than by association and the clothes I had last seen her wearing. Her head is a mutilated bloody pulp. Charlie had been using her as a human battering ram, the top of the trap door is covered in dark splashes of blood.

He lets her body fall to the floor—a deep guttural laugh issues forth from his foul being. For a second, I see her face and it is Lucille. Suddenly, Charlie lunges at me. He comes toward me, the flesh from his fingers falling away as he reaches for me. His bones clicking— black tongue lolling loosely in his open mouth …

The dream cuts to another scene: the Ford now parked in the garage surrounded by the drums of explosives. The sound of an old tune echoes eerily through the dark confines of the garage—a single dull light bulb illuminates the scene. I can see a figure in the front seat. The green glow from the dashboard casts a strange effect upon Charlie's stony face. The flesh surrounding his mouth looks as though it has dissolved, revealing his teeth in a weird grimace. One bony finger taps the chrome steering wheel in time with the music. Two pinpricks of light stare back at me from the black crevices of his eye sockets. He looks completely demonic.

The Ford growls as he gives it some gas, a transparent black mist of carbon monoxide drifts up from the rear of the car and seems to reach out towards me with its vaporous tendrils. He revs the vehicle again and I notice the plumes of exhaust fumes are inside the vehicle as well.

I see the car from the driver's side. Charlie's deathly glare follows my every movement. He revs the Ford again. A length of garden-hose runs from the back of the car and in through the rear window. His head begins to slump forward as the music continues its ghostly dirge.

I am inside the vehicle now, Charlie nowhere to be seen. The subtle but nauseous stench of carbon monoxide floods my senses. I choke back bile and the oily taste in the back of my parched throat, as I look at my reflection in the rear-view mirror. My eyes water profusely as I gasp for breath. A greasy film coats my skin as I watch the veins in my neck and temples bulge.

The music is deafening now.

I scratch at the door locks, my muscles incredibly weak—the door handles have been removed.

I pound the windows until my fists bleed.

My sight begins to fail as an unusual feeling of calm eases my weary head down onto the steering wheel.

My mind and body numb, now fading ...

Charlie's face suddenly appears at the window. I can't move. He smiles at me and waves—he looks ten years younger again. He motions toward me in a half bow as if showing me a range of products he is selling. Instead, I see he is directing my attention towards the drums of explosives—smiling insanely all the while, like a crazed used car salesman.

He looks knowingly at me and removes a lighter from his pocket. His face darkens and his thin lips peel back from his bared yellow teeth in a maniacal grin.

He puckers his lips very deliberately and mouths Lucille's name three times, until he knows that I know what he is intoning.

I watch his hand with the lighter.

I can't scream, let alone move.

I watch his thumb roll across the striking wheel, as the flint ignites the lighter fluid ...

I sit bolt upright, body covered in sweat—my breath coming in short strangled gasps. I can't get back to sleep. I get out of bed to check the garage below to reassure myself it was only a dream. The image of Charlie hunched over the steering wheel of Pa's car impressed firmly on my mind. Everything seems strange—like a jigsaw puzzle with all the pieces stuck in the wrong place. I try to go back to sleep but give up, instead spending the next endless hours flicking through screeds of mindless infomercial channels on TV. My mind twisting and turning with the knowledge that Charlie knew about Lucille.

The next night I had another dream, more profound and disturbing than the others. In this dream, I am dressed in a black soldier's uniform, in a huge empty warehouse at night, a single light bulb dangling from the rafters overhead—throwing light down on the concrete floor in a white oval shape.

Queues of faceless personages stand to one side of the circle of light, shuffling forward. I stand at the center. As each one enters the light, Charlie who stands on the other side of the circle on the edge of the light—also dressed in a black uniform –barks an order as the faceless entity, prone in front of him, visibly trembles.

"Aim …"

"FIRE!!!"

I perform my terrible duty. A single shot from my chrome plated .45 automatic, directly to the ashen temple of the humanoid in front of me. Then another enters the circle of light and the process repeats itself, the queue shambles forward with each shot and another lifeless corpse drops to the bloody floor. The smell of spent gunpowder and the coppery perfume of blood fill my senses.

As I perform my mechanical task, I notice that each time I execute one of the beings, a portion of Charlie disappears.

I fix my gaze on him and fire randomly into the queue.

Three different sections of Charlie's body consecutively vanish into darkness—his left arm to the elbow, his right ear and right leg to the knee.

I keep firing into the crowd.

After what seems an eternity, his floating head minus an eye, an ear and the tip of his nose, is all that remains.

"Aim. Aim. Aim. Goddam you, Caleb!" He pleads, tears tumbling from his black eyes.

I draw a careful bead, sighting the automatic on the pale forehead of one of the minions and slowly squeeze the trigger.

Charlie had disappeared again. With the house to myself, I went on a three day drinking spree searching for oblivion. With only myself for company, Bourbon seemed the most logical way to dull my thought processes for a short while. On the morning of the third day, I finally managed to drink myself into a deep state of penumbra and had a dream that the Police had found Charlie dead in the garage. It went something like this:

The black uniformed officers, who looked very similar to SS officers from the Third Reich, had searched the house from gable to foundations, their boots creaking on the concrete floor of the garage as they stripped black polythene from the veiled Ford. They unearth a bloated blue corpse, wedged between the steering wheel and the seat, the hose still jammed firmly in the back window, trailing to the exhaust system at the rear of the vehicle.

The detectives at the scene appear to discuss what they had found. In my dream, I catch short bursts of conversation. The general thread of their dialogue is that the case is one of those phenomenal events that defy logic or ready answers. It wasn't that Charlie had topped himself, they had a problem comprehending how the body came to be wrapped tightly in a quilt and secured fast with a seatbelt, especially with the doors all locked from the inside. Blood and saliva secretions were found on the outside of the windscreen as well. The dream falters at this point. I see a close up of Charlie's bloated face— his blue lips blistered, his eyes glazed and open, the whites the color of nicotine-stains. The dream begins to fade. Charlie's face switches to Pa's except Pa is alive and laughing hysterically. His eyes are completely black, his gray tongue lolls from the corner of his mouth and his stained yellow teeth are sharp—very sharp. He continues to scream with laughter, black blood now bubbling from his mouth.

I float up from the scene through the roof of the garage and look down on the property. I see the long geometric shape of the rooming house set amidst the crumbling factories and bars on Artaud Avenue. I see the cemetery across the road—all the white death markers, askew like broken teeth. I see the North Shore and smell the blood. As I rise higher and higher, all I see is a black sky and smoke-cough clouds on the horizon. The stars in the sky morph into shimmering skulls that seem to cackle and chatter amongst themselves.

The dream jumps and continues back down into the abyss. I am back in the garage and it looks as though a dance party had smashed its way into the place the night before—dirty footprints and overturned containers and tools are scattered everywhere. The cops roam around the room like hunched gargoyles, poking through the debris until they tire of their search and exit single-file out the side-door.

They never found the 'red room' in the corner of the garage. They found the cash and the firearms in a backpack under Charlie's bed and later matched one of the revolvers to an outstanding multiple homicide at a bottle store on the other side of town.

The dream cracks and breaks into a frenzied onslaught of multi-media clips like on the TV crime shows. News reports reveal that the authorities didn't find the fertilizer residue or the blood between the cracks in the concrete floor of the hidden chamber. A press conference shows the feds scratching their heads over the whereabouts of our mother and as to the reasons why Charlie had apparently gassed himself in the rundown old Ford parked in the garage.

Everything gets weird and the past and present merge into one. The report continues, that after looking through their records they found that Pa had set the ball rolling twenty years earlier, by gassing himself in the same garage. The report ends and I am alone in my dream. There didn't need to be a past or a future, here it was—just a big shitty mess in the here and now. It was just a big filthy old city with blood and guts splashed all over, interspersed with absurdity and the odd glimpse of naked humanity, crawling along in the eternal now of everything and nothing. People like Charlie, disintegrating on every street corner. The dream fades to black …

It was a day later, I woke and realized only half the dream had been illusion.

28

Charlie waits, crouched low in Lucille's wardrobe, his face nestled amongst her few dresses and nightgowns. He can smell her scent on the clothes—almost taste her subtle smell on his tongue. His hard-on throbs in his jeans, aching with need, blood pumping with every loud heartbeat. He thinks of Lucille entwined with his brother. He thinks of Caleb's lack of loyalty and his blood boils. His breathing comes hard—the air in the closet is stale and damp. He opens the door slightly and winces as light cuts through the darkness in a shaft of swimming dust particles. He fondles the cold-steel barrel of his automatic until it grows warm with his touch.

In his mind he can see her breasts peeking through a torn white blouse, a slick sheen of maroon covering her tight young belly, her honey thighs quivering in fear, her blue eyes pleading, her full red lips mouthing *'Save me. Save me ...'* over and over and over.

He hears the key unlocking the front door and scrambles quickly to his feet, his knees aching from having crouched for so long in his hiding place. He feels the barrel of the automatic again and slowly tucks it into the back of his jeans under his belt. He withdraws the switchblade from his back pocket and releases the nine-inch stiletto blade with a flick of his thumb. It gleams like a sliver of glass in the faint light of the dark closet. Stars flash and dance around the blade as he turns it, admiring the sharpness of its shape, the coldness of the steel. He thinks about his brother again for a brief moment, about the day when he presented Caleb with the switchblade, told him its history. Ticked off each carved notch with graphic narrative. The power in that knife was electric—this, Charlie had said to Caleb, was his legacy.

He hears footfalls ascending the stairs. Certain haste to their measure. He crouches again, ready to spring forward in attack. He knows she is coming home for the last time. He knows she will be packing her meager belongings in the old cardboard suitcase under her bed and taking the first bus out of town. He knows he won't get another chance to hurt Caleb in such a way. He knows he cannot let her go.

Lucille starts to undress as she reaches the narrow landing at the top of the stairs. The house seems so empty, her mother now dead and buried. The former tenants evicted after Lucille's recent decision to sell the house. Lucille manages a half-hearted chuckle to herself at the sad irony of her situation. Ironic in that, after all the years of neglect and abuse at the hands of her mother's countless 'boyfriends' and her mother, she is now better provided for by her dead mother than when she was alive.

She looks around the hallway and the stairwell and shudders as she remembers the times she has been flung down the stairs, or molested in the various rooms of the house. The old stale house with peeling wallpaper and stained floors is a tomb filled with bad memories and she would be damned, if she was going to spend another moment in it. Anger rises inside her as she thinks about Caleb, she lights a smoke and watches the flame dance intently at the end of the lighter.

'I could just torch this place and be done with the whole mess,' she thinks to herself. *'I could walk across the road after and torch Caleb's house too. See how he and his freak brother like that! Give him something to remember me by. Fucker!'*

Lucille thinks about the money she stands to inherit from the sale and manages to push back the rage building inside her. She puts her hand on the doorknob but hesitated, pausing to remove her sweater, before entering the room where she had spent her childhood.

Charlie stifles a gasp as he watches Lucille enter the room and toss her sweater on the bed. Her beauty still leaves him breathless every time he sees her, even if it is through a crack in a door. She is dressed in a pair of tight-fitting black slacks and a bra. Her firm full breasts and smooth flat stomach crowd Charlie's brain. He waits. She leans down and drags the suitcase out from under the bed and throws it on top of the covers.

She takes a drag on her cigarette, inhales deeply and blows out a stream of blue smoke, then busies herself throwing belongings into the open case. She drops the spent cigarette on the floorboards and grinds it viciously with the heel of her boot, turns and heads in slow motion towards the closet door. Hand outstretched. Her body looming larger by the second.

Charlie burst from the closet, knocking her backwards onto the bed, the half-full suitcase scattering its contents across the room as it crashed to the floor. He holds the blade to her neck, catching the soft skin and drawing a slight trickle of blood. Her eyes are huge, the blue irises shocked with surprise and fear. Her full chest heaves beneath his weight, breath warm against the palm of his hand as it covers her mouth.

"Don't make a sound little angel," Charlie instructs quietly.

He strokes her blonde hair with his other hand, looking deep into her frightened eyes, smelling her fear stronger than any perfume.

"You're leaving aren't you Lucille?"

She tries to shake her head, her eyes pleading.

"You're not leaving, Lucille. Never!"

Charlie removes his hand from her mouth, her breath releasing in short gasps as she gulps for air. His breath fast and deep now.

"Don't hurt me Charlie. Please don't hurt me?" Lucille begs.

Charlie stands up and looks down at Lucille. He sees her body. He cuts her bra strap with his knife, watching her breasts sway as they are released from their supports.

"Stay still bitch!" he commands, as he tears her slacks and panties from her trembling body.

"Please Charlie? Please don't do this? Please?" she implores.

Her voice fades to a dull roar as Charlie's mind disengages.

"Why are you doing this to me? Why?"

Charlie's vision reddens to a murky hue.

Her body looks stark white, almost floating on the bed.

Charlie's hands feel numb, his chest tight, groin pulsing. He almost feels as though he is watching himself or someone who looks like him—Caleb maybe—as if in a film.

The female body scrambles across the bed on all fours. He sees a rough hand grasp her bare ankle and tug her with force back onto the bed, into a prone position. He sees a hand raise a pistol, glowing luminous gold in the red haze, turning it this way and that. Holding it to the body's head. The dull roar changes to a high-pitched scream. Charlie realizes it is himself screaming, at the very instant the shot reverberates around the small bare room.

The smell of sulfur and blood fills Charlie's senses. He feels empty. Numb. He slumps to the floor, his back against the wall as he watches Lucille's pale legs twitching at the end of the bed. He looks slowly under the bed. Lucille lies whimpering on the other side, her eyes rolled back in her head, her blonde hair matted with dark blood.

Charlie's heart begins to race. Images fill his brain to bursting point, voices chatter deafeningly in his head. His skin itches, his gut wrenches. He pukes on the floor and feels slightly better. He wipes his stubbled mouth with the back of his hand, still holding the automatic.

He takes a deep breath and closes his eyes.

Lucille inhales a sticky bubble of blood, gasps, and coughs simultaneously. He hears her toe nails clicking on the wooden floorboards as her body convulses.

Charlie closes his eyes, forcing the image of Lucille's death throes from his mind. Soon he slips into an exhausted deep sleep, half conscious of the pitifully painful sound of Lucille moaning through smashed teeth and a mouth full of blood. He dreams the strangest dream.

In the dream, Charlie lay in a field at night on a bed of crushed maize and moonlight. A man stands above him, axe held in two fists. His menacing form is a silhouette against the dark blue night sky. He has no face but his body cast a familiar shadow. Charlie can hear him breathing slowly.

In the dream, he cannot move. His fear grinds his bones to air. His breath is like so much dust in his mouth. The cold night air chills his blood as he waits to die. He cannot move.

The man has on a black leather jacket, his dark hair slicked-back. He slowly leans down towards him, a bone pendant clicking around his neck. A Cop badge shining in the moonlight on his black shirt. What appears to be blood—glistens on his shirt. He has no face. In the darkness, the pig's eyes sparkle like polished coals.

Charlie can feel the crushing weight of the man's boots on either of his pinned arms. The odorous smell of lanolin and animal fat permeates his senses. Fear swallows him—he cannot breathe. He cannot move.

The Cop with slicked-back hair and eyes like polished coals, effortlessly runs the blade of the axe in a cross pattern across Charlie's forehead. Charlie feels warm blood trickle down his sweating temples.

The man steps slightly away from Charlie, axe swinging gently at his side and says, "I have you now."

In the dream, the words fall like axe blows—deft cuts—each word exaggerated in Charlie's petrified mind. The full white moon now haloes the man's head—the moonlight shining on the blade of the axe and on the truncheon hanging from his belt. On his other hip gleams the butt of a chrome .357 magnum revolver.

Charlie is suddenly very thirsty and tired at the same time, as if he had not slept for a long slow century or had just walked across a vast desert. His thirst is insatiable, every vein and vessel in his being aches to be filled with the sweet warm blood of eternal life. Every sense of his intellect, cries out against another minute of his existence.

The man with black hair leans down towards him again, holding the axe blade before him as if measuring the center of his breath. The moonlight plays upon the blade of the axe, reflecting light up upon his grim countenance.

Charlie saw the face of death and it was horrible to behold. His heart stops in his dream, his eyes locked with his maker who was Caleb, who raises the axe high above his head in the cruel moonlight.

For an instant, time ceases its merciless infinite countdown, and then the blood came in torrents. A deluge and the dream drowned and everything became nothing, but slow dark peace, much like sleep. Then he heard Lucille and the last gasp of breath she would ever take.

Charlie rubbed his eyes and looked around the room in a panic. Lucille had managed to struggle into an upright sitting position in the corner of the room thanks to the curtains, evident by their blood-smeared coating. Her head is slumped against the wall, which is also streaked with dark blood. One bare leg stretched out accusingly in Charlie's direction and her left hand lay curled palm-up in a pool of blood at her side. A glazed blue iris gazed out between matted clumps of hair, a tear of blood trickled from her eye. Her naked body is so white, but stained with maroon patches of coagulating blood.

Charlie turned away and promptly threw up in the opposite corner of the room. He kneels and heaves and heaves all he can onto the bare wooden floorboards of Lucille's room. Charlie steadies himself and stands, his back to Lucille's lifeless form, and wipes his mouth with the back of his sleeve. He tucks the front of his sweater into his jeans, shuts his eyes, breathes deeply and, avoiding the sight of Lucille, walks sideways out of the bedroom and into the dark light of the hallway.

Charlie lights a cigarette and inhales deeply, he breathes the nicotine deep down into his lungs and sighs. He runs bloodied fingers through his hair and adjusts his black hoodie. Charlie explores the other rooms and finds an old pile of curtains in a spare room. Along with the curtains, he fills the linen closet under the stairs with as many flammable items that he can find. Turning on the gas taps on the stove in the kitchen and the heater in the living room, he lit a corner of the curtain in the open closet, turned and closed the backdoor behind him as he made his way out into the night.

Looking over his shoulder, he sees a flash of orange light as the ground-floor windows burst outwards with the force of the gas explosion. Charlie lights a cigarette and weaves his way through the tombstones in the cemetery next door. He doesn't care if anyone sees him. Reality has swallowed Charlie whole and it is a terrible thing. He can taste death creeping up on him. Big, black and omnipresent now—there is no escape.

I knew Charlie would try to get back at me via Lucille. I knew in his psychotic state of mind that he wouldn't think anything of finishing Lucille. I felt his fear and his release before I saw the flames from her house explode and twist into the night sky. I knew he made her suffer for our indiscretion. I heard the sirens approaching in the distance and checked the locks on all the gates and doors. I knew Charlie was home but I didn't attempt to locate him.

As I watched the fire-crew battling the blaze across the road through a crack in the fence, I thought it wouldn't bother me and it didn't at first but after a while, it invariably did. I filled my thoughts with her beautiful face. My heart filled with something I assumed to be guilt and I did what I could to dampen my emotions. I drank myself to sleep that night, not wanting to confront the inevitable. The following day's headlines and the CSI team picking over the charred ruins, confirmed what I already knew. I made a phone call, packed a bag and rang the car-hire company. I'd prepared for such an occasion, although one more substantially predictable than this one.

This after all was the year, amongst other things, that I plotted to disrupt the present government by Coup d'état. I would assassinate the President. Not because I had any political motivation, other than a biased opinion towards gun control legislation, but more to do with the fact that I could. The fact that no one was beyond my reach, I would touch the untouchable. I breathed life into a debt-free identity, free from conviction or commitment. I did my research carefully and chose my target. The city is full of them. The lonely ones with nobody and no-one to give a rat's-ass about them. No one knew or gave a shit that the air was short a breath, when they kissed their lives' away. Lucille's death was the final motivating factor behind my pursuit of a new identity and a change of scenery.

Charlie disappeared again. I was glad that I didn't need to confront him about Lucille as I wanted to erase her from my mind and heart. I had important things to do. Plans to put into effect. A new Hertz Toyota Camry was my chariot, complete with a visitor's visa and accompanying passport and other legal travel documents.

According to my forged documents, I was an Irish tourist on a three-month visitor's pass and a transfer with another good three months in Canada before my belated return home to the place of my birth—'Limerick ' and the sweet river Shannon.

It would be a while longer before I returned 'home' to Limerick. Europe beckoned. The world was suddenly a small place and nowhere was beyond my reach. The cities of the world were engorged with breeders of every nation. I felt drawn and tired at the same weary moment, there was more than enough work in my own country before looking elsewhere for inspiration. Besides, I had an immediate job at hand. The timing was perfect.

The small town of Forked, in the northern most western state, was the President's last stop on his whirlwind by-election campaign trail. He was at the height of his popularity and set to take the county by storm as he swept into town on the balcony of a colonial steam train. He wasn't winning the green vote but people up there hated tree-huggers anyway. Gun control was his meal ticket in most other states but here he would have to push his labor schemes and logging export referendums to win votes.

My plan was to make sure he died a martyr and wipe that oh-so-perfect shit-eating grin off his face. I would be caught of course, as I knew I would have to be up close and personal to do a proper job. I would be remembered for the assassination and go down in history, as had all those who had done the same before me. My mind was racing a million miles a minute and I knew it was a crazy incompetent plan. I thought of my dead family and spat on the ground. I thought of Lucille and felt hollow like an empty coffin waiting to be filled with sweet death.

Despite my misgivings, I locked the garage up and hit the road. I looked at the oppressive façade of the house as I pulled away and considered torching the place before I left. Thought about transplanting a suitable cadaver as a placebo doppelganger before I incinerated that hellish place that was also my home. Instead, I drew a deep breath, refrained from my paranoia and good sense, wished Lucille well with a psychic communiqué, and kept driving.

I headed north into a harsh winter and spent the next few weeks staying in cheap motels and burning up miles of asphalt with my futile quest. Turns out the president caught a dose of something and had to cancel the last leg of his spin-tour. I knew my plan was doomed to fail and was almost relieved that nothing had eventuated from my travels. I chose to see it as a sign that I needed to complete my work in Portvale and then move on. I viewed my trip for what it was—I had seen a boring part of the country, bagged some trophies and blistered my hands on the unfamiliar steering wheel before I hit Portvale turf again. With no expectations, other than inevitable death. The break away had not served any purpose, other than a brief respite from the destiny that awaited me at home.

Once back home, I begun to feel very removed from reality, to the point where I didn't care about anything. Not Charlie, not Lucille and not that parasitic detective Ray Truman who I knew was now watching the house like a hawk. He had taken to parking directly across the road and leveling his thumb and forefinger at me whenever I ventured out, mimicking the shooting of a pistol. My headaches grew worse by the day.

I pretended to ignore him, I knew he was clutching at straws with his intimidation tactics, just waiting for me to slip up and make a mistake. I realized that perhaps my biggest mistake was to let him continue to breathe. Maybe I should have hunted him down like a dog, instead of an entity like the president, who was way beyond my grasp. My fucking headache was building to a migraine. Something needed to give.

30

As a young recruit, Ray Truman attended his first homicide on a particularly hot summer's day in a trash dump, on one of the many vacant lots spread across Portvale. Ray had just turned eighteen and had graduated from cadet school with first class honours. On his application form for the position of police officer, Truman stated he wished to become an officer of the law to carry on a family tradition. Ironically, his first homicide investigation was one of many that would be carried out by a family steeped in murder. Ray remembered his first flush of nausea hitting the back of his throat as he stared at the pale blue corpse. The deep crevices hacked into the putrid flesh, gaped black with rotten flesh and coagulated blood. The whole body was covered in gaping wounds; the remaining flesh, shrivelled and burnt in the hot summer sun.

After emptying the contents of his stomach, Truman pulled on a pair of latex gloves and dressed his feet and uniform in a set of coveralls. From a slight distance, he clinically looked at the body, aware of his training and his purpose. He stopped counting the knife wounds after fifty. He noticed the black, grease stained rope embedded in the female's neck. He confirmed the corpse was female, noticing the two severed breasts lying on the dirt beside the corpse and the mutilated genitalia. The senior detectives swarmed around the cadaver before the coroner arrived. Truman watched intently over their shoulders, before he went back to combing the blades of grass in the vacant lot for DNA or material evidence. Such was Ray Truman's introduction to the Cunningham family, in particular the 'Dockside Ripper,' or Errol Cunningham as was later discovered.

A decade later and Ray was the lead investigating detective on the scene of the first official homicide by Errol's progeny: Charlie. He witnessed the chaotic violence of a Cunningham unleashed on an unsuspecting world. In this case, on a thirteen-year-old boy, who had been battered to death with a concrete block. The intense rage of the act filled the abandoned warehouse with violence. Ray couldn't help himself, a shudder running up the length of his spine, as he contemplated who could commit such a heinous crime. It wasn't until Charlie Cunningham committed his next sick act that he would be caught, red-handed.

Ray realised that the Cunningham family had become an obsession for him. He felt without a doubt that the Cunninghams, from Errol through to his twin boys, were a bloodthirsty family of prolific serial killers. Ray had realized Errol's crimes through the discovery of his son's violence. Truman had questioned the nature of Charlie's upbringing, knowing his father's criminal background and his own suspicion that Cunningham senior was the 'Dockside Ripper.'

Charlie's conviction and the growing knowledge of the Cunningham clan, including the grandfather who is also suspected of multiple homicides, led Truman to look at the remaining member of the family, namely Caleb. The 'Portvale Slasher' was the name given to the phantom killer of over thirty victims. Truman had done his own investigations and had attributed over sixty murders to whoever was the Portvale Slasher, dating back over two decades.

With over twenty years of homicide investigations under his belt, nothing prepared Truman for the first official Portvale Slasher murder. The mutilated, badly decomposed body was found beneath the North Shore Harbour Bridge, on the Portvale side next to the river. A city council worker discovered the corpse in the cold winter months of 1988. The headless corpse was nude and stripped of most of its flesh by feral animals. The body was found under the massive concrete bridge foundations, amongst piles of trash and debris, nothing remained but bone and frozen viscera. The pathologist's report suggested that the victim had died of multiple stab wounds, with over forty separate deep cuts found in the brittle bone structure of the corpse. The head had been separated from the neck with a large sharp knife similar to a machete or bowie knife. The same knife that decapitated the corpse had caused the deep cuts in the bones of the corpse.

The pathologist estimated death occurred before the victim's body had been dumped beneath the bridge, approximately three months before the remains were discovered. Truman stared at the grim remnants and felt sick to his stomach. It had all the hallmarks of the Dockside Ripper victimology, same M.O., same overkill, but different location. Ray noticed that the surrounding concrete was covered in graffiti, including pentagrams and other satanic references. Truman thought of the pentacle arrangement of the internal organs of some of the DR victims. He shuddered and looked back across the harbour mouth towards Portvale. He could make out the police precinct building, a hulking four-storey bunker of gray cement, and the cranes down on the wharf.

Ray pulled his coat tight against the bitter wind and felt the blackness and despair of the surrounding location. He felt sick because not only did the crime scene closely resemble that of the earlier unsolved serial killings of the Dockside Ripper, but it also meant that his suspicions about Errol Cunningham were incorrect and the killer was still at large. It dawned on Truman as he lit a cigarette, shielding the lighter with numb hands as he inhaled deeply, that it could be the work of another sicko. He hoped, almost to the point of prayer, that this was a one-off dope deal gone bad. A jealous lover's quarrel that got out of hand, a mafia hit on a nark. Anything, but another fucking serial killer's handiwork. As it was, the first official victim of the killer was never formally identified as anyone other than a 'Jane Doe.'

Ray made quick scribbles in his notebook and watched the squad clean up. Another tag-and-bag.

How many more to come?

No matter how hard he tried, Truman couldn't shake the image of Errol Cunningham's black evil eyes. The name Cunningham echoed in his fatigued mind—haunting him. It was this case that would turn Ray into an alcoholic and break another marriage in two. The same thing had happened to Ray's father, part of the sacrifice of the job. Despite all the shit, blood, and violence of working the homicide division, he loved it. He loved busting heads in the wee hours and putting sickos behind bars. He would live and die a cop, it was in his blood and he was going to die hunting this latest sick piece of shit if it killed him.

Truman placed the dumbbells on the floor and shook his arms to release the tension in his biceps. He took a towel off the back of the kitchen chair and mopped the sheen of sweat from his half-naked body. Breathing out hard, Ray made his way to the bathroom and ran the shower. Soon, steam filled the small room as hot water stabbed his fatigued muscles into submission. After washing thoroughly, he dried himself and dressed in jeans and t-shirt. He poured a whisky and swallowed his tablets, after the death of his third wife, it had taken years to admit he had a problem with depression. It wasn't until he found himself sitting alone in the dark, with the cold barrel of his service revolver in his mouth, that Ray finally sought some help. He decided to go private and saw a shrink on the other side of town. One consultation was all it took for him to get a prescription for Prozac. The drug wasn't a cure-all but it gave Ray enough headspace to get him out of the deep dark hole he'd got himself into.

It took three marriages before Ray felt like he'd found true love. Maria was an attractive Italian brunette from the North Shore, who worked with the victim support team out of the Portvale Police Precinct. It was the end of nineteen-ninety four and they met at the Police Annual Christmas Party, with the help of numerous shots of scotch and good cheer they had woken up in the same bed the next day. Ray remembered lying in bed watching Maria as she slept peacefully. He felt hypnotized by her subtle beauty. She had soft olive skin that enhanced her dark features. When she let her hair down it was a beautiful lustrous waist-length that sent Truman wild. And when she fluttered her long eyelashes at him and looked at him with those dark brown eyes, Ray knew he'd fallen head over heels in love with her.

Maria stayed for breakfast and never left. After a year they were married in a ceremony at the downtown registry office, followed by a celebration at a local police bar with a small group of friends and family. Ray and Maria bought a small two-storey villa in a middle-class suburb on the outskirts of Portvale. They tried not to bring their work home with them too often, but inevitably it intruded with an occasional argument but usually they got on well. Ray had feelings for Maria he'd never experienced before. She softened his hard heart and he felt happy for the first time since he was a child.

In the second year of their marriage, Maria passed the Police exams and was admitted as an officer to the Portvale precinct. At work, Ray and Maria maintained a professional relationship when they crossed paths but still managed to have a few romantic liaisons without any of the other staff members noticing. There was talk of a family and a new home. Their two-year anniversary was spent in each other's arms at home with a bottle of expensive wine and news of Ray's promotion to lead Detective in the Portvale Slasher investigation. It was with mixed emotion that Ray accepted the position. He knew it would mean more time away from Maria and home life, but he also knew the extra hours would fatten their bank balance and allow them some financial security for the future.

The next year went by quickly and the marriage began to feel the strain of the long hours and gruesome experiences involved with the case. Maria had her own problems as a Patrol officer and had been threatened by some local goons who tried to get her on the payroll. It wasn't until Ray had paid them a visit and busted a few heads that they left her alone. Maria had become upset with Truman when she found out about his intrusion into her affairs and coupled with the other stress they were under, the incident had nearly split them apart. Ray and Maria took a week's leave and the two had a much-needed holiday in Hawaii. Despite being a short sojourn, it was enough to rekindle the passion in their relationship and set them back on track with their marriage.

Once back in Portvale they settled into work again. Ray had a new homicide to investigate in relation to the Portvale Serial Killings, while Maria continued her work as an officer patrolling the mean streets of Portvale's seedy red-light district. Ray received the dispatch call while on a suspect stakeout outside the Cunningham residence on Artaud Street. He was alone in the beat-up undercover Ford Crown Victoria, when the call came through that there was an officer down near the dockside strip of bars and strip joints. Ray rang Maria on her cell phone but it immediately went through to her voice mail. He knew something was wrong. The sick feeling in his gut grew worse as he drove furiously towards the docks, running red lights with the siren blasting full-noise.

Four squad cars surrounded the entrance to the 'Crow's Nest,' a notorious bar situated right next to the entrance of the main wharf. An ambulance pulled up as Ray leapt from his vehicle. He pushed through the gathered crowd and saw what he hoped he wouldn't. Maria lay crumpled in the gutter, one of the officers had propped her head up with a folded police jacket. She was dead. Her usually olive skin was chalk-white, her lips blue. The gaping wound in her throat made her head hang to one side as the muscles in her neck, along with the main carotid artery, had been shot to pieces. Her dark brown eyes reflected the street light overhead. Truman dropped to his knees beside his dead wife and cradled her in his arms. He couldn't believe it. His breath came in short gasps and he realized he was convulsively sobbing. She was still warm as he stroked her long blood-matted hair, usually kept back with a ponytail but now splayed across her face, the hair-tie disintegrated when the bullet passed through her throat.

He looked up and saw her partner, Tom Cranford, sitting on the curb sobbing as well as clutching a stomach wound. The perp lay spread-eagled on his back on the ground, a skinny Hispanic junkie with three bullet wounds spread across the front of his blue t-shirt. From where he crouched, Truman could see the tracks on the junkie's arms. Ray wanted to get up and kick his dead body until he couldn't kick it anymore but he couldn't move. Ray was faintly aware that ambulance officers were helping him to his unsteady feet, as they carefully strapped Maria to a stretcher. He felt completely numb as though he'd been underwater, very cold water, for a long time. He wished he were dead as he sat next to Maria in the back of the ambulance, holding her cold bloody hand in his own.

Three days later, after Ray had buried her in a small family plot on the North Shore, he went back to work. The inquest revealed that Maria and her partner Cranford, were on a routine call-out to a bar fight when Maria attempted to arrest the perp who then shot her. She didn't see it coming. She had one of his thin arms bent behind his back while Cranford took the other brawler into custody. He made a break for it and lashed out wildly, Maria caught a glancing blow to the side of her face and she released him for an instant. In that second the perp withdrew a small 9mm automatic from the waistband of his jeans and fired a volley of rounds in the direction of the officers.

The first shot hit Maria directly in the neck and dropped her to her knees outside the bar. The next shot hit her partner in the stomach, doubling him up and forcing him to let go of his arrest. The next shots struck the other handcuffed brawler and fell him where he stood. Cranford squeezed three quick shots from his revolver as he lay on the pavement; each shot hit the perp squarely in the chest, as the already-dead junky fell backwards, arms outspread like Christ. The sound of his head smacking the ground made a sickening thud.

Cranford dragged himself to his knees, gasping, and radioed in the call for help as he tried to stop his intestines from spilling through his blood stained fingers. The patrons of the bar scattered while some remained, watching Cranford try to crawl towards Maria, as the sound of squad cars approached in the distance.

Ray lasted two weeks at work before his drinking kept him home with the blinds pulled shut. Venturing out only to make a trip to the nearby bottle-store, Truman's despair began to eat him up inside. He couldn't get Maria's sweet dead face out of his thoughts. He didn't think about the investigation of the Cunninghams. He didn't wash or eat; he just drank until he couldn't drink anymore.

On the last day of a two-week drunk, he found himself sitting on the end of his unmade bed in the dark. The same bed where he and Maria had slept for the past two years; where they had made love and planned their futures together. Now Ray sat with his shoulders slumped, reeking of alcohol and self-pity, the cold steel barrel of his .38 Smith and Wesson in the back of his throat, his finger trembling on the hair trigger. He thought of Maria and heard her voice from the dark recesses of his dying heart. Her gentle voice told Ray not to pull the trigger. He dropped the revolver to the floor and drank half a bottle of scotch before lying back on the bed and collapsing into a deep intoxicated sleep.

When he woke he felt sick but better. He knew what he had to do before he even thought about it. Ray stepped under the scalding water in the shower and stood there for half an hour before he turned the faucet off and dressed himself. He rummaged in the kitchen cupboards until he found a tin of food that he heated and ate. There was no more booze. Ray's body screamed for it. His mouth was bone dry, he smoked a spliff he had sitting in an ashtray in the pantry. It took the edge off the day but didn't kill the thirst. Truman felt like smashing his head on the wall just to get rid of the tension in his brain.

The cannabis kicked in and his thoughts finally calmed. From that moment forward, Ray sunk his whole being into the investigation. He might not have found the killer, after nearly twenty-five murders, but Ray began to envisage Maria's head on each decapitated corpse that he discovered. In some small way, it offered hope to Ray that he would meet her again one day, in a righteous way. Truman replaced alcohol with weight lifting and his depression for anger.

Maria never went away, even after Ray sold the house and moved into the heart of the Portvale Slasher enquiries, only three blocks from the Cunningham residence. Ray didn't see the Cunninghams as guilty of Maria's death. Nevertheless, they were definitely murderers and so was the little fucker who shot her life away. Ray wanted to kill him. Kill him, real fucking badly. He was dead, of course, so Truman focussed his anger and sense of injustice on the Cunninghams.

Ray walked past the supermarket and his taste buds roared for the sweet taste of alcohol. Every atom of his will fought the urge to open his wallet and buy a forty-ounce of bourbon. But he didn't, instead he thought about what was left of the Cunningham family, what he'd like to see happen to them. The two brothers dead under a fucking bridge somewhere. Ray fumbled with the cap on his medication and popped a handful of Prozac into the palm of his hand, threw his head back and drank a whole bottle of mineral water, as if it were a cold beer. He kept walking and the medication slowly took effect, as his thought processes began to plateau.

Truman stood in front of a store window and lit a cigarette. He heard sirens, the revving of vehicles and the sound of drunks on the main strip. He looked at his dark reflection, catching the glint of a streetlight on his cornea in the dark face that stood staring back at him. He stood wide, his large shoulders framing his tall muscular form. A solid head with a decent chin and full head of hair, Truman stood strong, despite his despair and seething rage. In fact, he thought, he looked bigger than life and frightening. Ray never remarried or replaced Maria with another. He had no room left in him for anything, except rage.

31

Charlie gunned the Ford, weaving like a snake between the cars that lined the interstate. He checked the fuel gauge and felt confident he had enough gas to get him where he was going. He lit a smoke and began to feel sick in the pit of his belly. He noticed his hand tremble as he took a drag on his cigarette.

He knew there was a happening with his name on it, just around the corner. He thought of Lucille and tried to push her face from his mind. An image of her face appeared suddenly in the windscreen, coming headlong at him as he sped into the night. Now her twisted face loomed over his shoulder in the reflection of the rearview mirror. She was everywhere.

This was the Devil's own forked tongue in the road.

The V8 throbbed with power, as it flew past blurred buildings and stunned pedestrians. He eased back on the accelerator and watched the unmarked police car pull into view in the rear-view mirror. Charlie steered the vehicle with his knees while he snapped a fresh ammo clip in his automatic. He can see clearly the cop's face screwed up in anger. He instantly recognized the pig.

Ray Truman.

If there was one motherfucker Charlie wanted to cap, it was Truman. He knew the pig had mutual feelings about him.

Charlie knew the on-ramp was half a kilometer away and he desperately quickened his speed. The needle climbed to a ton as Charlie hit the on-ramp at the last minute.

Ray hung on, he knew the off ramp pointed toward the lower east side and Charlie was heading home. Ray swung briefly between calling for backup and continuing the chase solo. He chose solo.

Ray clenched his service revolver between his thighs and inserted a speed loader into the empty chambers. Holstering his .41 Smith and Wesson, he checked the clip on the M9 semi-automatic Beretta he kept strapped to his ankle.

He wanted Charlie badly. -

That snot-nosed piece of dirt is the end of a legacy that extends back to the old man, Errol Cunningham.

Ray remembered the bitter taste of defeat in his mouth after finding Errol gassed, in that very same old shitter of a Ford that Charlie hurtled towards Armageddon in now.

Ray knew all about evil.

He had seen it in many forms and he knew his own capacity brimmed over on occasion. The Cunninghams were an evil breed. There was no doubt in his mind that they were all tainted with the same bad genes.

Charlie looked in the rearview his heart pounding as he watched Truman gaining on him. He knew couldn't shake his nemesis. The filthy cop bastard that killed his old man, had him nailed. Charlie panicked and hit the freeway, heading nowhere fast, pulling away from his freedom. He knew as he headed northwest that if he had just turned home and got that pig in the basement he would be in the clear. He knew if he just had him down in the damp cold haunted abattoir, he would've had him ...dead.

But he didn't.

He fucked up and became the hunted instead of the number one mother-fucking hunter.

And he knew he was going to die that night.

He sent Caleb a message. He focused all the hate he could muster and sent him a blood soaked message of rage with all his might. He pushed the car further towards the outskirts of the city, aiming towards Grandpa's place in the small town of Repose, some five hundred miles west. The calf muscles strained in his leg as he tried to squeeze every drop of speed from the black Ford as it growled into the dusk.

He flung the Ford down a side exit with a squeal of burning rubber and into a dimly lit road that fed into an abandoned block of factories. He checked the rearview mirror and saw the bastard cop still hot on his tail. Barbwire fences, burnt-out derelict buildings and bulldozed lots flash past as Charlie sped down the industrial strip into the darkening night.

He heard a shot like a faint firecracker over the roar of the engine, then another and the rear windscreen burst in a hail of glass across the back of his neck. He kept his gaze forward and gripped the steering wheel tight as the next shot blew one of the rear tires out. In slow motion, the car started to twist into the center of the road in a spin. The motor howled hopelessly in unrestrained fury as the car leapt the curb, tumbling twice before hammering into the side of an abandoned building in a cloud of smoke and dust. Charlie's head smashed against the door pillar, his shoulder simultaneously ripping from its socket as the car hit with a huge impact.

Charlie hung suspended upside-down by his seatbelt, blood pouring from his wounds. The sound of glass tinkled as it cascaded through the car from the broken windscreen. He could hear the hissing of the wheels as they spun uselessly. The motor pinged and cracked as engine oil and fuel leaked from the carburetor. He started to panic, thinking about the possibility of fire. Everything had been in slow motion, now everything was moving very fast.

Charlie wiped blood from his eyes and looked out the smashed windscreen. He could see Truman's car parked down the street, the engine running, exhaust smoke clearly visible under the yellow streetlight.

Charlie fumbled with the seatbelt and managed to pop the clasp. He fell in a heap onto the roof of the Ford, wincing as pain shot into every part of his wrecked body. He searched helplessly for a weapon, anything. Then he saw what he feared most, Truman's boots walking quickly towards him.

I never saw Charlie in the flesh again. I knew he must've returned home at some point because the Ford had disappeared from the garage. I felt strangely calm and unperturbed by anything. I didn't read the papers or follow the news. I wasn't even aware that he had officially been suspected of Lucille's murder.

I cleaned out the garage and moved my things into the main house, leaving the explosives sitting under a large tarpaulin in the garage next to the van. I found Charlie's plans in the old suitcase under his bed, along with an eclectic collection of books—*Crime and Punishment* by Dostoyevsky; *Mein Kampf* by Adolf Hitler; Nietzsche's *The Will to Power*; *The Anarchists Cookbook*; Bunyan's

A Pilgrim's Progress; Aleister Crowley's *White Stains* and so forth and such like. The plan itself outlined a detailed schedule and layout of the federal building located uptown.

He had written in detail how the van would be parked in the service entrance under the pretense of servicing a reported 'bug invasion.' The size of the explosives and the incendiary nature of it all would turn the buildings and grounds into a Roman candle of death and destruction.

The second half of Charlie's plans involved a simultaneous demolition of the main hydroelectric dams across the country, followed by an extensive campaign of random bombings of iconic capitalist institutions ... and so on it went.

I knew it was impossible.

There was no resolution of the eternal now. Infinite things would carry on consuming themselves, as they always had and always would be. The stars were burrowed deep in the sky and nothing Charlie or I could do, would ever bring them down.

I, however, had a simpler plan.

A small house on the coast.

Find someone—settle down.

Maybe fly to Europe and lose myself on the Riviera.

Just forget about everything. There was nothing else for me, just this present moment. The eternal now.

I lit Charlie's plans with my lighter and let them tumble from the upstairs window to the ground below. I watched the sun going down all red and bloody like an engorged eye staring over the top of the black hills. I felt my body, mind, and soul, merge as my own plans began to ferment in my brain. The next two weeks were spent tidying up the property. I loaded the van with the forty-gallon drums after much effort and filled in the 'red room' with fresh concrete.

I was tempted just to burn the whole place to the ground and try to collect the insurance. I knew that would be a waste of time. A quick check would find my felony convictions as a teenager, in particular a previous conviction for arson. I still considered torching the place as part of my overall plan. I considered selling the Econoline as well, but decided there wouldn't be much of it left, as it was due to be destroyed along with the explosives. I would need a new vehicle to head west to Grandpa's ranch in Fey County, something reasonably non-descript and easy to dispose of like a motorcycle. I had been planning this moment for months now. With the completion of my latest installation, I would also need a new identity. I knew exactly where I was going to find one and where I could score a vehicle at the same time.

The house was completely empty and strangely lonely. The hollow rooms where so many screams and ghosts lurked began to haunt my sleepless nights. A couple of times lying awake in Ma's old bed, I thought I heard someone coming up the stairs, forcing me to sit bolt upright in the dark, my pistol held out in front of me pointed at where I had imagined the noise to be. I thought it was Charlie, returning for something he forgot to take with him.

My paranoia multiplied its negative intricacies within my addled brain. My fragile state of mind was not helped by the presence of two plainclothes detectives, one of which was Ray Truman, knocking at the door on more than one occasion. I saw them coming towards the house as I looked from the upstairs window. I made sure to stay well inside, quiet as a mouse, sucking on a forty-ounce of whisky. My .45 Automatic trembled in my sweaty hand, wet with nervous anticipation. They soon left but returned a week later, catching me by surprise as I hosed down the back yard. I turned and saw Truman looking at me over the top of the fence, aided no doubt by a boost from another accompanying pig.

"Open the gate or we'll dismantle the whole fucking house with a court order," he ordered. I had no choice but to let them in. Once inside, the other cop revealed himself, bald as an egg with a thick moustache, his tall frame bristled with violence. I looked at them both with disgust. Thankfully, Truman remained silent while the other cop assaulted me with a barrage of questions as he stood there eyeing me curiously, as though I were a freak at a carnival.

"Is Mrs. Cunningham home?" The one with the baldhead and thick brown moustache asked.

I told them she was away.

Visiting relatives.

Out of state.

I wanted to force feed these maggots a handful of grade-A rat poison. Especially Truman.

Send them to a different hemisphere.

They asked me if I had heard about the fire at Lucille's and if I had ever seen any suspicious characters in the neighborhood.

I remained calm and said 'no' while Truman approached the garage. The other kept talking to me, trying to distract me. I watched Truman try to peer through the blackened windows.

"Why are the windows painted over?" he called out in a dumb fashion.

I lied and told them my father had a workshop inside with many valuable tools and the painted windows were to prevent neighborhood hoodlums casing the joint.

"Fair enough" he said, without a hint of belief in his voice.

Baldhead showed me a picture of the Mayor's daughter and asked if I had seen her round the neighborhood.

Fuck, she looked like Lucille. I shouldn't have killed her. Jesus, I miss her bad. Lucille, that is.

"No," I replied.

I turned and headed up the steps and stood in the doorway of the rear entrance, ready to close the door behind me.

"What's *your* name?" Truman asked abruptly. I knew he wanted to see if he had rattled my cage. He knew my fucking name already and I knew he knew everything about my family. The pig asked me again with a dead look on his face. Ray Truman, the curse of my father's existence and the pig who'd put Charlie behind bars for killing the old broad in the drugstore, all those years ago.

"You Charlie's brother, Caleb?" he asked in reply to my silence, as he approached the rear doorway where I was standing.

I said nothing.

"You know your brother's dead?" he asked as he mounted a step.

He's talking shit, I told myself.

He's trying to fuck with my head.

I lit a smoke, nearly dropping it with my trembling hands.

"We know he did more than just the old woman at the pharmacy."

"You wouldn't know anything about anything would you, Charlie? I mean, Caleb?" he asked, with a smirk on his face.

He stood level with me on the top step and looked directly at me, unflinchingly. He laughed a low deliberate sound like death coming in a slow train. I pictured a carving knife deep in each of his eye sockets. I cut his nose off with an imaginary razor and watched blood pour like an elephant's trunk from where it had once been.

He leaned in close, trying to position himself to look through the opening in the doorway as I tried to block his view, never letting his steel-blue stare leave my own. I shivered with hate and held back the adrenaline coursing through my veins. I wanted to kill him with every bone in my body, burn his corpse, and kill every member of his family and everyone who had shown that scumbag a moment's kindness. Then I wanted to kill him all over again.

"I killed your brother and you're next you sick bastard!!!"

His whispered words hit me like a sledgehammer.

"I know what and who you are Caleb. You're just like your fucking sicko father and brother and like them, the end of the road is where you're heading!"

He looked me up and down and adjusted the collar on his brown trench coat, lit a cigarette, turned and made his way down the steps to his partner and then walked out through the gate to the unmarked car parked at the curb. My heart hit my ribs like a jackhammer. My temples throbbed as a headache swelled my brain.

He knew.

The fucking pig knew.

The fucking pig was dead.

His words still rang in my ears, as I walked through the dark empty rooms of the house, amongst the ghosts of the dead. The pain building behind my eyes, felt like someone had cleaved my skull in half with an axe.

Archive transcript from Channel 9 2009, TV Doco: 'Hunt for the Real Portvale Slasher.'

Evidence suggests that upon his release from prison in January 2008, Charlie Cunningham began a systematic campaign of terror. Police surmise he abducted women and held them captive in a makeshift basement in the garage of his parent's large boarding-house in Portvale, a semi-industrial suburb of Eden Park.

The discovery of the basement along with other forensic evidence, found after a suspected arson that burnt the hostel to the ground in 2009, suggests that both male and female victims were tortured and possibly murdered in the makeshift garage basement and the large basement that ran the length of the hostel.

Replicating his father's example (who was the prime suspect in the Dockside Ripper murders) he would use the city's viaducts and subterranean passages to hunt and capture his victims. Over a ten-year period Charlie apparently kidnapped multiple young women, sometimes up to five at any one time, imprisoning them separately in a makeshift cellar and in reinforced rooms in the family's disused hostel, before torturing and executing his targets, coup de grace style. Circumstantial evidence suggests that when his first captive died of neglect, he dismembered her body with a chainsaw and distributed it to various places around Portvale. After a few more killings, Cunningham's suspected foul deeds were attributed to the 'Portvale Slasher.' This was the name given by the media to an apparent serial killer, operating in Portvale County from 1986 to 1996.

Another man would be wrongly convicted of the murder of one of the nine homicide victims, which led police to believe they had caught the Portvale Slasher. Despite their belief that they had the right man in custody, the other eight murders remained 'unsolved.' All the victims were sexually assaulted and stabbed to death with unusual brutality. Some of the victims were seen with a Caucasian man with a shaved-head shortly before their death and many other suspected victims remain missing.

Local and Federal authorities list the 'Portvale Slasher' case as still open and unsolved, although most of the evidence points towards Charlie Cunningham as the prime suspect. The killings that took place after and during Cunningham's incarceration were thought to be the handiwork of a copycat killer who was reputedly more prolific than the Portvale Slasher. A distinguishing feature of the later killings was that each victim was found decapitated. The heads have never been recovered.

VI
Sick Urges Manifest

The murderer is the last man who still seeks human contact; the remaining members of the species merely continue to ride past each other on escalators. In such a world, murder and conflict govern humanity.

Heiner Muller

Acts must be carried through to their completion. Whatever their point of departure, the end will be beautiful. It is because an action has not been completed that it is vile.

Genet, Journal du Voleur

32

When Charlie died, he sent me a telepathic message as his spirit left this world. Yeah, he sent me a message so beautiful that I knew he was really a god. He glowed in my mind and spoke with profound words, so eloquent and honorable, despite his base deeds and the legacy he left behind.

He told me he died at the hands of that maggot Ray Truman.

I didn't know whether to believe him at the time.

Truman had now personally admitted to me that he had killed Charlie. There is no room for doubt.

I'm driving aimlessly in the van now.

Cruising for a message of my own to send that pig.

I'll send fucking ravens to pluck his eyes and dead men dreams that'll haunt his sleep, I'll make sure he sees my knife blade above him twisting in the moonlight, before I rip it across his throat ...

I see her flash past and jump on the brake so hard, I peel rubber as I stop and a blue cloud of burning tire smoke drifts past. The weight of the drums in the back sway the van, I grit my teeth waiting for the explosion to rip me to smithereens. My heart smashes against my ribcage as I realize my psychosis has led me to another dangerous place. I start thinking about the cops and the van full of explosives and realize I don't give a shit ...

I reverse the van and pull up at the curb and look straight into the most perfect set of breasts I'd ever laid eyes on. She leaned on the side of the van door, tipped her sunglasses at me, and smiled.

Here was the message Charlie sent to me, just standing there waiting for me to use, on the side of the street. They all look like Lucille now. They all glow with death.

Two ten notes and she was mine.

'Ray fucking Truman, I'm gonna leave you a little present for when you get home.'

I smile at the bitch now sitting in the passenger seat and pull back onto the interstate, heading back towards the Lower East Side.

She starts to whine about the smell of the explosives.

I turn the stereo full blast, Nine Inch Nails grinding out *'The Perfect Drug,'* pumping in my ears.

I pull my Buck knife out of the sheath and look at it.

She cowers in the corner of the passenger's seat, trembling hands raised towards me. My large knife blade glints in the streetlights flicking overhead through the windscreen.

She starts to scream.

I turn the music up louder, take a slow drag on my smoke and let out a bellowing devil laugh. I catch a flash of my eyes in the rear view and am shocked to recognize myself. My eyes bleed together and blacken and they are my Grandfather's eyes, Pa's eyes and Charlie's eyes, all staring back at me.

Murder—deep deep deeply in those black eyes.

"Let my role define you," I said to her, just before I stabbed with a backhand thrust straight through her bare sternum.

Everything froze in that second, as the tip of the blade punctured her heart in a gasp of blood and a crack of bone.

The warm dark fluid covered my hand, squirting between my clenched fingers across the dashboard. Her head dropped forward and I raised an elbow quickly to catch her, before she makes a mess of her face on the expensive stereo system.

I keep one hand on the steering wheel and flip the side-lever on the passenger's chair. The chair tips backwards and she rolls into the rear compartment, an arc of blood splashing across the roof of the van as she tumbles lifelessly to the floor, her head wedged between the 40 Gallon drums. I wiped my hand with a towel I keep under the seat for such occasions and pull over to a lay-by that runs down towards the Upper East Side River.

Ray Truman would know this one's for him.

I worked on her for over half an hour, before putting her back in the van and then dumping her in the stairwell on the ground floor of Truman's apartment building. It was two-am and I knew Truman was pulling hours on the graveyard shift. I looked at the mutilated corpse lying naked at the foot of the stairs to his apartment. Her naked body lay in a cruciform shape, her innards displayed around her headless corpse like writhing snakes. In the dim light of the stairwell, I could see her decapitated head sitting on the third step up, the JT clearly visible, carved deep in her forehead.

I stood staring at it in the half-light, marveling at its austere aestheticism. I must have stood there for at least five full minutes as I considered my next move, before I left. The head was still warm against my shoulder, safely hidden in my backpack, I was unable to leave it behind.

Three days before I executed my plan, I woke from a fitful insomniac night lucky to have achieved forty hours of rest over the last month. It was clear as day what had to be done. I had to get rid of the van and its dangerously laden contents. It seemed like such a waste, all the hard work and anxiety that came with our revolutionary plan of liberating the free world.

However, Charlie was dead and our plans would no longer be the same. That morning, I rose to the vision of the same skull I had witnessed in the mall, hovering in the bedroom doorway.

Its voice boomed around the room.

Its grim words resounded in my tired brain.

"Assert yourself Caleb. Do one damn thing to tell the world who you are."

I could hear its foul teeth clacking together as it hovered at head height. The white bone of skull housed two burning red orbs in its dark eye sockets. It spoke to me, pitch perfect Charlie.

"Make your mark, Caleb. Now is forever, you have the power. You have the power," it reiterated.

The apparition flickered then disappeared.

I got out of bed, shaking badly. The words still bouncing around inside my mind. I felt totally disconnected from myself, as if I was asleep dreaming. Like I was Charlie. All I could see was the vision's skeletal face and the cold eyes of Ray Truman bearing down on me.

I spent the morning packing my bag and getting rid of any personal effects from the property. Aside from the furniture, the house was now bare.

I drove the van carefully. The smell of fertilizer mixed with gasoline, burnt my nostrils. I was hanging out for a smoke, badly.

The windows all wound down to let in fresh air.

I was on autopilot.

I looked in the rear-view mirror at the blue tarpaulin covering the drums. I thought of the broken black-suited cadaver, lying crumpled between the covered drums. I couldn't get Ray Truman, but I got myself one dead member of the Portvale Police Department. He was on a short road to hell in a hand basket if ever I saw it.

Actually, I could have probably fit him in a 'hand basket,' what was left of him after an accident he had with a hedge-trimmer. A routine traffic stop the night before had landed the recruit in the back of the van, unconscious with one Taser strike to the left temple. I took him back to the house and employed the basement one last time— tied him to the altar with duct-tape and cut him down to size.

Soon, I saw the advertising billboards and rows of parked cars stretched around the outside of the huge shopping mall. It looked like a gigantic pastel stadium from the outside. I cruised very slowly over the judder bars as I entered the east entrance, heading towards the underground car parking. After twenty minutes of careful navigation around reversing mothers and their screaming cargoes caged in overpriced SUVs, I finally found a parking space directly next to the lift chambers in the center of the basement car park.

My hands were sweating.

My temples pulsed as adrenaline coursed through my wired frame.

I switched the ignition off, pausing for a brief second before climbing over the front seat into the rear of the vehicle. The dull overhead fluorescents in the car park cast a jaundiced light through the lower level—each vast concrete pillar creating dark limbs of shadow everywhere. I rolled the blue tarp tentatively off the top of the yellow drums. The eight drums were bound tightly together with ratchet straps. I had to leave two drums behind as the van couldn't carry the extra weight without attracting unwanted attention. The middle drums had a plank mounted across them—screwed to the timber was a wooden box with a series of ignition fuses trailing in various directions out to individual drums. I lifted the cover on the box, turned on the cell phone resting in a hollow in a foam-rubber pad and checked the electronic connections to the primer kit. I checked all the wires again and unscrewed the air release valve and the main filling cap from each drum. I topped each one up with fresh fuel—a jerry can's worth for each drum—and screwed the caps tightly in place. I looked down at the cop's severed mustached head, staring lifelessly up at me from the center of the drums.

I felt nauseous. The smell of the gasoline, mixed with the pungent aroma of the fertilizer, tasted bitter in the back of my throat.

My eyes were watering constantly.

Meanwhile, behind me in the passenger's seat, I could hear the constant rasping breath of the disembodied skull—watching my every move like some omnipresent spectral fascist. Now beside me, floating above the cop's decapitated head, like a ghostly spirit leaving its bodily form. The apparition cackled and then disappeared.

I exited the van from the rear doors, wiped my hands on my jeans, pulled my baseball cap low over my eyes, opened and shut all the van doors, locked them and then broke keys off in each lock before walking through the dark, mausoleum-like concrete car park, out into the sunshine. Making sure of course, to flip the bird at the security camera mounted on the wall next to the car park building exit.

33

O utside a rundown motel a few blocks away from the mall, I waited for the bus. I watch the Hispanic and Asian girls hanging around the bus-stop selling their wares. The motel provided cheap beds for the johns, while the pimps sat in their blinged-up cars in the motel car park, smoking ice and watching their whores do business.

One of the crack whores approached me.

"You want comfort?" she asks. Her big brown eyes dilated and huge, no blinking.

She whispers again. "You want comfort, boy?"

I don't understand the question until she leaves.

"What?" I ask her back, as she slides past as if in a dream.

I picture her head sheathed in slick varnish, perched on top of one of the conductors in my lair. Her decapitated body walks off into another world.

There is a small group of shops next to the bus-stop so I go to the bakery for a pastry. A Vietnamese girl with long straight black hair, red lipstick and a sexy hard-bitch style brushes my arm on the way past as she whispers, barely audible, "You want to have some fun?"

I freak out — the first come-ons I've had for ages and both in the same afternoon by fucking hookers. It's almost tempting, but not enough, as my breath quickens and my fingers dig into the cold steel blade of the knife in my pocket. . .

I buy a pastry and leave the bakery. I stand at the bus-stop eating and watching a gaggle of short old Greek women bitch and moan about the bus timetable. An old guy about fifty shuffles past, with an alcoholic pallor and ruddy red bulbous nose to match. He sucks his gray moustache with his bottom lip in between drags on a crumbling hand-rolled cigarette. Across the street, I see the Vietnamese hookers hustling their butts, jostling for curb-space with the whites and Hispanics who are doing the same thing.

A tall skinny white dude with a goatee beard and a big silver belt-buckle holding up his leather pants, whispers to each of the white girls and winks at the Vietnamese chicks as he walks up the strip. *These fucking pimps all look the same,* I think to myself. He motions them over and they all meet in front of a shithouse burger bar for a conference. The Vietnamese girls look at each other then watch the cars sliding by for tricks. A bunch of hooded teenagers do homey greetings: flipping fingers, butting fists, slipping palms, then exchanging handfuls of plastic for cash with passers-by who try to look nonchalant and non-committal ...

A tall Greek man about fifty-five with a pawnshop suit on begins waving his hands wildly — screaming in Greek at the hookers, pimps, dealers, freaks, passers-by. He walks frenetically, head in hands, hands upraised now, yelling across the street pointing at them. Screaming. He is mad and without love, but perhaps the sanest person on the whole fucking block. I think I hear him screaming, *"The Horror. The Horror. Look — look everybody — there they are — there is death personified ... "*

The bus pulls up with a gasp of hydraulics, and the doors swing open.

The ride home is hot and uncomfortable. There are a few freaks on the bus—a yellow haired woman with bulging doughy breasts dangling from gaps in her floral-print dress. Some old black dude sucking his stubbled lips, leaning on a cane. Some young white trash, making out with his equally white-trashed acne ho in the back seat of the bus. A chubby Mexican dude drove the bus, his dark eyes glazed with last night's liquor—trundling along.

Halfway home I take my cell phone from my jacket pocket and a scrap of paper with the phone number on it. I look out the window at the car and the shops and people crawling by like some grotesque carnival parade. All their faces seem elongated—distorted.

My heart skips a beat as I notice the skull hovering at the front of the bus behind the driver. It seems to be moving very fast in one place—its definition blurred, just two burning orbs and the black cavities of its nose and mouth clearly visible—the rest of it shaking uncontrollably in fast-forward.

Everything else on the bus seems to be motionless. Stationary.

The vision twitches and speaks—

"Charlie is waiting for you Caleb. Charlie is waiting," it hisses ominously, dark blood now running in streams from the black hole where its mouth should have been. I watch the black blood splashing on the floor of the bus, counting each drop as it hits the spreading pool of blood, ticking off time like a metronome.

I look at the old man opposite—he is looking at me as though I have a third eye. He quickly turns his gaze out the window and resumes sucking his toothless gums.

I run my finger absent-mindedly across the length of the deep scar on my face as the bus pulls up at the lights of a large intersection. I look at the front of the bus again and the apparition has disappeared again, as I knew it would. I look out the window to get my bearings and spy a trench-coated bum on the sidewalk with a cardboard sign hanging from his neck. It reads *'The End is Near—Repent.'* He wears a lopsided cap but I can still make out the black glinting orbs of his deep-set eyes glaring at me from his sallow face. His mouth hangs open, a trail of saliva cobwebbed from his stubbled chin to his filthy coat front. One arthritic hand stretches out towards me, pointing accusingly. He rises awkwardly to his feet and lurches between the cars to the side of the bus, beginning to smash his knotted fist against the window, mouthing curses and garbled accusations at me.

The other people in the bus gaze moronically ahead. They look like frontal-lobotomy patients on a field trip. Like Jack Nicholson's freed sanatorium pals, in 'One Flew over the Cuckoo's Nest.' The bum keeps punching the window as the bus continues to idle at the lights. The thuds of his old fists grow weaker as the bus starts to pull away. I stare straight ahead, aware that the skull has resumed its position, hovering midair at the front of the bus. It suddenly twitches, flickers, and then disappears.

'Fuck Charlie,' I thought.

I dialed the number.

As I look out the window in the direction of the mall in the distance, I notice smeared blood on the outside of the glass where the old wino had pummeled his fists. On the horizon, I see the light of the blast and a massive cloud of smoke mushroom into the sky. The strange thing is, it is probably about 10 kilometers where I thought it should've been, in the opposite direction of the mall. Maybe what I saw was just an industrial fire? Maybe Lucille was up to her old tricks? I was sure I heard a rumble and saw an eruption of smoke a few seconds after I dialed the cell phone number. In my mind's eye, I could see the light flash on the detonator unit, sitting on the barrels of explosive in the back of the van. I knew it had worked.

I felt cold, almost frozen.

I pulled my jacket tighter around me, despite the sunshine and dusty downtown day outside.

How many people were slaughtered?

Babies? Women? Old people? Anyone?

How powerful was the explosion?

Banal thoughts doubting my handiwork clouded my brain, until I arrived home. Once safely inside, the house was deathly quiet. I tried remembering if I had cleaned all incriminating evidence from the van. Everything had been bought with cash many months before. There would be no fingerprints. The whole van would've been incinerated. The bike was fueled up and sitting in the garage ready to go. My bag was packed and I was on schedule to leave in the morning.

Would it look suspicious if I left the next day?

Fuck it! I couldn't stay here any longer.

I felt like I was going insane, Charlie's words banging around inside my tired brain. I opened a bottle of bourbon, collapsed on my bed and turned the television on. I switched it on just in time for the evening news. There it was, except it wasn't. The reporter announced that: ". . . a whole city block was nearly leveled today in what police describe as an unwarranted and cowardly terrorist attack on public safety ..."

The news report went on to describe the effects of the blast, showing a main city street with a crater the size of an Olympic swimming pool. All the store windows had been blown out, broken glass and bodies strewn across the sidewalk. The images showed cars still smoking—blackened husks. Beirut had come to downtown.

Apparently, a tow truck had been towing an illegally parked service vehicle from a shopping center when the blast occurred. So far, the fatalities stood at thirteen dead with many more reported with 'serious-to-critical injuries.'

I turned the TV off and sucked back another fifth of the bourbon. An hour later—a packet of smokes and the bottle of booze were both gone. I felt empty and full at the same time. Almost as though there was nothing left inside and that nothing more could be put in. A heavy black aura enveloped me completely. I felt sick to my stomach.

I kept beginning sentences in my head:

'Why did I ...?'

'I shouldn't have ...'

And so on.

I needed sleep desperately if I were to hit the road running tomorrow. I stood up and nearly fell over—my legs were gone. I descended the stairs to make my way outside to urinate but gave up, exhausted. I sat on the bottom step and lit the tail end of a cigarette butt.

I heard something behind me at the top of the stairs—a deep hissing sound. I turned around and sure enough, there in the shadows above, the disembodied gray skull peered down at me, a low chuckle on its foul breath. In my state, it seemed as though the vision was alternating between the boned face of a skull and Charlie's lost countenance. The sound of its rasping breath and guttural laugh reeked of evil malevolence and threat. It addressed me directly:

"Virtues are lost in self-interest Caleb, as blood is lost to the earth."

I couldn't stand it any longer and stood up, heading out of the garage. Tears began to flow freely with the strain of it all. By the time I got outside and released my bladder against the back fence, I was consumed with self-doubt and fucked nerves. Until now, I had never been troubled by a conscience or the lack thereof. In fact, nothing I had done in the past until now had attracted emotion of any sort, other than sheer dumb pleasure. I had evolved from a sub-human to an overload of death or ubermensch. Now, I could see my headstone very clearly before me in a vision. No name or dates. Just a simple obelisk on some lonely gray windblown hill, overlooking a cold unforgiving ocean. There I would remain forever—the worms twisting around my bones. So much mulch.

That's all I was now.

Coffin fodder.

I was death.

I had lost my way.

I had compromised my art.

34

After regaining my composure, I ventured back inside the garage. I couldn't even walk up the stairs to the loft. Again, I sat on the bottom steps, my mouth dry as cotton wool—head spinning. There was nothing left in the garage save for the black Ford parked menacingly in the center of the empty space. I staggered to my feet and closed the garage door. For a moment, I couldn't understand why the car was there.

In the shadows, something moved behind the steering wheel.

A grinning skull stared back at me, rotted flesh peeling, revealing gray bone. My weary brain reasoned with what remained of my good sense that maybe I should split now, before the cops came knocking on the door. I looked at the Harley covered with a tarpaulin and tried to focus my thoughts. I closed my eyes and then looked back at the rest of the garage space. It was empty, save for a mass of oil stains on the concrete floor. No car. No horrors sitting in the front seat leering at me.

I stumbled out of the garage again, grabbing a shovel on my way out the door. Sure enough, the money and firearms were still buried behind the garage in the paint tin. The cash was slightly damp but still worth as much as when I buried it.

I had a long drink of water from the faucet on the side of the garage, which made me feel better. I took my haul inside the garage and managed to make my way up the stairs to the loft—the short exercise sobering me up somewhat. I struggled into fresh clothes, put the money and the weapons in my backpack, bundled up my few possessions in a quilt and made my way back down the stairs.

My head spun and waves of nausea washed over me.

I couldn't think as I steadied myself on the bottom step. I felt exhausted as I sat on the step in an attempt to regain my senses. My thoughts started to race and I felt as though I was dreaming for a second. My surroundings flashed around me and a vision appeared before me.

The Ford was parked back where it had been for so many years.

The garage had become very cold.

The single yellow light bulb over the Ford flickered briefly.

I hesitated, expecting it to blow, but it settled back to a steady dull glow. I got up and opened the car door and looked inside. The car was empty. I was exhausted—too tired to even think bad things. I sat down in the driver's seat to collect my thoughts. I looked through the windscreen at the garage where I had spent a considerable amount of my life. Memories came flooding back. The old days, before Charlie's plans began to dominate our lives, then the violence of the past years eclipsed the good memories.

I started to drift off, still half-drunk from the night before and very tired.

My fear gave way to fatigue as I resigned myself to leave at first light, when my hangover had worn off and the morning traffic would provide adequate cover. The last thing I needed was to be stopped by the cops on my way out of town. I tilted the front seat back and closed my eyes.

I awoke with a gasp. My body was rigid, as if bound by tight rope. There was a sickly sweet smell in the car. Small phosphorescent blue dots flashed in front of my eyes. The engine was idling low. I couldn't remember turning the ignition on. I couldn't move.

I looked down. I was cocooned in the quilt, the seatbelt tight across my chest.

My arms were dead. The light in the garage flickered wildly and then Charlie appeared as if from nowhere, standing in front of the car, a wide grin spread across his skeletal face. Then Ma emerged from the shadows like some ancient reptilian hag. Behind her, came the Mayor's daughter riddled with bullet holes. A becoming look on her haunted face, still looking like she could've been Lucille's twin sister despite her advanced state of decomposition. I began to choke on the carbon monoxide now flooding the interior of the vehicle.

My breath came in short strangled gasps.

The storeowner and his wife shambled forth from the dark. Smoke drifting from their blackened peeling bodies—charred fingers leveled at me accusingly. Then came the old woman from the bottle store, a gaping hole in her forehead giving the impression of a bloodied third eye. Then the two customers ...within a minute, the garage was full. A ghoulish procession of corpses seemingly intent on an equally gruesome revenge.

I panicked as I tried to free myself from the quilt that had constricted tightly around me like a giant snake.

Sweat soaked my clothes as my anxiety levels peaked.

I looked in the rear-view and saw the vehicle was surrounded.

The fear in my eyes flashed back at me for an instant and then shifted. Suddenly, I was looking into the eyes of someone else staring back at me from the rear-view mirror. It was unmistakably Pa. His lips blue, eyes glazed, white orbs, pupils rolled back in his peeling skull. His black hair slick with what looked like a mixture of blood and engine oil.

Terror welled up inside me as my brain fought to preserve my sanity.

Suddenly, Charlie mounted the bonnet of the Ford on all fours, peering through the windscreen intently, a trail of saliva and blood dripping on the glass. His black eyes more evil than ever, bulging from his cavernous eye-sockets, hungry with anticipation. My vision became blurred, the car now thick with the blue suffocating haze of exhaust fumes. I could hear his thick laughter through the windscreen. Something snapped in my brain and I slipped into unconsciousness, a whimper on my dying lips.

I woke with a start, my heart thumping like a jackhammer, sweat pouring from my forehead. I searched blindly for the car door handle, but there was none. I had been asleep on my bed in the loft. Sunlight glowed through the blacked-out windows and I quickly made my way down the stairs and out the back door for a breath of fresh air.

My heart was still racing as I caught my breath. I used the tap on the side of the garage to splash water on my face until I regained control again. I cursed myself for my weakness. It was all just a nightmare. That's all. I made my way back into the garage to get the Harley ready to go and stopped dead. The Ford was definitely gone but in that moment, I knew it had been real enough. I became acutely aware of the sickly taste of carbon monoxide in my mouth. As I stumbled back outside into the bright sunlight, I vomited heavily against the fence and repeated to myself, *'I have to leave this place. I have to leave this place. I have to leave ...'*

I thought about the cops and the feds who would now be crawling all over the city, looking for the terrorists behind the latest 'Ground Zero' event. I thought about Ray Truman and his bullish determination to destroy my family and I knew that he would not rest until he caught up with me. He was the only person who had ever implicated me in any crimes. I knew that the security camera footage in the mall car-park would reveal me to the world and I knew that it would be Truman, who would recognise the way I walked, the way my jaw line met my collar, the scar that would be visible with the digital enhancement of the security files.

The only reason Ray Truman suspected me of any of the unsolved murders in the Portvale region and surrounding city boroughs, was by way of association. Crime by association. That is, my family legacy—tainted with the same lust to kill, the same burning urge, passed on down from generation to generation. And I am guilty. Guilty of the crime of being a Cunningham, and an exceptional killing machine. Truman's suspicion made it interesting. From that point forward, after the bombing, my life changed. I thought about my actions from a different viewpoint. I had failed on a mission for the first time. My subject, or subjects, in this case had not been realised. I had changed my MO and stepped outside of my own true mission. The bomb was Charlie's idea and like every fucking plan of his, doomed to failure from the start. I vowed to stay true to what I knew. My art was perfect, it needed no adaptation, no interference.

I had experienced what would happen if I stepped outside of my realm of existence. If I catered to the whims of others. No more fuck ups. No more distance. Everything would be personal now—a subjective experience direct from my essence. From conception to completion, there was no substitute for absolute perfection. I did, however, need a new playing field. As far away from Portvale as humanly possible, but first I had a few things to clean up before I left for good.

35

Ray Truman sat hunched over his desk in his cluttered office, one hand shielding his tired eyes from the solitary lamplight. The files on his desk were stacked high and another cardboard box waited on the floor for him to read. These were his father's files and his grandfather's. Dossier upon dossier in manila folders, arranged chronologically according to year. Each file was marked on the cover in the top-left corner with the Cunningham name in black marker pen. As Ray worked his way methodically through the piles of papers, he couldn't help but feel his stomach turn at what he was reading.

The victim files were bad enough, but the photos were so graphic they could have made a stone puke. He had seen it all before and some of it in the flesh, literally. The files were in order chronologically, from most recent to some that dated back to his Grandfather's rookie days on the Portvale precinct. He'd concluded that the Cunninghams were a bunch of the most perverted twisted fucks, he'd ever come across. Ray spent his spare moments trolling for missed clues within the files. Looking for connections, events, patterns that could connect the last remaining Cunningham to a legacy of murder and mayhem. Ray knew that Caleb had bad blood running through his veins. He knew that there were victims that fell outside of Charlie and Errol's MO. Cold cases that were ten years old and new victims turning up on a regular basis.

He lit another cigarette and leaned back in his chair as he exhaled, stretching his back and checking his watch.

"Fuck it," he said to himself, as he closed the folder and stacked the files back in the cardboard box next to his desk. As he leant over to put the files away, some papers slipped from the centre of the pile.

"Shit," Ray muttered, as he picked the files up. He glanced quickly at the loose sheaves of paper to find the case-file reference number. He laid the papers on the desk under the lamp to see the reference codes better and noticed a transcribed statement on the top sheet, relating to an interview a local patrol officer had with Caleb Cunningham.

Interviewed subject: Caleb Cunningham
Approx. time of interview: 14.30 am.
Location: Eden Park Industrial estate, cnr of Maple and Dockside Avenues.

I questioned subject while on routine patrol. Subject was acting suspiciously and was attempting to cover his face as the squad car passed. I questioned Cunningham as to what he was doing in the area so late at night and he replied that he was 'looking for his dogs.' When I asked him about his dogs he replied that he owned two Rottweilers and they had gone missing from his home address on Artaud Avenue. Once I learned that Cunningham resided at number 7 Artaud Ave, I remembered the family history and criminal events/activity that had taken place there. He seemed nervous and obviously hostile towards my presence and questioning. When I asked him to remove the hood from his sweatshirt I noticed his head was shaved like the suspect sought in connection to the Arat homicide and other possible 'Portvale Slasher' murder investigations. Statement given by the subject follows:

"I have been trying to find my two dogs, 'Cain' and 'Abel.' They are good dogs but seem to have gone missing. I know nothing about any murders and I am on my way home. I haven't seen anything and I'm not doing anything wrong. I am just out looking for my dogs."
I had to let him go, as he had done nothing wrong. I would like the record to show that

I feel strongly that this subject should be interviewed fully if given an opportunity to do so. He seemed very suspicious and struck me as being someone capable of anything. I had not asked him any questions relating to the recent homicides in Portvale yet he mentioned 'murders' without any prompting from me. Due to the nature of his character, the suspicious manner in which he conducted himself and his family history I would recommend further investigation/ interrogation of this individual.

Ray rubbed the stubble on his chin and crushed the remains of his cigarette out in the over-flowing ashtray on the desk. What he read was nothing he hadn't suspected himself. The Patrolman's statement was an affirmation of his own suspicions that gave him a new energy. This cop had seen it, as Ray knew in his gut, that Caleb was a bad fucker just like the rest of them. What Ray didn't know was just how bad Caleb was. He grabbed his leatherjacket off the back of the chair and shrugged it over his muscular shoulders, locked the office door and stepped into the corridor of the precinct house.

The only evidence of life in the building was the sound of a short-wave radio crackling somewhere down the hall. The place was dimly lit as most of the office space stood empty at this time of the morning. Ray knew a few remaining senior officers and detectives finished off paperwork for the evening in their own dark recesses of the building. He thought of those cops lucky enough to have wives and kids waiting for them at home. His heart softened for a minute and then hardened instantly as he thought of Caleb Cunningham.

Ray longed to put the final nail in the Cunningham Coffin. He'd do whatever it took to bring the creep in legally, but if it meant bending the rules to get the slippery son-of-a-bitch then he'd do it. If that didn't work, then he'd so some more.

As he made his way to the exit, he thought of Charlie Cunningham, lying smashed and broken next to his busted-up hot wheels. He remembered the look on Charlie's face as he stared down the barrel of Ray's pistol. It was the unmistakeable look of fear, the same look that he hoped to see on Caleb's face before too long.

Ray remembered the kick of his .41 Smith and Wesson revolver as it parked a round clean between Charlie's black eyes. The shot blew the back of Cunningham's head off like a ripe pumpkin exploding. After Charlie's lifeless corpse had stopped twitching, he'd carefully extracted the spent bullet from the mess of blood and brain's on the pavement and shoved the body back into the overturned car. Ray knew the boys would see it his way, the scene that is. They wouldn't question his senior appraisal of the incident and the events that led to Cunningham's death. Despite the obvious tell-tale signs of overkill, everybody knew the creep got what was coming to him.

Ray stood on the steps outside the rear steps of the precinct car park and lit another cigarette. He'd tried to do things the right way in the past with the Cunningham kid, but time was running out. Ray didn't have much to lose anymore, except sleep and until Caleb was behind bars or in a hole in the ground that was enough to drive Ray forward. It was enough to make him want to take the last Cunningham down in a mess of pain. For himself. For his father and for his Grandfather. Most of all, for all those poor whores and sad victims, who could still be out walking the streets if it wasn't for that sadistic fucker. He knew that Caleb was the missing link in the brutal slayings, especially after they had continued following Charlie's death. He flicked his spent cigarette into the yard and made a beeline for his car in the darkness.

36

I found out that they buried Charlie in a pauper's grave on the outskirts of Portvale. A priest apparently read the last rites, as two underpaid laborers shoveled dirt on top of his cheap pine casket. I wasn't there for my brother's funeral, as I didn't even know when, let alone where he was being buried. After a rushed autopsy, he was quickly interred. Winter was well underway and rain and sleet froze the canal banks near the cemetery. It would have been a cold gray miserable day when he was put in the ground. Before I found out what happened to him, I made repeated calls to the city morgue and the precinct house. No one would give me any information about my brother. Most people I talked to even denied that he existed!

Ray Truman's sneering face burnt a hole in my mind as my hate for him boiled over. In order to find out the truth, I decided to break into his office to get the information I needed. This proved easier to plan than to execute, but was finally achieved with less trouble than I would've believed. I chose a quiet and rain-soaked Wednesday night for my mission. I carried two semi-automatic handguns and a razor-sharp machete concealed in a back sheath that hung between my shoulder blades. I used the tunnels to work my way towards the precinct house. I felt invisible, dressed in a black waterproof trench coat, ski mask and patent leather gloves. He would not see me coming unless he was wearing the same night-vision goggles I was wearing.

It was exactly 3am as I exited the tunnel into an alleyway behind the precinct house, ankle deep in rainwater and floating garbage. A concrete perimeter wall was my only obstacle to the rear car park and the loading bays. A single camera with a blinking red LED light hovered on a post mounted on the corner of the east wall. I slipped silently down the alley, found a suitable object to make a wedge and hoisted myself onto the roof of an abandoned car, bringing myself eye-level with the top of the wall. I could hear the whirr of the camera as it oscillated slowly on its mount, surveying the rear of the precinct house and surrounding area. I waited until the camera passed, then wedged the broken shard of timber I had picked up into the base of the camera mount. It effectively jammed the camera into a static position. I scanned the area and froze.

Truman stood in the shadows on the rear steps of the precinct house. I could see the red ember of his cigarette glow as he inhaled and then flicked the butt onto the asphalt. I watched him make his way across the car park to his beat-up sedan. He lit another smoke and I saw his face in the glow from the flame of his cigarette lighter. He looked old and bitter. I knew he was thinking about me. I knew I was eating him up inside like a slow deadly cancer. I stifled a laugh as he gunned his shitbox out through the exit gates.

I lifted my bodyweight up and over the wall and dropped silently to the concrete below. There were a few patrol cars and unmarked vehicles parked in the yard. I knew every inch of the precinct house as Charlie and I had previously planned an 'invasion' and cased the joint for two months, calling off our plans at the last moment due to more pressing matters at hand. I spied the large roller doors that led to an underground car park where they bought prisoners to the holding cells. I made my way across the car park to a ledge under the loading bay platform next to the roller door.

I waited for ten long minutes under the concrete platform until I heard the mechanical grind of the roller doors as they started to rise. A minute later, a police van exited slowly, the windshield wipers working overtime as the rain came down thick and fast. I could see the pig's face inside the vehicle, illuminated by the green glow of the dashboard lights. I lowered my 9mm as he steered the van towards the exit gate. I seized the opportunity and ran quickly inside the entrance, into the dark shadows of the underground car park, as the roller door hit the concrete behind me and shuddered to a stop.

I knew Wednesday was a quite night crime-wise in Portvale and, consequently, there were usually less staff at the station house at this time. This proved to be true as I made my way quietly towards the stairs that led to the upper floors. There was no one in sight as I made my way up to the ground floor and then up to the first floor. I knew Truman's office was on the second floor, but I paused briefly to double-check a directory notice board inside the foyer entrance on the first floor. I could hear voices coming from the other end of the building in the direction of the staff cafeteria.

I quickly looked around. To my immediate left was a fuse box. I pulled open the front panel and realized that it was the main electrical circuit breaker. I grabbed a handful of cables and ripped them out of their sockets. Immediately, the lights went out as a shower of sparks burst from the power box. I shut the fuse panel, ducked into a cleaner's cupboard, and adjusted my night-vision goggles. The sound of running feet echoed down the hall as the night-duty staff scurried along the corridors, trying to find the source of the power shortage. I figured I had at least ten minutes before someone fixed the destroyed electrical cables and got the power back on. I opened the door slowly and looked up and down the hall. Seeing the stairs to my left across the hall, I moved quickly into the stairwell.

The green glow of the NVGs illuminated my way as I climbed the stairs towards Truman's office. If he returned tonight, I would kill him. I would put a bullet in each of his knees and break his arms with my steel-capped boots. I would use my machete to sever his head from his spineless shoulders and I would bury it in Charlie's grave, once I found out exactly where it was located.

A police officer fumbled his way into the stairwell and headed towards me in the darkness. I stopped dead still as I watched him tapping his standard-issue night torch in the palm of his hand. Obviously, the batteries were as dead as he was about to be. I let him come towards me, watching while he desperately grasped the handrail as he tried to make his way down the stairs in the dark. I could see beads of perspiration on his forehead and could smell his cheap aftershave.

At the same moment he realized I was with him in the stairwell, I quickly stepped up above and behind him and wrapped my arm around his neck in a choke hold. His torch clattered to the concrete steps below as I lifted him off his feet, his legs kicking wildly. I held him like that for maybe two or three minutes as his body twitched against mine and I felt his life force leave with his last shuddering breath. I let him slip to the steps below, listening as his lifeless body thudded and flopped for a few seconds before coming to a halt with a bone-snapping crack as his skull slapped the hard concrete.

I checked the magazine in my 9mm and stepped from the stairwell into the hallway of the second floor. Ray Truman's office was directly in front of me. His name boldly stamped in gold lettering on the glass window set in the door.

Once inside his office, I pulled the blind down to cover the window on the door and set to work. It took a minute to locate my brother's file in a cabinet next to Truman's desk. I adjusted the infrared settings on my NVGs and searched under C for more files relating to our family. I found nothing. I noticed the top drawer on Truman's desk was locked so with the aid of my machete blade, I levered the drawer open and there they were. Two separate dossiers on both Pa and myself were bundled together with crime-scene tape. I put the files in my knapsack and looked around the office.

The walls were quite bare apart from his framed commendation and graduation certificates and a massive wall chart of Portvale peppered with different colored pins and garish photographs and post-it notes. After closer inspection, I realized it was a map of national homicide locations accompanied with annotated autopsy photos of murder victims with joining arrows to the pinpointed crime scenes. An early black and white mug shot of my father was pinned next to one of my brother's color portraits. Above the two of them was an enlarged photo of me from a Portvale Preparatory School class photo.

Truman's desk was covered in papers and files but amongst them were pictures of some children and a somber, but pretty, middle-aged woman. Another picture showed all four of them together on a picnic blanket in the countryside, smiling contentedly at the camera. I slipped the photo out of the frame and tucked it into my breast pocket along with the address book from his top drawer.

Before I left Truman's office, I gathered all his commendation certificates, the photos and map off the wall, into a shredded pile along with the papers on his desk, and set them on fire with my lighter. I watched the flame dance and take hold for a minute before I left, locking the door behind me as I made my way to the stairs. Five minutes later, I had made my way through a side door on the ground level and out into the car park. The rain had slowed to a drizzle and the asphalt was slick with moisture. I waited for a minute, making sure the exit route was clear across the car park. I noticed a water-main on the west corner of the precinct building. After ensuring that the fire sprinkler system would not be pumping water to extinguish the fire, I climbed the rear wall of the compound, careful to avoid the camera mounted on the east corner wall.

The autopsy photos clearly revealed Charlie's gunshot wound. Despite the other injuries from the car accident, the bullet wound reeked of Ray Truman. His involvement in Charlie's death was obvious from the surveillance photographs and the Internet map printouts of the location where Charlie's body was found. The printouts were dated, via annotations, a week before he died. Truman knew where Charlie would run. He knew the area was a barren industrial landscape—a perfect place to commit an execution.

The autopsy certificate had been signed by the coroner and verified with Truman's own signature. Cause of death: death by accidental violence, despite the obvious bullet wounds. Another signed statement from Truman said that he shot my brother in 'self-defense' as Charlie had apparently fired at Truman with a 9mm. He went on to say that he only wounded Charlie and that my brother had shot himself. This was bullshit, as I knew Charlie didn't own a 9mm. It had to be a plant. After more investigation, I found what I was looking for—a letter recommending burial in the west Portvale cemetery, located on the canal banks of the West Side River. Charlie's name was not on the death certificate. I was looking for a 'John Doe,' which meant I was looking for a fresh grave in the pauper's section.

I never did find my brother's grave. I searched the cemetery for three days until giving up and breaking into the groundskeeper's office to steal the gravesite maps. There were over three hundred 'John' or 'Jane Doe' burial sites, too many to possibly excavate on my own. Even after carefully studying the map and the dates of burial, there were still too many buried the same week my brother would have been put in the ground. In despair, I walked the streets in a blind rage with the dogs, feeling hopeless and very much alone. I was the last remaining member of my family and I knew that my time was limited in Portvale. Cain and Able clung to my shadow as I paced the streets but there was no blood between us, just misery. Like Charlie's Rottweilers, I felt lost, without purpose or place, just another animal roaming the night. There was nothing to keep me in this stinking shithole of a city anymore. I stopped at a corner store and bought some cigarettes, while I contemplated my next move. The night was still young and I decided I had time for one last kill, before I moved on.

From Portvale Daily News:
'Suspected Serial-Killer found dead at scene of road accident after police pursuit.'

After an anonymous phone call, a local man by the name of Charlie Cunningham was arrested and charged with the vicious murder and arson of the residence of one Lucille Cassandra. Due to the horrific nature of the crime and the similarities of the victim's injuries to other unsolved homicides, police are looking at potential connections between Cunningham and unsolved Portvale slayings. Residents of the Portvale area were relieved to know a suspect was now in custody, under suspicion of multiple homicides.

Residents and local authorities were confident that their neighborhood could return to normal activities with the capture. That is until Cunningham promptly escaped from police custody this morning.

Due to overcrowding in the state penitentiaries, Cunningham was remanded in custody to await trial at the Portvale Precinct Police station, which sits directly in the epicenter of most of the Portvale slayings.

He apparently crawled through a loose ceiling panel and escaped via the central heating ducts in the old building, immediately accosting a young mother and stealing her car.

The woman was later recovered, bruised and badly shaken but alive, in the lower east-side dock area. Cunningham was later spotted heading west on the freeway in a black Ford sedan, traced back to the suspect's father, Errol Cunningham.

Taskforce investigator, Detective Ray Truman later discovered the lifeless body of Charlie Samael Cunningham, 600 kilometers west of Portvale. The accused was found propped up against an alley wall in an industrial area after apparently crashing his vehicle at high speed nearby.

The county coroner determined the cause of death as a single gunshot wound to his left temple. Forensics recovered a 9mm Semi-automatic pistol and various weapons from the wreckage of his car, including three large hunting knives.

It is believed that the accused died from self-inflicted wounds at the scene of the accident. Authorities are carrying out a full investigation into the suicide and in-depth analysis of the weapons that were found at the crime scene to determine whether they may have been involved in any of the Portvale Slayings.

37

When I fixed my sights on a medium I would lock down everything else around me. My primary focus was the mark. Nothing could impede my attack.

Not men.

Not dogs.

Not guns.

Not Satan.

Not the police.

Not the fucking nuclear regime.

Not god.

God was dead, but art was alive. Very alive. Running down the dark subterranean tunnel in front of me. I am away from the reality of my existence at this moment in time. I float above the shit in the shallow stream below. She is screaming loudly. The shrill piercing noise of her fear-laden cry hurts my ears. I blink and the silver blade in my hand gleams like a diamond as it lunges wildly in front of me in the dark, striking the back of her blouse as she scrabbles ahead, running blindly into the black light. The LED miner's light on my headband cast a digital clarity to its illumination. Ribbons of blood cascade from her back, matting her long blond hair. I stop running, forcing my hand to lower gently to my side.

She keeps running.

Still running.

Stumbling ahead.

Splashing in the shit and trash amongst the sewer rats. I whistle quickly and Cain and Abel appear at my side like two ghost dogs from hell. They hunch forward, shoulders bunched with muscle and steroids, straining in the direction of the woman's screams. Drool hangs from their sharp bared teeth. They growl loudly, barely containing their bloodlust. "Go" I say quietly, but forcefully. They launch themselves into the dark and I hear her screams grow more frantic, bouncing off the concrete walls as the dogs splash toward her. One hundred and eighty kilos of death and fur. She screams one final time and then I hear her bones snap as they are crushed in the jaws of the dogs, the noise cracking through the tunnel like a whip.

I don't need to see the body. It's not aesthetically important. The dogs were hungry and she fell into my lap, literally. This is what helps me to evade capture. This kind of activity, it's not part of my M.O. It's the 'Tunnel Rat's' modus operandi. He is my subterranean brother. When I enter the ground he wears my boots, shoes, trousers, flesh … When he exits the tunnel, The Tunnel Rat tries to cling to my boots with his blood-caked claws as he slips back down into the underground. My knowledge is as complicitous as it is unavoidable. Across the grim city, other demons stalk the street like The Tunnel Rat. No finesse. No logic. No art.

When I'm above ground in Portvale, I am 'The Portvale Slasher.' When I'm traveling upstate I'm an "unknown killer or killers." Most of the time, I'm a faceless enigma whose work goes largely unnoticed. I choose to remain unknown—I don't crave publicity like other colleagues. I fly beneath the radar until I choose to fly above it.

My philosophy is simple. Violence is essential to population control. To democracy. To dictatorships. To human nature. To the media. The demons that stalk the streets have been bred from television. Youth inseminated with ideas, middle-aged males disillusioned by desire and selfish sensory lust. Too many ideas find traction in the shallow end of the gene pool. TV babies have gone mad with the desire for fame and bloody action.

I distinguish myself from these other barbaric monsters and give my work the dignity of aesthetic bestowment. The works I leave behind remind the minions that beauty is horrific. That reality cannot be sensationalized if the aesthetic is at its full potential. How can the media sensationalize the sublime?

I have spoken too much of things that don't concern others. I need to leave. I need to leave this filthy city. To quote a tired old cliché, 'I need to find my roots!' With the house empty and Charlie dead and rotting in the poisoned earth of the pauper's boneyard, no reason was left for me to stay. My thirst for travel beckoned me to far shores, to the wonders of the earth and all its realities. To all the places and things, I had read about in the old books and magazines at the Portvale Public Library. To all the art I could create.

Each piece, a new muse.

A new idea.

A new world.

Another installation.

I wanted to leave tonight, despite things left unfinished in Portvale. There were people I needed to say goodbye to, who I would no doubt catch up with later on.

The dogs, Cain and Abel, are busy with their prey. I won't be taking them with me; the mode of transportation for the next part of my journey does not afford passenger room. Mine will be a solitary flight from the city. I checked the garage and made sure everything was as I had left it. The Harley Davidson sat waiting with the key in the ignition under the tarpaulin, my backpack lay propped up on the rear wheel. That was all I was taking with me from this place, apart from some bad memories burned indelibly upon my brain. I pulled the garage door to and made my way across the yard to the rear entrance of the house.

I entered the house, lit a cigarette and sat down at the kitchen table. I looked around the filthy room and felt my stomach do a lazy flip-flop as what looked like blood, began to leak from the fly-marked light-shade in the ceiling. From the top of the barren walls, blood dripped blackly, streaking the grimy wallpaper. I screwed my eyes shut tight and inhaled deeply on my cigarette, until the scene had righted itself.

I opened one eye and looked around me, everything was static. The house was as it had been; nothing had changed. My mind was clear and empty of confusion now. I ground the cigarette out on the kitchen floor and walked from room to room, having a good look around the house once again before I left. I approached the stairs and stopped suddenly, a vivid memory of Ma hunched in her easy chair assaulted my senses. Her skeletal face void of life, twisted mouth pursed with exposed teeth. Her eyes deep wells, flyblown and blackened with decay. I decided to leave. I knew enough of what memories lived on in these walls.

In the basement.

In the garage.

Everywhere the memories burned their screams upon my brain. I had to disappear to escape the black depression of this place. I need to recreate myself in order to become myself. This place could be discovered for what it once was and always will be. I didn't care, I knew my brother had fucked things up for good with his stupid plans; I knew it didn't matter anyway.

Everything that could be traced back to me would shortly be destroyed beyond measure, never to be found again. My world had just expanded immeasurably. Then I thought about Lucille and my heart dropped. I thought about the short time we'd spent together and it felt like we had a lifetime behind us. She had the potential to make me love, to cease time, to feel things I'd never felt before, even now. I thought about Charlie and how he'd taken that chance from me and I was glad he'd gone.

I walked back though the ground floor, past the empty rooms, my footsteps resounding upon the wooden floors in the hollow space of the hallway. I walked above the basement, the abyssal room sitting hulked in the darkness below like some sleeping giant, hungry for blood and new flesh. That dark cavernous space held more than bad memories and the crimes of my family. It reeked of evil and sickness and I knew it had to burn. I reached the farthest west wall of the house and entered the former tenant's rooms one by one, touching my cigarette lighter to each filthy curtain as I made my way back to the front door. The tinder dry structure behind me, was now engulfed in curling black smoke and the crackling noise of a ravenous fire on the quick burn.

'This one's for you Lucille' I thought to myself, as I closed the door and made my way across the barren yard to the garage and my perceived freedom.

38

Ray Truman tucked his white vest into his chinos and bent forward to crack a cold can of lager from the fridge. He rubbed the can across his bloodied knuckles and shook his head as he assessed the damage to the kitchen wall his fist had made. He was fucked off and frustrated at being without the resources of the precinct house because of some arsonist with a grudge against the cops. With no leads on the fire and no office to work from, Truman was officially on leave whether he liked it or not. Despite being on a mandatory stand-down following Cunningham's death, he had been allowed full access to all his files and his office. Now he was in limbo, it was officially an arson enquiry and with the death of a police officer, who was found in the charred stairwell, the burnt-out building was uninhabitable and an ongoing crime scene. Truman had been advised that his office and most of the second floor had been completely gutted by fire. He was glad that he'd got into the habit of bringing his work home with him, especially the photocopied files relating to the Cunninghams.

He walked into the living room and looked at the east wall covered in maps and charts, mug-shots and scrawled black-felt tip annotations. He knew if anyone from the station saw the inside of his apartment his head would be on the chopping block, so to speak. Files were strictly off-limits outside of the precinct-house unless needed in court or on some other official business. He had all he needed on the Cunninghams filed away in his memory plus a closet full of Xeroxed files just in case. Despite all the file-copy, Truman knew that he would not need any paperwork for what he had planned for Caleb. This one would definitely be off the books.

Despite his frustration, he didn't care about the office but he did care about the cop who was found dead at the scene. The poor bastard who died in the fire had been murdered—arson was arson. They had no leads and Ray hadn't suspected Cunningham at that stage, his focus was too tight. Cunningham had been tried, convicted and sentenced in Truman's mind a long time ago, for other matters. The IA boys and the forensics team could deal with the precinct fire; it was time to prepare, for the culmination of years of intensive investigation into the Portvale Serial Killings.

It was a stinking hot Portvale night and he breathed hard as he cooled the sweat off his forehead with another cold can of beer. He forgot about the arson and his throbbing knuckles for a minute and thought about Charlie Cunningham, realizing that when he thought of that psycho he couldn't help but picture Cunningham senior. He looked at the only mug-shot on the wall he had of a young Caleb and saw both Charlie and Errol in his dark eyes. He thought of how Caleb looked the last time he'd seen him. The scar that ran from his forehead to his chin had changed his face so he looked like his brother but not like his father, it was kind of hard to explain. Charlie was more like his old man than Caleb was. Caleb was a different beast altogether. Suddenly, Truman didn't feel so hot anymore as a shudder ran up his spine. He grimaced as he thought of Caleb and what he was capable of.

Ray lit a filter-less cigarette and hoisted a 30kg barbell off the floor with each hand, sucking up the pain as his bruised fist throbbed. He stood in front of his apartment window and started to do sets of curls, watching his taut form in the reflection of the large bay window. As he pumped his biceps with a deep burning grind, he looked directly up the main strip of highway that ran through the heart of Portvale. He could see the ember-red glow of taillights cruising the strip. Looking to score. Cars full of pimps, spics, coloreds, wops—all looking to score or fuck some shit up.

Ray had seen it all too many times before. This was his town and sometimes Ray felt like all roads converged here on their way to hell. He pumped each bicep slowly, gritting his teeth as his muscles burned. Ray was hot with a seething anger tonight. He was burning up inside his head. He looked past the last liquor store on the left and there was Acacia Avenue. Ray saw red. It was one of the very gates of hell and by no mere coincidence, the path to the Cunningham's residence.

Ray had inherited a dossier from his father, Michael Truman, on the Cunningham clan, dating all the way to back to his good old

Granddaddy. Ray's grandfather, William Truman, had been a long-serving traffic patrol officer who had eventually made captain before disappearing mysteriously. He had been on patrol, supervising an undercover operation concerning missing itinerant farmhands on the highway leading into Portvale from the west. Then he vanished. After the disappearance and eventual registration of death, Ray's father had inherited his father's possessions. Michael found the dossier amongst his father's belongings. Other finds included a meticulous diary and a .41 Smith and Wesson revolver, plus ammunition. Samael Cunningham had been listed as the main suspect in the case notes and in the diary he had been portrayed as a prolific serial killer. Upon further reading, it was revealed that he also included his son, Errol, as a participant in the butchery. Ray's father firmly believed that the 'Cuntinghams' had killed his own father.

Michael Truman had carried this conviction to his death and had in turn passed the torch to Ray. It was no less than a family feud, one side perceiving the other as evil as each other. Ray turned his thoughts back to the present as his muscles screamed with exertion under the weight of the barbells. Ray let the weights hang for a minute and rolled the back of his sweating skull against his thick neck. He looked at his reflection, dissected in the window alive with the busy lights from the strip below.

He saw Charlie's face laid broken against the glass-strewn pavement. He remembered the lifeless eyes flickering and finally looking up at him, just before he pumped a single round into the shitter's temple. He knew that Charlie always packed heat but this time he wasn't carrying a thing. Ray had to drop a piece he had tucked away in the boot of the car, reserved especially for such occasion, next to Charlie's twitching corpse after he'd made a few adjustments. Ray remembered the feel of Charlie's cold dead hand as he pressed the 9mm into his palm and squeezed a round into his temple, directly into the same entry wound that Truman had made with his own piece. Ray rolled the end of Cunningham's fingers on the barrel and the butt before letting the corpse's knuckles rap on the pavement, as the first patrol cars arrived on the scene.

Self-defense, always a fail-safe alibi for a cop with Ray's

seniority, would cover any questions if they were ever asked. 'Death by misadventure with probable suicide' was the official cause of death on the coroner's report. Ray pulled a few strings and Cunningham's corpse was cremated before burial. Effectively burying the evidence of Truman's actions along with another member of the Cunningham family.

Ray pumped each bicep twice more and set the barbells on the floor beneath the window. He stretched, yawned and thought about sleep. Something made him hesitate as he went to pull the blind down. He opened the window so that his view was unobstructed and felt his adrenaline begin to rise until it hit his brain and his mind went into overdrive.

The flames climbed high above the Cunningham house. Embers danced into the black sky as plumes of smoke billowed from the inferno. Ray rubbed his eyes, still not quite sure of what he was seeing but knowing exactly what he was witnessing at the same time. A massive ball of flame burst from the burning building as the propane tanks in the basement exploded. Ray could hear the explosion from his window and then the sirens of the City's emergency services began to howl into the night, as they made their way to Portvale and what was left of the Cunningham's house of horror.

Ray quickly buttoned his shirt and holstered his service revolver before he made his way down the stairs and out into the street. He walked slowly along the street, past the whores and the junkies and the bums, past the bars and the strip clubs, past sin of every conceivable type. He thought about the burning house and he imagined what they would find the next day. He walked slowly as he lit a cigarette and watched ash falling like dead leaves from the night sky. A thin veil of smoke began to drift across the strip as he neared the entrance to Acacia Avenue. The fire service hadn't yet reached the house and this made Ray smile. With every passing second, answers to Ray's questions were being burnt in the blaze. Secrets were being incinerated and evidence destroyed. Despite these things, Ray continued to smile, taking some small comfort in the destruction of the Cunningham residence.

Ray stood on the street watching the building burn, as the fire services turned up with sirens blaring. Before he had a chance to relish the destruction of the Cunningham residence, he would be reminded that his office, along with all of the original case files and pre-trial evidence he'd accumulated against Caleb had been destroyed. A fire investigation officer at the scene of the Cunningham fire had reminded him about the fire at the precinct house and Ray intuitively connected the two events. *Cunningham! Why hadn't he considered him as a suspect?* After all, he knew Caleb was capable of anything. He knew that he was the fucker who'd torched the station, just like he'd torched his own house. Truman suddenly lost all desire to stand and watch the house burn. He turned and made his way back to his car parked outside his apartment and then drove across town to the police precinct.

As he drove, he knew exactly what had happened and who had set the fire. He knew that it would've started in his office before any of the other investigators confirmed it. He knew that Caleb would've read his notes and now knew that Truman suspected him of serial murder. Ray's heart alternated between severe depression and uncontrollable rage as he pulled into the station car park, the building cloaked in darkness, a jagged silhouette against the night sky.

As he sat in the car with the window down, he could smell the damp burnt stench of the gutted building waft across the empty car park and he knew that he had nothing on Caleb now, except his suspicions. The evidence bags and DNA samples that filled the boxes stacked against the wall of his office would be destroyed along with three decades of copious case notes relating to three separate Serial Murder inquiries, directly related to the Cunningham family. Truman thought about the copies of some of the notes in his apartment and he knew it wasn't enough to convict Cunningham, let alone raise a search warrant.

Ray knew what he had to do now and it wasn't a good feeling. He got out of the sedan and lit a cigarette. He felt like drinking himself into oblivion, leaving his badge on the wet curb where he now sat with his head in his hands and just walking into the night never to return. He thought about pulling his service revolver from its holster and blowing his brains out right there in the deserted car park. Instead, he stood and got back in the car and headed in the direction of the nearest liquor store.

Truman knew that Caleb would run. He knew that he would slip away into the night when the heat was raised, just as his cowardly father had. Just like his brother had. When Ray witnessed the fire at Artaud Avenue all he could do was laugh, as he knew it was an attempt by Caleb to cover his tracks, hide evidence, and evade capture by faking his own death. It was no surprise to Ray, when burnt human remains were discovered in the burnt-out building. Two of the charred corpses were found buried in a wall cavity in the basement and another body was discovered amongst the smoldering ruins in what remained of the kitchen on the first floor.

Ray needed more information and he had to find out whether his suspicions about Caleb were accurate. Maybe the stress of the case and the booze had caught up with him and he was just being paranoid. He approached the captain about reinstatement and after a cursory reprimand was welcomed back to active duties. Truman was the only one with the background to deal with any developments relating to the Portvale Murders and as the Cunninghams were primary suspects throughout the investigation, he was an invaluable resource.

As the fire investigators and forensics team sifted through the smoldering remains of the house, Ray soon learnt that the house held more than a few secrets to confirm his theories about the Cunningham clan. The corpse found on the first floor was identified as a white male aged in his thirties. Along with the two corpses in the basement, investigators later found the charred remains of at least ten bodies in various states of decomposition and dismemberment buried beneath the burnt out building. Some of the bone fragments dated back almost sixty years.

Truman personally investigated the identity of the male corpse found on the first floor. All the evidence pointed toward it being the remains of Caleb Cunningham. The DNA tests showed the body to be the right age, the correct height and so on. Truman almost believed that it could actually be the remains of Caleb lying in the city morgue, when he received confirmation from dental records that it was apparently Cunningham. He felt frustrated as hell at having been denied the chance of exacting his own punishment on Caleb. As Truman was leaving the Central Portvale dentist's office, the dentist asked him a question.

"Before you leave—who do I speak to about a trespasser?"

"Huh? What do you mean?" asked Ray impatiently.

"Well, we reported a break-in a week ago and haven't heard anything back from the police. We had an intruder in the clinic," said the dentist emphatically.

"Go on," Ray prompted.

"Well, it was strange really. Whoever broke in didn't steal anything or force entry. The only way I know we had an intruder, is because I saw him on our surveillance footage."

Truman thought carefully for a second, halfway between walking out the door and telling the guy to stop fucking wasting police time. Something made Ray pull back.

"Could I have a look at the surveillance video?"

"Sure. I have it rewound to where the guy enters our office," said the Dentist, with a perfect smile.

For the next half hour, Ray sat in the Dentist's office reviewing the security footage. He watched the guy enter the office through the street-side window, obviously using the fire-escape landing to make his entrance. It was hard to make out the face of the man in the video as it was shot at night, but the dentist had taking the precaution of installing an expensive system with a night-vision lens. After watching the footage a few times, Ray was in no doubt it was Caleb Cunningham. At first, Truman joked to himself that Cunningham was a one-man fucking crime wave. Then, after the realization the intruder was there to fuck with the confidential patient files, rather than steal a prescription pad or drugs, he knew something was amiss.

"What's he doing with those files?" Truman asked the dentist.

"I can't work it out but he was messing with the files that you were asking about!"

Truman nearly jumped out of his seat.

"Is there anything missing or tampered with?"

"Well, I can't really tell in the video, but it looks like he's replacing the file he stole the night before!" said the dentist, flashing another blinding smile.

"WHAT THE FUCK! What do you mean, 'the night before'?" Ray screamed at the spectacled white-cloaked dental surgeon.

"Well, the same guy was in here the night before. Look."

Sure enough, there was Cunningham in the footage shot the night before, playing with the files. This time there was a shadowed but revealing profile shot that showed Caleb's face. Truman was at the filing cabinet in two quick steps before the dentist could protest. He pulled Cunningham's file from the drawer and placed it under the light on the desk. Without asking, he fished around in the top drawer of the Dentist's desk until he found a magnifying glass. The name and details appeared untouched but the x-ray files attached had been tampered with. The name on the x-ray prints had been carefully altered to read 'Caleb Cunningham' as had the birth date.

The dentist, who had been looking over Ray's shoulder, suggested the x-ray was not even for one of his patients as it had a different surgery address imprinted on the side of the negative. The surgery was across the other side of town and Truman wasted no time contacting them. Calling from the dentist's office he discovered that the other surgery had a similar break-in except all that had been taken was a patient's file. Truman wrote down the details, thanked the dentist for the file and made his way out to his vehicle. As soon as he had lit a cigarette, he radioed in an APB on the patient. He knew they wouldn't find him—he was the burnt stiff lying on the slab in the coroner's morgue. Cunningham had switched the x-rays, obviously intending the dead guy to literally take the heat for him.

The precinct had been temporarily relocated to a warehouse by the docks while the burnt station was being rebuilt. Ray was glad, despite it being against regulations, that he'd had the foresight to copy many of the Cunningham case files. He'd brought them in to work and put them in a lockable filing cabinet that was already nearly filled with new case files and paperwork. He looked across the warehouse at the rows of desks and the bustling activity of his colleagues. From his vantage point in the corner at the rear of the building, Ray made sure that he kept his head down and transcribed as much of the old case file notes he could remember into the growing stack of notebooks on his desk. New information surfaced and Truman found out the dentist's patient had been missing for the last two weeks. The victim's mother, who he lived with, had reported him AWOL the first day he'd gone missing. Apparently, he was an accountant by day and a queer biker-type by night that liked to frequent seedy bars, looking for slum-rats to pound his ass into the early hours. No trace of his expensive Harley-Davidson motorcycle had been found either. Truman ran the plates and placed another APB out to all national traffic patrols. He knew it would be unlikely that Cunningham would be picked up. He had probably ditched the bike by now and jacked some new wheels, but he had fucked up once before. It was quite possible he would screw up again. Ray felt the adrenaline course through his veins and he felt like a real man again. He was the great white hunter—hot for blood, the scent of his prey fresh on the wind.

Ray pulled an overflowing folder out of the filing cabinet. The Cunningham file had grown to the point where Truman now used one whole drawer specifically for his copious notes. He updated an incident report and filed it chronologically with all the others, detailing the latest developments. He had separated the files into separate folders, each marked with the names of the individual Cunningham family members. On a hunch, Ray opened Samael Cunningham's file to be greeted by a photocopy of a black and white crime scene photograph of the Cunningham family ranch in the small mid-western town of Repose, Fey County. He knew all the remaining files inside-out and he knew that Caleb had only one place left in the world that had a family connection to him.

After gaining access to court documents, relating to the Cunningham family affairs, Ray knew all about the inheritance and the fact that Caleb officially owned the run-down ranch. Caleb was taking care of business, setting the family home on fire—disappearing off the face of the planet.

Ray knew the ranch would be next on Cunningham's list. Possibly, even a place where Caleb could stay or bury his bloody secrets. Truman also knew that Samael had been suspected of more than one murder in the past and that Errol had used the ranch on his travels. It occurred to Ray that a full search warrant would be needed as he suspected the farm would be the mother lode of evidence he required, to put to rest at least a few of the cold cases connected to the Cunninghams.

He considered the search warrant again and thought better of it. That could come later, he would take some unused leave he had owing to him, rent a car and fill the trunk with an assortment of weapons from the armory. Fuck the warrant!

What Truman planned to do would be off the record.

He pulled the latest incident report from the file and put it through the shredder next to his desk in the temporary office he'd been assigned. He looked at the single sheet offender profile he'd sent to the Fey County Sheriff's Department months before and put it through the shredder as well. One call on the short-wave radio cancelled all APBs on the perp and Cunningham was now his for the taking. Caleb was a dead man. Dead on paper and, in a few days, dead for real.

39

The lair was always cold which was perfect for its usage. For it was essentially a mortuary, as well as a tomb. The long concrete room had the entrance centred in the middle of the south wall. The east and west walls were lined with 24 old electrical conductors that stood man-height and were fastened symmetrically along each wall. Twelve on each side. The north wall housed a recess with a concrete slab that stretched from one side to the other. The slab stood a meter and a half high and was wide enough for an average sized body. My guess was that the slab was a makeshift workbench built for the service technicians, who used to maintain the electrics and various plumbing fixtures.

On top of each of the twenty-four electrical conductors, I had originally placed a large red candle. It became a ritual that I would light each one as I entered the lair. The candles cast a red glow throughout the room and gave a certain amount of warmth to the damp stale air. As time passed, I added new ornaments to the lair. With each new piece of art went with it a place for a candle. And with each candle annexed, went with it another slice of light. I stood now in my lair in the half-light and stared at the three remaining candles burning back near the north wall. I wiped my hands with a damp rag, working the detergent between my fingers and up and down my shaved arms. My new addition was prepared, dried, cleaned and ready for the final process before beatification.

I finished cleaning and slipped on a new pair of latex gloves from the box next to the paint thinner and tins of cleaning solvent. I checked my watch and carefully raised the head out of the bucket, my fist clenched tight around the long brunette ponytail. I was always amazed at how heavy the head was, like holding a twenty-pound bowling ball with one hand. The excess polyurethane dripped like honey into the bucket beneath. I turned the work toward me and nearly burst the zipper in my pants as the red glow of the remaining candles glistened off the side of her immortalised features. I stared transfixed for minutes as I watched the solvent coating, harden and set like ice. The red glow of the candles shimmering on the slick polyurethaned face rendered it wet, with blood.

Before the polyurethane had hardened completely, I walked the length of the cavern with my arm outstretched before me, bearing the head like a zombie's offering. I raised it up high and replaced one of the remaining candles on top of the conductor box with the art. Once set, it would eventually weld with the rust-covered top of the conductor and become part of the lair, effectively a representative piece of a complete oeuvre. I took care of my installation, brushing their scalped wigs and even applying makeup on occasion. However, I digress, time was knocking on the entrance door now. When the work was complete, I would move on … to the next one, a completely new installation in a fresh location.

I zipped up a fresh set of overalls and stepped into my wading boots. I reached under the decapitated corpse and lifted the rigid eviscerated remains off the slab. I placed her carefully on the gurney and rolled her to the entrance beneath her own head perched above on top of the conductor. The dead glazed eyes looked lifelessly ahead, as if ignoring the sight of her own headless body stretched naked beneath her.

As with the others, I had a prearranged site etched into my brain. On autopilot, I would arrive. The time would be right each time. The site would be perfect for the second half of my installation. The final work would be done underground, beneath the manhole cover. No blood, no viscosity, no mess. I would wind the slick coils of intestine around the limbs and arrange all the major internal organs in the hollow cavity of the belly. Once completed, I would make my way through the tunnels and open the man-hole cover and quickly scout the area.

After relieving the gurney of its passenger and hiding the trolley for collection at a later date, I would cradle the sculptured corpse in my arms like a lover, as I made my way carefully up and out into the night. Always at night, the darkness concealed my art-crime as I deposited the rendered corpse in the area under some pre-arranged debris. Once outside, I would make my way to the next area, stopping briefly to san-wrap my boots while sitting on a fence or dumpster.

I would NEVER return to the lair immediately. It would always be from a location at least three blocks away from where I had exited.

Once again, the location of the entrance to the tunnels would be familiar to me and I would make my way home, either on the bus or through the underground tunnels to avoid detection. By the time the body was found, it would be a day or two after and all trace of my scent would have disappeared from the area. Not once did I witness the authorities use tracking dogs, but my measures still ensured my anonymity.

Tonight, as I walked briskly in the bowels of Portvale once more, I realized I had forgotten the last one's name already. I had seen her ID, yet the only face I could remember was the glistening polyurethaned head, which sat like a totem piece in the lair. I felt like a rabbit that needed to come up for some air. Now the end was in sight, I could almost taste the fresh clean air that I craved. I thought about my family ranch in rural Fey County and the trees and clear blue skies and I longed to be away from the stench of the city.

My work was near completion and I knew that I would have to leave my trophies behind. I thought of the pyramids and tombs of the Pharaohs and knew that what I was leaving behind was something akin to an archaeological time capsule. Once the installation was complete, I would cement the entrance to my lair closed forever. Or at least until someone discovered it. This would ensure the protection of my work and give me time to complete my oeuvre, offering the world a cipher to interpret as they wished.

40

It was a dark winter's evening and I was bored, but on the trawl. It was starting to get dark as night approached. I had been on the North Shore for an hour, cruising the tree-lined avenues, checking out the mansions and stately homes of the nouveau-rich. Then I spotted the blonde walking a dog through the schoolyard, next to a closed shopping mall. She was five-feet ten inches and weighed approximately one hundred and fifty-four pounds. She was a perfect ten, her voluptuous chest encased in a navy blue mohair sweater, complete with a tartan scarf. The short pleated skirt covered her black tights that looked like they were painted on her shapely legs. She would do nicely.

The twelve hundred volts from my Taser knocked her out with the first jolt. Her long blonde hair seemed frizzled at the ends. I hefted her over my shoulder and ducked into the bushes next to the schoolyard. Concealed by the darkness of the unlit school field, I dropped her to the ground and dragged her across the field. She started to murmur and move her arms so I let her go and zapped her with the Taser again, this time with two thousand volts. She shuddered and blacked out again.

I looked at her lying there prone, the faint streetlight illuminating her shapely form like a store mannequin. I grabbed her ankles and dragged her for a few minutes until I reached the van in the parking lot. I opened the side door and grabbed some plastic ties, strapping her arms behind her back and her ankles to her wrists. I duct-taped her mouth and covered her with a light army blanket after hefting her onto the floor of the van. Before I shut the door, I gave her another shot with the Taser to ensure her compliance.

I drove across the North Shore Bridge, heading south to Portvale. The moon was full and hung in the night sky like a medallion, I lit a cigarette and checked my speed. I thought about my installation in the lair and the candle waiting to be extinguished with the arrival of a new work. I drove down the strip; looking at the street trash lining the boulevard, glad to have a clean specimen on board. I pulled up to the house, parked in the garage and locked the gate and garage door.

She was still unconscious when I zipped her up in a large black plastic bag and dragged her out the garage, to the corner of the section where the drain-hole cover was. I tied a rope around her stomach and lowered her doubled-up form to the floor of the storm-water tunnel. The gurney awaited and gave me the means to transport the medium to the altar in my lair. Before I discovered the Taser, I used to use blunt-force trauma to subdue my prey. Technology had awarded me the ability to preserve my canvas to create with what I would. It was with my acquisition of the Taser that I could finally create my latest installation. It was my most complex and biggest work so far and required perfection and numbers and this tool was perfect for easily rendering someone compliant, without aesthetic damage to the features. This latest woman was very compliant as she motionless on the gurney. I checked her heart and realized she was dead.

I slowed my pace and lit a cigarette before opening the door to my lair and trundling the gurney to the altar. I slammed the door and sat on the concrete ledge that served as my altar. I lit a smoke and looked at her still form with disgust. *To just give up on life like that was weak and weakness was no fucking excuse ...*

I sighed and leaned forward, running the razor-sharp blade of my Buck knife across her face, slicing the shape of a pentagram on her forehead. Black blood painted her white face; she looked like she was crying, although the blood was mere seepage due to the lack of a pumping heart behind it. I stopped myself from going further, I needed to conserve energy; I would have to hunt again tonight. I felt exhausted already, but committed to the task. It was my art of course; I could never let it die. I quickly wiped her naked corpse down with white spirits and covered her with a plastic tarp. I wheeled the gurney back through the tunnels to the foot of the exit in the rear of the rooming house and brought her limp corpse to the surface again.

For the first time in my life, I used Pa's furnace in the basement of the main house. As my father had done before me, now I found myself doing exactly the same thing. My rage allowed me to watch her burn, the rush of the furnace igniting. Instant white heat forced me back from the mouth of the oven. I thought about my mission and slammed the furnace door, as I heard flesh popping and lipid fat igniting. My heart smashed in my chest, as my adrenaline levels sharply increased. I quickly lit a joint and made my way back outside, the faint smell of meat burning in the air, down into the subterranean tunnels to the lair, to change my clothes and gather the contents of my night kit.

As I made my way back underground, the grass had kicked in and I was feeling more relaxed and serene. I took the back panel off the disused electrical conductor closest to the altar and removed a duffel bag, being careful to replace the panel again. Inside the bag was a change of clothing and my night kit. I changed into the black suit and put a slick hairpiece on my shaved scalp. I slipped on a pair of patent leather gloves and some black sneakers that looked like formal footwear and counted off ten thousand cash in hundred notes into a billfold clip. I laid my night kit out on the concrete ledge, and itemized the contents as follows:

```
Rope
Ice pick
Tyre iron
Ski mask
Handcuffs
Pantyhose mask
Torch
Two leather belts
Plastic ties
Bag of heavy-duty black plastic trash bags
Crow bar
Heavy-duty wood-handled awl
22. Luger with silencer
NVGs (night vision goggles)
```

I took a black briefcase from another hidden panel behind the opposite electrical conductor box. Inside the top of the briefcase was a flap with a pocket and my set of lock-picks. I put my Buck knife in and removed the picks, putting in its place a small key-chain with a smiley face key ring and a single key, careful to wrap the blade in my ski mask to prevent it from blunting. After placing selected items from my night kit inside the brief case, I covered the contents with a black liner and placed a newspaper and a towel over the top. I was ready, if I was seen on the North Shore I would be just another business Joe, on my home from a business dinner at a wine bar downtown.

I started the van and pushed the remote on the garage door opener, punching the remote again for the automatic gate. I eased the Econoline out into the stale night air. It was a Monday evening, not a night of the week I would usually choose but tonight called for something different, this was my twenty-fourth and final piece needed for my installation. This was my offering to Apollo and Dionysus, my gift to the universe.

I crossed the bridge and watched the lights of Portvale disappear behind me. Once across the bridge, I turned right off the freeway into Worthington, the first suburb of the North Shore and perhaps the wealthiest. No hookers or abandoned buildings here, just luxurious houses set apart on their lush green sections. I found the house I was looking for and parked the van down a side street before returning on foot, briefcase in hand. A single light was burning in the east corner window on the top floor.

I knew where she would be, the colour of her bedspread, her nightclothes, the shared ensuite, joined by an adjacent spare room. I knew her parent's vehicle was not in the garage because they went away gambling every other weekend. She looked strikingly like Lucille, in fact all the women after Lucille died, looked like her. This one was a post-graduate student at the North Shore University. I saw her on campus three-months ago and she immediately struck me as a candidate for my final work here in this hellhole. I followed her home and then tracked her movements until I had a firm idea of her daily routine and schedule.

I inserted the key I had cut two months ago in the garage door and slipped inside silently. Once in the dark security of the interior I pulled my ski mask and NVGs on, grabbed the length of rope and my Luger from the briefcase and made my way into the foyer. I flicked the illuminator switch on my NVG headset, the darkness mutated into light green brightness. I made my way up the soft-carpeted stairs, to the landing and to the east wing of the house. I saw the crack of light from under her door and caught my breath before removing the NVGs. Swapping green-time for real-life living colour as I opened the door and pumped three quick shots into her ample chest, I moved quickly to place a pillow over her squirting wounds, careful not to let too much blood stain her beautiful hair.

Tonight she would be the last piece of my work here, and tonight I would change my MO deliberately with as much purpose as I would for any of my so-called crimes. Tonight I would just take the head. I took her head off clean with one slash of my Buck Knife, it dropped to the shag-pile carpet at the foot of the bed and I gently but quickly moved her head away with my shoe, from the flow of blood now spewing from her decapitated body laying naked on the bed.

After rinsing the warm head in the ensuite shower, cleaning it free of blood, I placed it in the black trash bag I brought with me before I finished arranging her room. Tonight I was 'The Messenger.' I created this persona as I created all my works of art, with carefully planned precision. I was what you might call an organised type character. I would definitely leave a message tonight for you, Ray Truman. Before I left, I carved a JT on her thigh and hacked the lower half of her body from her torso. I left her shapely legs on her blood-soaked bed and hung the torso upside down, from the chandelier that hung above the stairwell in the foyer. I bunched up a pillowcase and soaked it in her blood before writing a message on the wall and a few pentagrams for good measure. I stared mesmerised before exiting out the front door, watching the torso slowly turn on the chandelier until it finally stopped moving. The only noise was the hypnotic sound of dark blood dripping loudly from the gaping wound in her neck, as it splattered on the marble tiles below.

Once back in the van, I turned the stereo on and turned the volume up on the *Natural Born Killers* soundtrack as I made my way back towards Portvale. When I eventually opened the rusty steel door of my lair I worked quickly to preserve the 24th and final piece of my installation, I replaced the final candle on the last electrical conductor with the lacquered head. I gathered up my belongings in the lair and dipped a brush in the can of fresh blood on the altar. I wrote 'I AM The Messenger' across the end-wall above the altar and the blood-painted pentacle. The candles on the altar sputtered and flickered as I turned the last head directly towards me. I could clearly see the 'JT' I had carved on her forehead, one day Truman might see this.

Maybe he would get it?

Maybe he wouldn't?

I stirred the ready mix concrete in the bucket next to the entrance. Within twenty minutes, I had the door sealed and my hands clean, I smoothed the last of the cement over with the trowel, effectively burying my patent leather gloves. I looked forward to buying a new pair in Paris soon, or Venice, maybe even Prague? I held my breath for a minute and filed the last image of my home and studio for the past twenty years. I could playback every last image of each of the pieces in my latest and greatest installation.

I can see the scrawled words next to the pentagram above the altar, painted with the blood of each visitor. I can smell the dried blood of the pentacle and taste the fear in my mouth. I can recall every inch of my lair, and I would have another sometime soon on a new island, with new memories.

As I exited the subterranean world of the tunnels, I closed the lid on both the tunnel and that space in time. It was as if I was folding my world up behind me, until eventually, I could fit it in my pocket and hit the road.

'More Portvale Slasher Murders Discovered' from Portvale Daily News, Aug 3, 2008

Today, the half-clothed body of Candi Clarke, 24, of no fixed abode was found near Interstate 18, 7 Kilometers North West of Portvale. County coroners were unable to determine the cause of death because of the advanced state of decomposition, decapitation and disfigurement. Estimates were made that suggest the woman had been dead for near on 3 months before she was discovered on the banks of a river, half-buried in a shallow grave, by a real-estate surveyor. This latest killing is reportedly linked to a series of unsolved homicides over the past two decades in and around Portvale.

Widespread panic has spread amongst young women and the large itinerant population, particularly on the Lower East side where more residents have mysteriously disappeared or been found murdered over the last five years. Nineteen prostitutes have been found decapitated with at least another thirteen female victims of various civilian occupations from Portvale and surrounding boroughs.

Other unsolved murders in the area have similarities in M.O. to the frenzied slayings of the young women. However, because these other victims have been older homeless males, it is presumed that another serial killer is operating in the same vicinity as the 'Portvale Slasher.' A spike in the number of unsolved homicides on the North Shore over the past decade also indicates the presence of a sadistic serial killer, whose MO is significantly similar to those on the south-side for Federal profilers to suggest they are the work of the same killer or a copy-cat serial killer. The *North Shore Chronicle* named these particular murders 'The

Messenger' killings due to notes found at the scenes and letters sent to the newspaper from the apparent killer.

Entry for the 'Portvale Slasher' and 'The Messenger': From The Encyclopedia of Modern Serial Killers (London: Blackmark Publications, 2009)

The homicides, which quickly became known as the Portvale Murders, earned the killer the dubious nom-de-plume of the 'Portvale Slasher', took place over two decades during the 1980s thru to 1996. There have been out-of-state unsolved homicides that also bear a striking resemblance to the Portvale Murders. Due to the lack of DNA evidence at the murder sites, no substantial connection has been established by the authorities other than the similarities in the way the killer or killers disposed of the bodies and the horrible injuries inflicted.

After the third victim was found, similarities between homicides revealed that a serial killer was at large in the dockside county of Portvale. As the body count increased so did the frustration of the local authorities. It seemed that every lead, related to the violent killings of local prostitutes, came to a dead end. With each decapitated body found, the killer's bloodlust seemed to increase with the mutilations becoming more frenzied. All the victims were decapitated.

Near the site of one of the earlier homicide scenes, in a dumpster enclosure at the rear of an industrial complex on Holmes Avenue, a man emptying trash recoiled at the sight of Michelle Arat's nude and decapitated body. She was the thirteenth official victim and had just celebrated her 22nd birthday two weeks before her death. This was the first victim of the Portvale Slasher who wasn't a street worker. After extensive investigations, it was discovered that a missing British tourist matched the victim's profile. Forensic analysis and dental records confirmed the victim's identity.

Slowly information was gathered as to Michelle Arat's movements since entering the country more than a year ago. Police were baffled that she had been missing for so long and only recently discovered. Interpol discovered, after interviews with her family and friends, that she had been employed as a model and as a designer in the fashion industry. Since leaving a once successful career behind her to travel, Michelle's creative nature had apparently led her into a life governed by her addiction to narcotics. The Federal investigators tracked her movements from the East City International Airport to various hotels around the city.

A pattern was detected and through credit card records, it was ascertained she managed to spend most of her substantial credit limit over the course of three months. Her whereabouts could be seen to deteriorate from swank hotels on the Upper East Side to run-down hostels on the Lower East side. The last known place of residence Michelle Arat lived was in a decrepit flophouse in Portvale on Artaud Avenue. The place had thirteen rooms and offered low-cost accommodation to mostly itinerant dockside workers and hookers.

The owner had been investigated on a number of occasions and was known to local authorities but wasn't considered part of any on-going investigation. Investigators had tracked the victim from a previous cheap motel whose owner had reportedly confiscated the woman's belongings after she failed to pay for her room two consecutive nights in a row. In the duffel bag, tucked into an inside pocket, police discovered her passport. The owner of the motel had provided police with a newspaper clipping she had found in the bottom of the bag listing 'Cheap rooms for rent' and the address on Artaud Avenue.

After the last apparent Portvale Slasher homicide, more than $500,000 had been spent on the long and fruitless search for the ruthless killer who had kept the city in the grip of fear for so long. According to the pathologist who performed the autopsy on the thirtieth and supposed last victim of the Slasher, Helen Clark, a divorced woman of 42, she "was tortured, murdered, decapitated and then cleaned with a solvent, then burnt with what appeared to be a blow-torch, presumably to get rid of any DNA evidence."

Her mutilated, headless, and nude corpse was found in a disused warehouse on the industrial outskirts of Portvale. Her body was arranged in an obvious manner in the form of a crucifix, her twisted arms affixed to an iron girder with electrical cord, her ankles bound with tape. The pathologist theorized that someone standing on top of a vehicle, possibly a van, had hung her from the girder. Faint unidentified tire tracks were discovered beneath the body on the rubble strewn concrete floor of the warehouse. Her head has still not been recovered.

Police were stymied. The clues led nowhere. They had no witnesses and in a city of more than 4 million people not including visitors, to match a faint tire track to a car without a suspect, meant the case would remain unsolved as long as they were without one. The only clues the police had were the victims and they weren't talking.

Aside from the obvious commonalities between victim type and the M.O. of the killer, there was no identifiable DNA residue from the killer on any of the victims. Distinct parallels between each homicide would remain buried within police files.

Some of the evidence was withheld from the press because of the unique identifying factors that could be used to match more victims to the same killer.

Other evidence was deemed too gruesome to unleash on a public already in the throes of horror at the nature of the slayings. The killer had not only used solvents to eradicate any trace of DNA from the bodies of the victims but he had also employed other equally effective, if not more horrific, methods of destroying his linkage to the crimes. Each victim had been horribly burnt internally, as well as externally, with what the pathologist described as "an instrument capable of delivering concentrated extreme heat. Namely, a blowtorch."

With thirty women dead, no apparent end in sight to the killer's insatiable bloodlust, and no clues to lead police to a suspect, panic spread from the city through the state. Police were flooded with letters and petitions demanding they catch the Portvale Slasher. A national television program profiled the killer and asked for the public's help in solving the crimes. Even with the national TV exposure and a record reward offered by the city, the killer managed to evade capture. After six months or so of no news, the Portvale Murders became just another bad memory as public interest dwindled. There had also been a gradual increase in homicides in the greater region surrounding Portvale. It appeared there were a number of multiple murderers operating within the city at any one given time.

'The Messenger' is a label assigned to a serial killer believed to have murdered and decapitated at least 24 people on the East Side and North Shore suburbs surrounding Portvale between 1996 and 2006. During that period, 14 other women are missing and presumed to be dead or linked to the case.

Similarities between cases are apparent due to the notes that have been left with the bodies. While different methods of death were employed by the killer or killers, the distinctive handwriting and content of the notes assume intimate knowledge of each of the separate cases, leaving authorities to speculate about the possibility of two serial killers operating within conjunction, if not cooperation, with each other. The following letter was recently sent to the office of lead Homicide Detective, Ray Truman:

Dear Ray
I am The Messenger. My message to u is death. I am The
Messenger. I am baneth u. I am above u. I am incide u.
My messages are writtin in the blud of the unwanted and
in the blud of the privlidged. My only diskriminatun is
sex-u-al, I like wimmin. Black ones. White ones. Red
ones. Green ones. Wimmin r the best messages to men. My
message is - HERE I CUM. I will not stop ripping and
killin til my message is herd all over the world. U can
not stop me. U can not stop The Messenger. If u do not
print this letter I will kill 3 more wimmin, one black
one, one white one, and one young one. They will
disapeer from the good places and the bad. They will be
found in the good places and the bad. I will clean the
streets of disease and filth before the end cums. The
end is cumming 4 u all. The end is cumming 4 u RT.

RT = ☘

I cent u a message downtown a while ago. No one was
blamed 4 it.

🚗 + ☄ + 13 + = ☘.

There will be more messages. I cent u a message at the
licker store.

2 + = ☘.

I cent u anutha message at the corner store.

2 + = ☘.

I cent u messages 4 the past 10 years.

🎞 + ☮ + ☦ x 20 + = ☘☘☘☘☘☘☘☘☘☘☘☘☘☘☘☘☘☘

I am losing my head. I am the messenger. U will lose ur
head if u do not lissen 2 my message. Stay off the
street. Lock ur door. Do not breeth. Be still the blud
that runs thru ur vains. Be still the blud that runs
like water down the sewar drayns under the city streets.
This is my message to u RT and the world. Ther will be
more blud in the streets. Ur ankles will be stayned red
with my messages. Watch out 4 me. C u soon. I am cumming
4 u.

My predikshuns 4 the futer -
SCH 🚗 + ☄ X 30 + = ☘☘☘☘☘☘☘☘☘☘☘☘☘☘☘☘
FaBIo QUANTICO + ☮ \ ☄ X 300 + = ☘☘☘☘☘☘☘☘☘☘☘☘☘☘☘☘

Remember I am The Messenger. I walk ur streets and paint
ur houses with blud, flud ur city with red death. Catch
me b4 I kill agin. If u can?
CCCCCCCCCCCCCCCCCCCCCCCCCCCCCCCCCCCCCCCCCCCCCCCCCCCCC
CCCCCCCCC

VII
Into The Wilderness

'Kill a man, and you are an assassin. Kill millions of men, and you are a conqueror. Kill everyone, and you are a god.'

Jean Rostand

People begin to see that something more goes to the composition of a fine murder than two blockheads to kill and be killed - a knife - a purse - and a dark lane. Design, gentlemen, grouping, light and shade, poetry, sentiment, are now deemed indispensable to attempts of this nature.

Thomas de Quincey

41

The town of Repose looked as though it had been excavated from the dust-blown earth on which it stood. It seemed a lot smaller than I remembered it as a child, as I entered the outskirts of the town I was greeted with a sign that proclaimed "Town of Repose, Population, 283." I slowed the bike to a crawl as I entered the town-belt. The wide main street was full of potholes and prairie tumbleweeds, lazily rolling in the warm breeze across my path. The houses that lined the main street stood apart from each other and were old and weather-beaten, save for a few that looked like they were still cared for. A handful of brick buildings signaled the approach of the town center.

I slowed to a stop just before the shops, at a gas station in need of a good paint job, with pumps that looked like relics of the 1950s. The mid-day heat was oppressive so I took the opportunity to remove my leather jacket and helmet while waiting for the attendant to appear. I scanned the shops for signs of life—the place was like a fucking ghost town. There was a hardware store, a food market, a drapery shop, a rural supplies outlet and a courthouse and tavern housed in the double-storied buildings. Down the street, past the shops, I could make out a police cruiser in front of a dark brick building with the words 'POLICE' emblazoned above the foyer entrance.

I peered into the grimy windows of the gas station but couldn't make out any movement from inside. I stepped down hard a few times with my boot on the bell-hose that lay across the covered drive-thru. I heard the sound of the bell's muffled clang from what I presumed was the workshop behind the forecourt. I started to put my helmet back on when suddenly an old guy appeared in the doorway wiping his grease-blackened hands with an oily rag.

He tilted back his STP Trucker's cap, filthy with grease, as were his once-blue coveralls, peered out of the shadows of the courtyard and spat on the dusty ground before asking me what I wanted. His toothless mouth emitted a voice cracked with age and years of whisky and cigarette smoke, the mass of wrinkles covering his leathered features spoke of a hard life.

After filling up the fuel tank of the Harley and paying for the gas and a cold Cola with cash, I thanked the unfriendly old timer and parked the bike outside the hardware store. After entering the store and waiting for what seemed like ages, a store clerk finally appeared from the back of the store as equally old and wind-blown as the guy from the gas station. They obviously didn't get many visitors from out of town in these parts, as much was evident by the suspicious stares that greeted me from the few people I met.

In the Food Market there was a customer being served by a young female clerk standing behind the counter, she was a typical country girl who managed to look extremely attractive and homely all in the same moment, despite no obvious signs of makeup or intent. The tall old guy she was serving looked like a farmer, he was wearing bib overalls caked with dry dirt and a worn wide-brimmed hat that would have looked at home in a wild-west museum. He looked at me like I was an alien with two heads; as he walked past, I caught an audible sniff as if he was trying to smell what kind of creature I was before he left the store. I tried to joke with the clerk by suggesting that we were the only ones aged less than forty years. She just looked at me with a vacant humorless gaze and asked me what I wanted.

I packed the food and tools that I had purchased in my backpack and put my helmet on, glad to be leaving this dump of a town. The place gave me the creeps and imparted a sad, lonely, feeling of emptiness that I had not experienced before. I flicked the electronic ignition and the Sportster rumbled to life, I tapped he kickstand with my boot and pulled away from the curb.

As I steered the bike away from the town center, I noticed a figure standing in the shadows under the awning outside the courthouse. I saw the light-tan uniform and the wide-brimmed Sheriff's hat and knew that he'd been standing there watching me for a while. His dark aviator glasses and white goatee hid his face under the shadow of the brim of his hat. He was tall and well-built but the slight stoop in his shoulders and the way he stood with legs apart betrayed his age. Judging from the whiteness of his beard, I figured he was at least fifty years old.

I headed out of the town center, watching him in the side mirror as he stepped into the center of the deserted street, staring after me, as he appeared to scribble something in a notebook. A chill ran up my spine and I considered heading back into the town and killing everyone in it but I kept riding, convincing myself that they didn't like outsiders and would figure that I was just passing through. I knew this cop recognized me from someplace and I knew that Truman had researched our family background and knew that we had family property in Fey County. I had seen his journals and notes strewn across every available inch of desk-space in his office before I had torched the place. I knew Ray would know this place would be on my itinerary when I disappeared. If my assumptions were correct, he would be coming for me as soon as that cowpoke Sheriff called in my arrival.

I remembered the town of Repose from when I was a kid but it had seemed a lot bigger then. One thing I knew was that I hadn't liked it back then and I liked it even less now. I was pleased to be leaving and I knew that to get to Grandpa's property I had to go straight through town heading west and take the first left past the small bridge heading south, towards the Prairie Mountains in the distance. As soon as I left the main street, the rural road turned to dust and gravel but the bike seemed to handle it well although my ass felt bruised from the long ride. I was looking forward to resting my weary body as soon as I reached the farm, as much as I was looking forward to putting Ray Truman in the dirt when he finally showed his ugly mug.

Half an hour later with the light starting to fade, I changed gear and eased the Harley Sportster to a chugging crawl. The surrounding farmland stretched into the horizon behind me and ahead rose to meet the brooding foothills of the mountain ranges. The land was a dull brown colour, bone dry with the early summer season. The dusk settled on the plains, twisting shadows flat into the darkening fields. The vaguely familiar sight of the dark pines at the end of the stretch of gravel road beckoned ahead.

The pines rose to cover a hill upon which sat the homestead, unseen from the road below. As I approached, I saw crows perched in the trees and on the sagging wire fences, tilting their black heads towards me as if they were sentries on guard. The twilight breeze blew warm against my skin as I pulled up at the mouth of the driveway to the Cunningham property. The looming pines lined the narrow dirt road and blocked out the remaining light from the evening sky.

I disengaged the clutch, climbed off the bike and kicked the stand down as I arched my back and stamped my boots until my leg muscles loosened and relaxed. I removed my helmet, savouring the unfamiliar rural smells of pine and manure. The bike idled quietly beside me as I recapped my journey, I switched the ignition off and the heat from the V-twin engine pinked the blue steel on the exhaust as it cooled slightly. Twelve hours non-stop from Portvale, save for fuel and food, and here I was finally after two decades.

In the fading light it was obvious that everything was overgrown—the Pines had risen from fresh saplings to giant trees; weeds cascaded from the shadows of the thick bark trunks; the road was littered with deep potholes and patches of weed and grass, but everything still reeked with familiarity. After stretching my tired muscles and surveying the area as the last dull strains of light were swallowed by darkness, I strapped the helmet to the sissy bar at the rear of the seat and threw my tired leg over the bike, switching the starter motor into life once again.

As I made my way up the dusty incline toward the farmhouse, the headlight from the bike revealed that the narrow road was growing thinner as the overgrown trees swelled and crowded my passage. The first signs of fog smoked from the shadows as I steered the bike south into the darkness. It was a ten-kilometre trek in from the main road and I remembered that this passage had always been the longest part of our 'family trips.' Pa would grow silent with each kilometre until he remained stone still as he stood on the porch, his clenched fist hovering above the peeling paint of the front door. Finally, he would knock solemnly and step back—as if he were a bible salesman expecting a dog attack or imminent rejection.

I turned the bike's headlight on high beam and a million silver sets of eyes blinked and disappeared into the shadows of the thick grove of trees. The place was crawling with feral cats and dogs and other rag-tag mongrels. The beam of light cut through the dark to illuminate the thick fog that now enveloped the way ahead. I kept the bike at a slow pace as the dirt track became even narrower and the crunch of the gravel grew louder than the deep throb of the Harley's powerful V-twin engine. I heard a barn owl hoot in the nearby distance and branches crack in the forest as animals scattered, as I continued toward the house.

Lower braches of the pines started brushing forcefully against my leather jacket, almost as if sweeping me clean of the outside world or vainly attempting to grab me as I passed. I feared that I would have to dismount as the fog and trees thickened to the point where I could hardly see a metre in front of me. As I changed down to the lowest gear in preparation to stop, the track suddenly widened and cut left behind a solid bank of overgrown Maple hedge and there, across a weed-strewn courtyard littered with rusted machinery, sat the dilapidated farmhouse glowing eerily in the dark.

I left the headlight on and parked the bike directly in front of the house and stood back to take it all in. The shadowed gabled roof sagged, as did the roof of the front porch. Once painted white, the house was now the dull colour of exhumed bone in the glare of the headlight. The front windows were smashed and jagged flashes of cobwebbed glass reflected the light from the bike. The decrepit balustrade around the porch looked like a broken set of teeth. The front door was missing and the dark space between the windows looked like the hollow nasal cavity of a skull. I looked at the house for a moment longer and then removed my pack from the back of the bike. I was glad to have a torch in my bag along with the nine-inch blade Buck knife I now held in my fist.

I kept the headlight on as I carefully climbed the decayed steps. The porch groaned under my weight as I hesitated briefly while I switched the torch on and then stepped forward into the darkness of my past.

The house smelled dry and musty, vines crept from the cracks in the floorboards and climbed the peeling walls. A few old pictures caked in dust hung from odd angles between the vines. I kept close to the walls to prevent my foot going through the old floorboards as I made my way down the long hallway to the end of the house and the kitchen. My torchlight revealed that no one had been in the house for a long time, the dust thick on the floor betrayed the presence of small animals—possibly cats or rodents but no human footprints were apparent. I found the kitchen and gave up looking for a place to put my bag as the vines covered every available surface. It was like stepping into an out of control greenhouse.

I holstered my knife in its sheath under my jacket and made my way back out the way I had entered. I remembered that the farm had many outbuildings that housed the horses and the pigs when I was a boy—strange ramshackle buildings, keepers of dark secrets then and god-knows what now. I remembered how the section flattened out behind the main house and stretched kilometres along the brow of the hill-top giving plenty of space to let the livestock roam and for hiding family secrets.

I started the bike, and walked it down the side of the house through the waist high weeds, using the accelerator to steer it effortlessly around the rear of the property to the old barn that rose up out of the darkness behind the main house. With considerable effort, I opened the large doors, parked the bike inside and closed the creaking doors behind me. The headlight revealed a cavernous interior; ivy had invaded the space and covered the timber walls, climbing blackly high into the rafters overhead. The old wooden stiles that had housed the pigs lay strewn in the dirt, rusty chains hung from the roof beams, as did the hooks and pulleys used for hanging and slaughtering the carcasses. I remembered the unforgettable sound of the pigs' high-pitched squeals and grunts as Grandpa threw buckets of blood and scraps into their pens at feeding time. The place was deathly quiet now, all I could hear was the faint creak of iron as the night air cooled the tin roof, and the old building's timber bones creaked with the weight of the evening.

I found some hay bales still bound tight and stacked high against the rear wall. I attempted to move a few but they crumbled hopelessly at the slightest touch—riddled with rat and mice nests. I resigned myself to the thin blanket I kept in my pack and a clear space on the dirt floor became my bed for the night. The dawn would bring some hard work with it I thought to myself, as I closed my eyes there on the hard bed of dirt and collapsed into an exhausted sleep.

42

Truman got the call just on dinnertime. It had been over six months since he had faxed the Sheriff's office in Repose, Fey County with a surveillance photo and description of Caleb Cunningham. The Sheriff, Tom Dewey, had called Ray to let him know his 'boy was in town.'

"He arrived in town at 5.30pm this afternoon and bought some supplies before heading south," said the Sheriff on the other end of the phone.

"Can you give me a full description of what he was wearing etcetera?" asked Truman.

"He looked like biker trash, full leathers and a Harley Sportster but when he took his helmet off he had a shaved scalp. He looked different than the photo you faxed through though, he's got a mighty scar that reaches from his temple to his jaw and he sure is an ugly sumbitch, I can tell you that much for free. Do you want me to pick him up for ya?" asked the Sheriff with a certain amount of excitement in his voice.

"No I just need to track his whereabouts that's all. And you sure he headed south?"

"Yep, in a straight line towards the Prairie Mountains where his family property is, is my guess."

"You have done your homework Sheriff," said Ray.

"Can you tell me anything about Cunningham Senior? Did you ever meet him?"

The Sheriff paused for a second before answering.

"Yep, I had occasion to talk to the 'ornery old bastard in town when he picked up supplies. A few years before Samael died, he was the lead suspect in a bunch of murders. Mostly illegals and border-hopping farm workers, who went missing before or after working at his pig farm. Rumour has it he used them to feed his pigs, couldn't prove nuthin' though. When he died, the disappearances stopped. He was a strange old fish, used to put the creeps up the wimmin in town when he came in but we only saw him a few times a year. That grandson of his sure is a chip off the old block, eh?"

Ray was taken aback at the revelation that Cunningham Snr was the prime suspect in a serial homicide investigation and wondered why he hadn't spoken to Tom Dewey a few years earlier. He scratched his stubbled chin and made some notes in the pad on his desk.

"Yeah. Yeah they do look the same. Did you ever go out to the pig farm?"

"Sure did. Most rundown place I've seen round these parts. I had to see Cunningham Snr about a firearms licence renewal and he was none too pleased having me show up on his doorstep. It would've been about six months before he died; the funny thing was it was deserted apart from him. I couldn't hear any pigs like you do at other pig farms and there seemed to be no livestock anywhere, although he did have a huge Alsatian that looked half rabid. That guy sure was odd; I guess that's why he lived so far out of town. You sure you don't want me to go and pick up your boy for something? I'm sure I could hold him on a charge of being an ugly sumbitch or just mess him up for ya?"

The Sheriff's voice was heavy with adrenaline and Truman could tell that the Cunninghams would've been the only bit of excitement the poor sap had seen for a while in bum-fuck, Fey County.

"No that's alright Sheriff. I just needed to confirm he was in town. It was a while back that I faxed you the information and we no longer need him for questioning now, but thanks for the info anyways," Ray said, trying to sound convincing enough to end the conversation as quickly as he could.

"That's all right Pardner, just happy to help is all," said the Sheriff with his southern twang.

Jesus, thought Ray, if I asked him to he'd probably go and hang the bastard just for a bit of fun. Fuck, now Deputy Dawg knew that he was interested in Cunningham, maybe he'd have to play it by the books and follow procedure? Maybe I should let him bring Caleb in and sort it out from there? Thought Ray to himself. No, he definitely wanted that pleasure for himself. He would pay to see the look in Caleb's eyes when he put him in the ground.

Truman couldn't believe how stupid Cunningham had been letting the Sheriff ID him like that. Ray thought for a minute that it might be a deliberate move on Caleb's part, but his taste for blood overshadowed his logic once again and he quickly set about packing an overnight bag, loading his utility hold-all with the tools he'd need to take out the sole surviving member of the Cunningham family.

Ray hit the road and drove west non-stop until finally taking a brief rest at a filthy roadside motel six hours from Fey County. He woke before dawn and left the dirty motel without a second glance, within five hours he hit the small town of Repose and knocked upon the Sheriff's door. Ray had given up caring whether anyone knew he was looking for Cunningham. The sheriff already knew that Truman had an interest in him and had witnessed Caleb's arrival. He would make it look like self-defence but somehow Ray knew that Caleb wouldn't be easy to take down.

The Sheriff's local knowledge proved invaluable and after describing a suitable vacant shelter near the Cunningham homestead, Ray knew he'd have a better chance of achieving his goal. Upon arrival at the small deserted farmhouse, Truman was pleased that it was just as the Sheriff had described. After looking around the small property, Truman realised how unnerved he was by the barren countryside. Amidst the burnt brown fields, the only greenery visible was the dark pine hedgerows that bordered the farms and dissected the land like stitched wounds.

After parking his vehicle out of sight at the rear of the property, he checked the surrounding countryside with his field glasses and spotted the flat section at the foot of the mountain ranges surrounded by massive trees. He couldn't see the Cunningham property or any of the farm buildings from where he stood but from the Sheriff's description, he knew he was looking in the right place. After cleaning and loading his various weapons, Ray took a nap on the old wire-sprung bed in the main bedroom. As he lay there gazing at the nets of cobwebs covering the whitewashed ceiling, he thought about Cunningham.

Ray could feel that Caleb was close by. He could almost sense the presence of evil lurking outside the house in the foothills, like some murderous beast or wild animal. He knew he wouldn't stop hunting and thinking about him, until he or Caleb was dead. Finally, Ray's eyes closed and he drifted into a fitful sleep full of nightmares and imagined violent scenarios.

43

I woke at sunrise with another stinking headache, cold and hungry, my back ached from the night's sleep on the hard soil. Morning sunlight cut through the cracks in the timber walls of the barn, illuminating the interior amidst floating clouds of dust. I brushed my jeans and jacket free from dirt and stretched my weary muscles. I opened the large doors and stepped into the blinding warmth of the dawn sun, only to be greeted by a guttural growl from a huge German Shepard standing directly in front of me, bristling with animal fury.

I froze then slowly drew my knife from inside my jacket; all the while watching the dog's every move. There was something familiar about the hulking wolf of a dog. I noticed the white foam bubbling from its bared canines, dripping on the dirt and its bloody paws. Each growl drew rasping breath from deep within its diseased lungs. Cataracts made its bulging eyes look ghostly as they intermittently rolled in the back of its bristled skull, revealing blood-filled orbs sick with rage. Its nostrils flared and it lurched forward slightly to the left of me. I realised this enraged animal was running blind, steered by a failing sense of smell. I used the morning breeze to my advantage and moved silently towards him.

Suddenly, with a sickening death rattle of a growl, the rabid animal jerked towards my scent. As he lunged forward, I stepped in and ducked down as it leapt, raising my Buck knife quickly with both clenched hands, the sharp blade sinking deep into the dog's chest as it passed over me mid-flight. The knife sunk deep between its ribs, cracking bone and puncturing organs in a shower of fetid blood as I carried the weight of the twitching dog to the ground.

I withdrew the knife with a twist and stepped back as the dog released a shivering death sigh and convulsed on the dusty ground with its last breath. As it died, its chest sunk as if deflated. The lifeless corpse twitched and shuddered with the sickness still swarming through its body. I checked myself for wounds and scanned the rear yard for the water pump that had once been there. I removed my jacket and shirt and walked the length of the yard in my hunt.

Amongst an overgrown bush of weeds the size of an automobile, I found the rusted arm of the water pump and the old well.

I put all my weight on the handle and pushed down hard. It didn't budge an inch. I soon found a length of hollow iron pipe and used it as a fulcrum to lever the handle. With a crack of old rust breaking, the arm shifted on its ancient bearing, as the handle finally rose and fell a few times. With a choking splutter, some brown drops of water spurted from the barrel of the faucet. I used my knife to free the pipe of years of accumulated debris and cranked the lever-arm again. An explosion of rust-coloured water burst from the faucet and then finally a stream of clear water gushed onto the ground. I soaked my shirt in the water and cleaned the dog's blood from my hands and face. I cupped my hand and drank the water; it tasted slightly muddy but cold and good.

I stood up and searched the yard and the tree line for any other signs of life. It occurred to me the dog may have been travelling in a pack. Judging from the state of it, I decided that it was probably an outcast. I thought of Cain and Able and wondered if they were still prowling the bowels of Portvale's underground sewer system. The German Shepard reminded me of my Grandfather's dog. It seemed implausible that it could still be alive but I couldn't help entertain the idea that it was the elder Cunningham's violent sidekick, still roaming the farm protecting it from unwelcome strangers, as only it knew how.

I gave Truman seven days to get to the ranch. Over the next few days, I made my preparations carefully. I decided to use the barn as a base as it had two exits—the main front doors and a smaller entrance at the rear of the barn that opened out into the camouflaged protection of overgrown shrubbery. As well as a safe exit route, I used up a few hours constructing a comfortable bed in the barn out of a few hay bales and an old horse blanket I found without too many moth holes. The long, winding gravel road that led to the main gates of the family homestead had two main chicanes, one at the bottom and one eighty meters from the entrance. I cut down a tall spruce tree that stood on the blind corner, it landed on an angle that effectively blocked the whole road and wouldn't be seen until too late. I made sure there was a track that bypassed the fallen tree, wide enough for me to leave in a hurry with the bike. I dug pits at strategic points on pathways into the property, lining the dirt-floor of each with upright sharpened stakes, made from various tool handles left in the barn. I covered each pit with branches and dead leaves to mask their presence. It would take two days for all the necessary work to be completed, to ensure my plan succeeded.

On the third day, I woke up with another stinking headache. I drained my bladder in the long grass at the rear of the barn then prepared a quick breakfast. I drank nearly a liter of water, had a can of baked beans, and then unwrapped Pa's map written on a piece of soiled bed linen. The map was simple; it showed the house, the barn and various large trees situated around the perimeter of the property. One tree had a crude circle with a cross drawn through it in deep red ink that looked suspiciously like blood.

I didn't know what was there. All I knew was that whatever was buried there would somehow prove important. So important, that I couldn't leave the country before I'd seen what lay buried under that cross. So I found the tree and I dug, and dug, and broke a spade, then dug some more.

Then I found it. A black suitcase wrapped in thick plastic sheeting filled with perforations. It took some effort to carry the thing back to the house, but I finally managed to heft it onto the deck of the rear porch and smash the rusted padlock from the handle with the shovel. I caught my breath and crouched down to open the lid of the case.

I paused and wondered for a brief second if Pa had booby-trapped it, but he hadn't. I counted over three million in used notes, perfectly preserved and legal tender, enough for an early retirement and a major change of scenery. I also found an old leather-bound journal covered in mold in the bottom of the suitcase, with the initials S. C. C. faintly embossed on the front cover.

After filling my backpack with the journal and enough cash to last me a few years, I buried the rest in front of an old oak tree settled amongst others on the south border of the property, being careful to make a sketch of a map on a white handkerchief. I considered the map for a minute and realized that it wouldn't do, I did not want to have to hide and protect it until the next time I needed it. Shit, it could be years before I returned to this spot, so I decided to tattoo the map on an obscure part of my anatomy.

I sharpened the blade of my knife to a razor edge on a flat stone and dipped the point of the blade in the ink I emptied from a ballpoint pen. I carved a simple, yet deep, map on my upper inner thigh. I wiped the blood from my leg with my t-shirt and admired my somewhat crude handiwork. It would do—five dots represented the trees along the boundary, an 'S' sufficed for due south, and a star next to the center tree symbolized the location of the suitcase.

I was ready for flight and for Truman. I had a special plan for him; he would die slowly and become my last sacrifice before Europe. He might be found eventually but it was obvious that no-one came to the farm anymore. The only visitors appeared to be the local wildlife that sheltered in the decaying farm buildings. If he was found eventually, they would only find the dust of his bones, scattered through the surrounding countryside by the feral creatures that roamed the rural badlands. I waited, sitting on the porch seat, listening to the things that move in the night and reading the disturbing annals of my Grandpa, penned so neatly in his bloodstained journal. As I read, visions started tumbling through my brain, trying to claw their way out.

44

I stared at my hands in the dull yellow glow of the kerosene porch light. I imagined my fingers slick black with blood. I thought of Charlie, now a worm-eaten mass of bones in an unmarked pauper's grave. I tried not to think of the ghosts, the screams, and the smell of blood and death. I tried not to think of the numbing pain from the migraine I'd had since waking this morning.

I thought of Ray Truman instead.

I imagined a perfect concentric bullet hole, drilled deep in the center of his forehead. His dead white skin. His lifeless cruel eyes glazed blue like a dog with cataracts. Pain, etched indefinitely, on his death mask.

I thought of Ma and Pa and they were dead to me too.

They were nothing.

I couldn't remember their faces.

I tried to think of myself and couldn't.

I just felt the dark and the pain in my throbbing temples.

The beating drum of my blood, pumping unrelentingly in my brain.

I tried to stop the inevitable images tumbling through my mind. Cascades of blood and gore, armies of haunted crushed souls, my stomach sick with it all. I cocked the hammer on my .38 and pressed the cold steel muzzle against my temple. The cool metal soothed my burning head. I closed my eyes and stroked the trigger with my forefinger, aware of my movements but completely removed from any sensation of control.

Distant—like a childhood memory.

I thought of my father, aimed the pistol at my foot, and squeezed the trigger. The pistol kicked in my fist. The reverberating blast deafened me for a moment as I blinked rapidly from the muzzle flash in the half-light. The smell of cordite and sulfur wet my tongue with its taste, as my foot burned with a numb heat. The wound had immediately cauterized with only a small trickle of blood bubbling from the hole in my boot. The smell of burnt flesh combined with melted rubber.

The pain in my head ceased.

I stuck a finger in the hole in the top of my foot, up to my first knuckle, and felt the warmth and heat. I could feel a pulse, strange and foreign, like the wet heartbeat of a frog. The night was suddenly deathly quiet after the shot, a few seconds passed before I heard laughter in the distance.

Pain crawled up my body from the wound in my foot, registering itself in my temples. At the same moment, I realized that it was the sound of my own hysterical laughter, echoing off the trees in the dark night.

I decided I seriously needed some sleep—I knew I was hallucinating, so I smoked myself senseless with the remains of my stash and collapsed on my makeshift cot in the barn. I needed my strength for the next day, my birthday and, all things going according to plan, Ray Truman's Death Day.

45

It was June 15, 2009, the morning of my thirty-fifth birthday and I had begun to doubt that Truman would arrive. I cursed my own stupidity as I strapped a makeshift dressing to my foot wound and thought about whether or not he would find me. Maybe he wasn't as intelligent as I figured? Maybe he had given up on me? Maybe I was safe and free from his relentless persecution for once? I checked the bike over and secured my pack to the rear of the bike before lighting a cigarette and closing the door of the barn. The morning light was strong and visibility was good so I made my way slowly to the foothills at the rear of the property, each step making me wince with the pain in my foot. After a painful climb of the hill to a level section that overlooked the plains below, I settled in and surveyed the burnt countryside beneath me.

The flat lands stretched to the horizon and I could see for miles into the distance. My vantage point allowed me to see vehicles approaching from any direction. I sat and smoked and thought about my next move as I waited. My foot ached with a tight pain but I knew it would be ok. I hadn't appeared to break any bones when the bullet passed through the webbing between my big toe and the next and the redness around the cauterized wound was not as bad as I had thought it might be. Still, I cursed myself again for my stupidity and wondered whether part of me was trying to subconsciously sabotage my escape.

Eventually, the afternoon turned to dusk and the waning light gave way to darkness as I made my way back down the hill to the farm. I was just about ready to believe that Truman was not about to show, but somehow I knew that he would and I was ready for him. I could smell his rage and fear and I could almost taste his blood. I reached the old farmhouse, sat down on the chair on the front porch, and waited, elevating my foot on the old banister to relieve the throbbing pain now shooting up my leg.

I held my head in my hands and sighed as if trying to exhale all the badness out of my tired body. My unrelenting headache pounded in my brain. Alone and exhausted I felt like dying, but I knew I had not seen my last sunset. I looked out across the valley to the dark flatlands from my vantage point on the porch. To the east, I could see the icy glow of the city lights on the horizon. My temples resounded with a deep throbbing pain. The migraine that had been plaguing my every thought for the past month was slowly killing me. Of that, I was sure. I seriously thought I had a tumor or an aneurysm. That a point of no return had come and gone, I was also certain.

My breath drew short as I pushed thoughts of suicide from my mind again. I had begun to feel unwell and realized I had a slight fever. My forehead was covered in a sheen of perspiration and I had a slight tremble in my limbs. I knew it was the wound in my foot telling me to rest and recuperate but I would force myself to carry on—to run like a dog and see another birthday come and go. I wanted to see the world. Maybe become a better person one day. God knows I had tried, but my urge to create runs deep. After all, killing's in my blood.

My mind begins to race again as my foot burns with a sickening pain that screams, 'INFECTION!' Time was running out and with it, my options. I would leave at first light tomorrow even if Truman didn't show. If my foot hadn't started to heal soon I would need a doctor, or an amputation.

I looked at the sun finally sinking to a line of silver and then as it disappeared in blackness behind the hills in the west I lit the wick of the kerosene lantern on the porch. I took a breath and heard a noise to my immediate right in the pines. In the dull light from the lantern, I saw a shape emerge from the shadows of the dark trees and sit in the tall grass next to the overgrown driveway. Watching me, two burning embers glowed red in its black eye-sockets. The unmistakably menacing shape of the lion, made my heart rush with adrenaline.

A deep low growl from the beast drifted ominously across the yard, as more sounds of movement caught my attention from the hedgerow at the driveway entrance. A large black leopard appeared from behind the Maple hedge and sat on its haunches in the center of the driveway. Two silver glints of light glistened from its eyes as it stared intently at me. I slowly raised myself up off the porch chair and stopped mid-action. A huge wolf stood at the bottom step, at the end of the porch to my left.

A rising growl broke from the wolf as its yellow eyes blazed at me with a primeval energy. Without thinking, I put all my weight on my wounded foot, and a sharp jolt of pain ran up my leg and embedded itself in my groin. I felt myself panic for a second as I reached for my .38 still resting on the chair next to me. The wolf threw back its massive head and howled a blood-curdling cry at the night sky. I could smell its sulfurous breath as its cry hitched and lengthened into a full killing scream.

Ignoring the throbbing pain in my foot I scrambled from the seat and crouched on the porch, covering my ears as the sound intensified. All the remaining front windows of the farmhouse exploded out across the yard as the wolf's howl reached its climatic pitch. Shards of glass and splinters of timber pierced the back of my hands and the shirt on my back, as I tried to protect my head from the blast. The kerosene lantern exploded in a shower of glass and molten flame, splashing small liquid fires across the deck and in the dry grass next to the porch. I frantically brushed flames from the legs of my jeans, my ears ringing with the sound of the blast, my eyes stinging from the fumes and smoke. The ringing in my ears and the smell of the kerosene intensified as the air surrounding the house condensed and thickened, almost crackling with an electric ferocity. I rubbed my eyes, trying to get my vision focused and realized the wolf was on the porch mere feet away from me now. A thick growl escaped from the beast's throat as it paced towards me menacingly.

I instinctively turned on my good leg and launched myself off the end of the porch, away from the wolf and the flames. As I hit the ground and rolled to a kneeling position, the front door exploded outward, sending more jagged shards of glass and timber across the yard into the trees, the rush of air accelerating the fire now blazing in the dry grass.

My senses reeled in shock as I saw the wolf preparing to leap off the porch in my direction. Strands of bloody spittle dripped from its bared teeth, as it looked down at me crouched in the long grass next to the house. I could see its black fur bristle on its muscular shoulders as it seemed to swell and grow with each passing second. In slow motion, I saw its muscles bunch and twitch as it launched itself at me. As it leapt into the air between us, I raised the revolver and fired three rounds through the drifting smoke into the wolf's chest and flank. The loud report of the shots cleared my thoughts and I quickly rolled aside, hearing the thud as the wolf hit the hard dirt ground behind me. I didn't wait to check its pulse as I threw myself into the sanctuary of the trees at the edge of the clearing.

I hobbled and crashed through the undergrowth until I could go no further. The pain in my foot overwhelmed the adrenaline coursing through my body. My lungs screamed for air as I swallowed mouthfuls of pine-scented oxygen. I sat with my back against the rough bark of one of the massive Pines, feeling my heart slam against my bruised ribs. I sat there breathing hard, my .38 held out before me with both hands, aimed at the flames twisting in the grass at the front of the house. My eyes ached with concentration as I scanned the burning yard, trying to make out the silhouetted shapes of the beasts.

I waited and counted the slowing beats of my heart, as my temples pulsed with expectation. Minutes passed without sound or movement and the fire began to burn brighter through the trees as it ripped through the old timber farmhouse. An hour passed and I continued to watch as the flames burned lower until finally they began to subside, billowing plumes of smoke rose into the night air and drifted through the trees like fog.

I waited.

No wolf came.

No lion.

No leopard.

Just smoke. I started to relax and made myself comfortable where I sat. I thought about what I had witnessed and doubted my sanity completely at that point. *'Fucking lions and wolves. Really???'* I froze, thinking I heard something move over my left shoulder in the woods. I flattened myself on the ground as I twisted my gun arm in the direction of the noise. I nearly screamed. Charlie's disembodied skeletal face smiled at me in the dark—and then there was nothing, as everything turned to white.

I woke as the soft morning light washed through the trees. I stretched my arms, arched my back and hobbled to my feet. Hesitantly stepping out of the shadows of the undergrowth into the full light of day. The front yard was black with the burnt remains of the fire. There was no evidence of the strange bestial trio I had battled the night before, but I was in no doubt as to how real they had seemed. The gutted remains of the burnt out farmhouse, still smoking, sat in front of me like some remnant of a bad dream. If what I had witnessed was real then I was ready to admit belief in things supernatural. I searched for the remains of the wolf in the charred stubs of grass, but found nothing. The fact that the farmhouse was burnt to the ground and that Charlie had visited me before I lost consciousness, led me to believe that last night had been a construction of my own imagination. I concluded that I probably needed sleep, antibiotics and anti-psychotic medication, in order to be on full alert for any attack Truman might throw my way. Not having the luxury of the last two items on my wish list, I decided that my best bet was to get as much sleep as I could during daylight hours. Truman was nocturnal like me and as such, it was logical that he would be making his move under cover of darkness. As it turned out, I was right.

46

Truman had used the days since his arrival to survey the Cunningham farmhouse and the surrounding territory. He had watched through his binoculars as Caleb made his way from his vantage point on the hill back down to the farm each night. The deserted farmhouse Ray was in was about a kilometer away from the Cunningham property and one of the few buildings in the immediate area that provided camouflage while he decided what approach to use. The day before, he had set out at first light and, using the cover of trees, made his way up the foothills until he had a clear field of vision down over the Cunningham farm.

He had seen Cunningham by the old oak tree at the back of the property, first digging something up and then reburying it in another spot next to another tree. Truman made an entry in his notebook to check out later whatever it was that Cunningham had buried. Ray had seen where Cunningham was holed up in the old barn at the back of the burnt-out house. He knew that he would have to move on Cunningham after dark to preserve the element of surprise and ensure maximum destruction.

Ray saw the tree across the driveway and had also seen Cunningham setting various traps around the main entrance to the property days before. He thought about taking Cunningham out with the hunting rifle and long-distance scope but decided that he needed to look him in the eyes before closing them. Ray woke that night to the sound of gunshots coming from the direction of the Cunningham farm. He stood on the porch in the dark and saw flames flickering behind the shelterbelt that surrounded the farm. He saw the red embers sparking in the night sky as they drifted in the plumes of smoke that rose from the burning farmhouse. Ray sat on the porch and sipped from a bottle of Vodka as he smoked and hoped that Cunningham was burning along with the farmhouse. Two hours passed before Ray realised no fire appliances were coming, no sirens approached in the distance. It was just he and Caleb, possibly just him alone out here in the middle of nowhere and he felt good about that. The flames died down and Ray turned in to dream of tomorrow and what he might find when he finally confronted Caleb or what remained of him.

Truman waited all day, plotting his movements and as the afternoon turned to dusk, he selected his weapons carefully and made sure they were in order and fully loaded before dressing himself in the borrowed SWAT outfit. Despite Ray's adrenaline-fueled bloodlust, he kept calm and reminded himself to control his breathing to conserve his energy. He strapped on a Kevlar vest before buttoning the black drill shirt over it and holstering his Glock sidearm. He pulled the flak jacket on and filled the pockets with spare ammo for the Remington 700P sniper rifle. The final item of equipment he took from the utility bag was a pair of night-vision goggles. Ray zipped his jacket up and shouldered the Remington as he made his way out into the twilight, fixing his sights on the foothills ahead.

It took Ray a good hour to make his way up the foothills to a vantage point behind the Cunningham property. He was short of breath and aware that he was far from being in peak physical condition. The light had now faded to blackness and the air was cool and silent, Ray took a moment to catch his breath. He adjusted the NVGs on his head and blinked as the eerie green vision revealed the white shapes of trees and the flashing bright lights of animal's eyes amongst the scrub and long grass. It took a full five minutes before his vision adjusted properly to the unnatural light. A slight wave of nausea passed as his body began to assimilate his surroundings and become used to the strange sensation of altered perception and motion. He caught his breath and made his way down through the trees.

As Ray approached the boundary of the property, he began to sweat profusely again. The years of alcohol abuse and stress had taken its toll on his body and he knew that he would only get one chance with Caleb. He hoped that the bastard had died in the fire but decided that to attack from a distance would be wise. He found a strategic place behind a tree that provided a clear view of the rear yard. He could easily see the old animal pens and barn, where he assumed Cunningham would be hiding. Ray assumed a classic sniper's pose and shouldered the butt of the rifle as he lay on the ground beneath the camouflage of the tree's foliage. He adjusted the range on the scope and centered the sight on the barn door as he set in to wait for Cunningham.

After an hour, Ray realized that he would need to draw Cunningham out of the barn soon if he were to maintain an advantage. His heart started to race as he searched for a projectile amongst the long grass. Finding a fist-sized rock, Truman hesitated briefly before pulling his arm back to throw. He thought about Cunningham and what he had done. He thought about all the peoples' lives the scumbag had destroyed, all the sickness he'd unleashed upon the world. He thought about his own life now in ruins. His dead wife, his career now destroyed, the mutilated body of the woman he'd found sprawled on the stairs of his apartment, the gutted precinct house ... Ray knew that if he wasn't already dead he would have to kill the son-of-a-bitch and that he would only get one shot at it. He was sick of waiting, now was the time to strike.

He raised himself to his knees and sighted the Remington once more before lowering the weapon, to throw the rock in the general direction of the barn. He watched the rock fly through the air, a white dot on a green background, and bounce off the side of the barn wall. He hadn't meant to throw it so hard and was hoping it would fall short and cause a subtle disturbance. Ray caught his breath as the rock thudded sharply against the side of the barn. The noise of the impact seemed amplified as it echoed across the yard.

Truman shouldered the rifle again and quickly centered the scope-sights on the main doors of the barn. He waited, his breath caught in his throat, his heart pounding in his chest as blood throbbed in his temples. He waited, wiping sweat from his forehead with the back of his free hand. The rims of the goggle lenses were cutting into the flesh of his cheeks as he realized the straps were too tight. An insect crawled across the back of his damp neck. His groin ached with the sudden sense of a full bladder and he felt old and tired. Yet he waited, forcing himself to fight the discomfort and keep his eye on the prize. Truman waited and waited ... *Maybe Cunningham had disappeared like he had in Portvale?* He considered approaching the barn or throwing something else at it, growing impatient with an uneasy sense of dread that he'd fucked up and missed his chance. Without a sound, Truman's worst fears were confirmed.

He felt the cold blade of Cunningham's knife sink between his shoulders, into the base of his neck just above the protective layer of the Kevlar vest. The blade passed through the collar of Ray's drill shirt and struck the vertebrate in his spine. Ray's finger tightened on the trigger and a shot exploded in the silence of the still night.

Ray's back arched and then he dropped to his knees, the rifle falling to the earth beneath him as he pitched face forward into the long grass. The lens of his NVGs broke as his skull hit the hard earth. Ray lay motionless as Cunningham removed the blade from his back with a twisting motion, before wiping it on Truman's shirt and laughing quietly. Ray could not move and he knew he was paralyzed. He could feel the cold moisture of the grass against his face, the warm blood curling down the side of his neck as it dripped on the ground, but he could not feel anything below his neck.

He could not move.

He could not breathe.

He felt Cunningham's cold fingers feel for a pulse on his neck. He was aware that Caleb was standing in front of him as Ray could see his legs at a right angle through the shattered lens of the NVGs. He watched as Cunningham leant down and looked at his face, his head cocked to one side like a bird. Caleb's black eyes glistened and his drawn face seemed the color of bone in the dark night. He reeked of death. Truman's heart skipped a beat as Caleb leaned closer and whispered in his ear.

"Fuck you pig. That's for my brother."

With those words, Caleb stood and kicked Truman viciously in the head and body a number of times before turning and walking slowly back to the barn. Explosions of light danced in front of him as Truman tried to blink the blood out of his eyes. His head throbbed where Caleb's boots had landed on the side of his skull, but he could feel none of the other injuries inflicted on him below his neck. He swallowed back unconsciousness and strained his eyes to see where Caleb was.

Ray watched as the headlights from the motorcycle illuminated the interior of the barn as the bike rumbled to life. He watched as Cunningham steered the bike out of the building and drove slowly towards him, the chug of the powerful v-twin engine throbbing in the night. Caleb slowed to a halt next to Ray's prone body lying motionless in the wet grass. He flicked the kickstand with his foot and let the bike idle as he approached Truman again. Ray tensed his mind, ready for the coup de grace, but it never came. Instead, he felt and smelt warm acrid urine splashing on his bloodied scalp. Cunningham's maniacal laughter rang out somewhere above him.

In Ray's tortured mind, he screamed with rage and helplessness. He thought about the countless headless corpses he'd seen and all the years he'd spent investigating the murders. As he lay paralyzed on the cold ground, Truman felt more useless and alone than he ever had in his whole life. He couldn't move and he didn't know whether he would live or die. He was completely numb apart from the blood pumping to his temples.

Through the one operating lens of the NVGs still strapped to his head, Ray noted that Caleb walked with a limp as he watched Cunningham's disembodied boots make their way back to the bike. He continued to strain his sight as he watched Caleb mount the bike, then the sound of the engine roared in the night as the Harley came to life. Truman watched him sit there, looking in his direction for a full minute, revving the powerful engine for what seemed like an eternity. Ray's vision started to falter. He took one last look at the specter-like image of Caleb staring down at him, as the bike passed by slowly. Then, with some relief, Truman finally lapsed into unconsciousness.

VIII
Final Installation

*You have just dined, and however scrupulously
the slaughterhouse is concealed in the graceful distance of miles,
there is complicity.*

Ralph Waldo Emerson (1803-1882)

*When once a certain class of people has been placed
by the temporal and spiritual authorities
outside the ranks of those whose life has value,
then nothing comes more naturally to men than murder.*

Simone Weil (1910-1943) French Philosopher

47

The headlight scattered small woodland animals into the shrubbery either side of the Harley's passage, as I steered the heavy motorcycle carefully down the slim trail between the gap in the hedge. I emerged from the foliage in front of the felled pine that blocked the driveway behind me; I rested for a second as the bike's engine idled. I briefly thought about Truman, a nagging doubt in the back of my mind that he was still alive. I reasoned that even if he was still breathing, he wouldn't be for long. The feral creatures that roamed the foothills of the mountain range would pick his bones clean in a few days. Part of me liked the idea that he might be alive. That somehow he might survive so we can continue to play our little game, but another part of me wanted to return to where he lay to check his pulse just to make sure he was dead. I brushed the thoughts away, figuring I was being paranoid and focused my mind on the next part of my plan, which was essentially to put as much distance between the farmhouse and myself. I was heading west to the coast, to an international airport with a one-way ticket with my new name on it and an as-yet-undecided destination.

Before I reached the main road leading back towards Repose, Charlie spoke to me again. His voice was muffled but distinctly his, as he told me to turn off on a small dirt lane twenty meters ahead. He told me to approach the small farm cottage tucked behind a grove of trees and that I would find a nice new rental car waiting for me behind the house. He told me to remove a sturdy plank from under the rear of the house and to securely balance it against the edge of an old stone well situated in the southeast corner of the small property.

Sure enough, I found the cottage exactly as and where Charlie described it to me. I pulled the bike up behind the building next to an old stone well covered in ivy and long grass. After clearing the mass of weeds from the top of the stone structure, I looked down into the mass of cobwebs strung across the black hole in the ground. I picked up a stone, dropping it down into the center of the well. I listened intently as there was a small gap in time and then the unmistakable sound of the stone hitting mud at the bottom of the dark cavern. I scouted around the building and once again, found a sturdy plank of timber under the rear of the house, exactly where Charlie had said it would be.

The mouth of the hole was roughly a meter and a half in circumference and just wide enough to push the Harley up the makeshift ramp and over the edge. I bit my lip as the pain from the infected wound in my foot shot up my leg, as I hefted the weight of the bike on its final passage.

Sparks jumped in the dark pit as the chrome and steel clattered down the stone walls of the well, dragging the mass of cobwebs and weeds with it as the motorcycle disappeared with a muffled thump into the depths of the darkness below. I threw my helmet in after the bike. As an afterthought, I gathered handfuls of weeds and bracken from under the trees around the property, to cover the bike below.

I turned my attention towards the small house and noticed the silver Toyota Sedan parked under a small tree down the side of the cottage. Truman had obviously attempted to camouflage the vehicle under some loose foliage and tree branches. It was perfect. I couldn't have chosen a more inconspicuous car if I'd tried. I brushed the debris off the car and looked in the driver's window. A flood of relief washed over me when I saw the automatic shifter between the front seats. This would make all the difference to my journey as I could use my good foot without needing the other for a clutch. The car was locked but the back door of the cottage was open. My uneven footsteps rang hollow on the bare floorboards as I made my way down the hallway. The house was completely deserted except for a bedroll and a black utility bag sitting in the corner of the south-facing bedroom.

There was a pair of binoculars on the windowsill and as I looked through the dusty Venetian blinds, I knew that Truman had been watching me from here. I looked up at the foothills and saw the familiar dark Pines that surrounded our property. The discarded food wrappers and half-empty bottle of Smirnoff alongside a jar filled with cigarette butts betrayed Truman's presence. It looked as though he'd been here for a few days. I gingerly tugged my boot off and doused my inflamed foot with the Vodka. The pain was sharp and intense but felt good, as decent antiseptic should. I took my other boot off and let my feet breathe. The wound already felt slightly better after being washed in alcohol.

In a small side pocket of the utility bag, I found the car keys. After cleaning all traces of Truman's presence from the deserted farmhouse, I threw his belongings into the well on top of the crumpled remains of the Harley. I wiped my patent leather gloves on my jeans and locked the back door as I closed it shut while contemplating whether to bring Truman's body from where I had left it and throw it down the well. I decided to leave it in the long grass behind Grandpa's barn, time was on my side now and I wanted to retain my advantage for as long as possible. I took comfort in the fact that nature would destroy his corpse, or at least shield it from discovery until I had left the country.

The Camry's gas tank was full and the air-conditioning worked well as I accelerated with my good foot and pulled away from Repose. I made sure to stick to the speed limit, taking the bypass to the outskirts of Fey County and exiting the rural back roads onto a main highway heading west. I relished the feel of the cool air-conditioning on my wounded bare foot. I turned the stereo on and laughed at the corny sounds of Truman's Country and Western CD. I began to feel like my old self again as the pain in my foot eased and my headache began to subside. I let the electric window down and flicked the CD into the blurred dry grass flicking past on the side of the highway. Preferring to listen to my own thoughts, I obsessively analyzed my plans and the unlimited possibilities that paved the road ahead. I still had a lot of art left inside me. Life was short and I had things to do, places to be, vermin to kill. I felt like a KING and I knew that feeling was as good as it would ever get.

Epilogue:

'Serial Killer Investigator Falls Prey to Assailant' from Portvale Daily News

Fey County Sheriff Tom Dewey discovered Portvale Homicide Detective Ray Truman, unconscious and badly beaten yesterday morning. Det. Truman remains in a critical condition in the intensive care unit of Eden Park District Hospital. Sheriff Tom Dewey discovered a paralysed Ray Truman at the deserted homestead of the notorious Cunningham family in the small farming town of Repose, Fey County.

The Cunningham family have been reportedly linked to three separate serial homicide inquiries over the past three decades beginning with Samael Cunningham, the father of Errol and grandfather of Charlie Cunningham, who recently died in a gun battle with police after the suspected arson and murder of one Lucille Cassandra from Portvale.

So far, police have been unable to release details of the events that led to the discovery of Detective Truman, comatose but alive, in a field behind the Cunningham farmhouse. Sources reveal that Detective Truman was suspended from active duty due to exhaustion and was off-duty at the time of the assault. Truman suffered severe blunt force trauma and a single stab wound to his spine in what appears to be an effective attempt at rendering him paralytic. No further leads are available but a police spokesperson has said that Truman was heavily involved in recent unsolved serial murder investigations into the 'Portvale Slasher' and 'The Messenger' murders.

'FBI issues all-points bulletin for apprehension of Serial Killer' from Portvale Daily News.

Portvale Homicide Detective, Ray Truman, who was discovered on a deserted Fey County property in a coma after a horrific assault, has been moved to the spinal unit of the Eden Park General Hospital in a critical condition. Recent intensive surgery has done little to correct paralysis suffered at the hands of his assailant. Medical staff are hopeful that Detective Truman will regain consciousness, but have suggested that his recovery will be a slow one if he recovers at all.

An all points FBI and local authority bulletin has been released for the apprehension of one Caleb Samael Cunningham, in relation to the serious assault on Detective Truman and for questioning in regards to the recent 'Messenger Murders' in Eden Park and the North Shore. He is also wanted for questioning into the unsolved 'Portvale Slasher' homicides.

Federal Authorities have notified Interpol and Scotland Yard, as the suspect is believed to have fled to Europe. Caleb Cunningham is described as armed and extremely dangerous and not to be approached by members of the public.

The FBI made their announcement after airport CCTV footage confirmed Cunningham's presence at one of the West Coast's largest international airports. Additional confirmation has been received that a rental car under the name of Ray Truman was discovered in the long-term car park. Authorities are still trying to determine if Cunningham did leave the country, as no record of ticket purchase or visa application has been discovered.

WILLIAM COOK

AUTHOR OF DARK LITERARY FICTION

Did you like this book? Please leave a review and visit William's Amazon.com author page for other exciting dark literary fiction and thriller titles.

http://amazon.com/author/william-cook

About The Author

William Cook was born and raised in New Zealand and is the author of the novel 'Blood Related.' He has written many short stories that have appeared in anthologies and has authored two short-story collections ('Dreams of Thanatos' & 'Death Quartet') and two collections of poetry ('Journey: the search for something' & 'Corpus Delicti'). William writes horror and thriller fiction mostly, but also ventures into literary fiction, a bit of sci-fi, Young Adult and, more recently, kids stories.

His work has been praised by Joe McKinney, Billie Sue Mosiman, Anna Taborska, Rocky Wood and many other notable writers and editors. William is also the editor of the anthology 'Fresh Fear: Contemporary Horror,' published by James Ward Kirk Fiction.

Member of the Horror Writers Association, Australian Horror Writers Association, SpecFicNZ & the SFFANZ.

Sign up for William Cook's VIP newsletter for new releases, promotions and free books: http://williamcookwriter.com/p/subscribe-now.html (copy and paste into your browser).

Thanks for reading.

CPSIA information can be obtained
at www.ICGtesting.com
Printed in the USA
LVHW092230150919
631156LV00001B/84/P